WHILE THE PATIENT SLEPT

BY
MIGNON G. EBERHART

Introduction to the Bison Book Edition
by Jay Fultz

University of Nebraska Press
Lincoln and London

♻ The paper in this book meets the minimum requirements of
American National Standard for Information Sciences—Permanence
of Paper for Printed Library Materials, ANSI Z39.48-1984.

First Bison Book printing: 1995
Most recent printing indicated by the last digit below:
10 9   8   7   6   5   4   3   2   1

Library of Congress Cataloging-in-Publication Data
Eberhart, Mignon Good, 1899–
While the patient slept / by Mignon G. Eberhart; introduction to the
Bison Book edition by Jay Fultz.
p. cm.
ISBN 0-8032-6726-6 (pa: alk. paper)
1. Women detectives—United States—Fiction. 2. Nurses—United
States—Fiction. I. Title.
PS3509.B453W445   1995
813′.52—dc20
94-44360   CIP

Reprinted by arrangement with Mignon G. Eberhart, represented by
Brandt & Brandt Literary Agents, Inc.

TO ALAN

*All of the characters in this book
are entirely fictitious*

INTRODUCTION
Jay Fultz

For Mignon G. Eberhart of Nebraska, the depression winter of
1930 was exhilarating. In February she won the $5000 Scotland
Yard Prize for her second novel, *While the Patient Slept*. Her de-
but mystery of the previous year, *The Patient in Room 18*, had
introduced Nurse Sarah Keate, who was received like a favorite
aunt—one with wry humor and convictions.

Mignon Eberhart appeared at a propitious time. American
readers, disillusioned by the first world war and deescalating
from the twenties, sought escape in tantalizing puzzles, chilling
conundrums, entertainments that made horror manageable. It
was the golden age of detective fiction.

In 1930 Agatha Christie introduced the fluffy but shrewd Miss
Jane Marple. Another English writer, Dorothy L. Sayers, made
Lord Peter Wimsey romantically vulnerable in *Strong Poison*. In
America the buffs stayed home on Saturday night to catch up
with Frances Noyes Hart's tour de force, *The Bellamy Trial*, based
on the sensational Hall-Mills murder case. Dashiell Hammett
arrived with the hard-boiled *Maltese Falcon* in 1930. And that
spring young Mignon G. Eberhart traveled from Valentine,
Nebraska, to New York City for the eventful publication of *While
the Patient Slept*.

Fame was sudden. By 1940 Mignon Eberhart was arguably
the leading woman mystery writer in America and, after Christie
and Mary Roberts Rinehart, the highest paid in the world. Her
reputation has grown, if anything, through more than six decades, possibly because of her influence on a new generation of

romancers who mostly lack her literate style and feeling for frisson. In 1989, when Mrs. Eberhart was in her late eighties, Random House published her fifty-seventh and last novel, *Three Days for Emeralds*. She lives today with a large devoted dog in a condominium in Connecticut. Hers is one of the great American success stories.

Born to William T. and Margaret Good in Lincoln, Nebraska, on 6 July 1899, Mignon Eberhart had an ordinary midwestern upbringing. The two-story frame house of her childhood, still standing in University Place, was far from the penthouses she would write about later—and from ugly violence. Bill Good manufactured ice and delivered it by horse-drawn wagons. He was extremely likable, a stalwart family man and friend who freely offered financial advice. Every business in Lincoln stopped for his funeral in 1937. According to a grandson, Margaret was a lady in the southern tradition, though her forbears had come from Illinois and West Virginia. Mignon inherited her gentility and love of storytelling.

What set the dainty Mignon apart was her restless mind. Playing dolls with her sister, Lulu, she wanted to know what happened to the figures after they were dressed. By the age of ten she was composing stories at her own desk. She read incessantly, graduating from Louisa May Alcott to Dickens, Thackeray, and Victor Hugo. Not even Nebraska Wesleyan University, where she enrolled in 1919, could contain her. After three years of testing its resources, she begged to quit without a degree. Her father persuaded her to apprentice under Miss Lulu Horne at the Lincoln city library. That was when she decided to write books instead of catalog them.

Evenings, a handsome blond giant named Alanson Eberhart, an engineering student at the University of Nebraska, waited at the library to walk her home. He was a talented Sunday painter, a cousin of the poet Richard Eberhart. The story goes that she bought a typewriter along with her trousseau and began writing three days after her marriage to Alan Eberhart in 1923.

"The Dark Corridor" determined her direction, though the novelette was secreted away and not published until December 1925—in the detective weekly *Flynn's*. The gentle Mignon was lured to murder mysteries because editors bought surprise or shock endings. A hospital was the perfect setting, offering sanctuary while arousing apprehension. Anticipating Sarah Keate, "The Dark Corridor" pits a nurse against a killer. The garish cover shows her training a flashlight on blood pooled from beneath a closed door. The white uniform fixes the setting, but the artist erred in supposing that nurses wear high-heeled pumps.

Mrs. Eberhart went on weaving mysteries while her husband built bridges and dams. His engineering assignments took them all over the West; for some years home was hardly more than a trunk and a car that was always collapsing. "Blessed be nothing" was their motto. By the end of the decade the Eberharts put down in the Sand Hills town of Valentine, where Alan engineered for the state highway department. Mignon wrote during the mornings and read her work to Alan in the evenings; his headshake meant that a dropped stitch in plausibility had to be mended. Even better than *The Patient in Room 18*, said the engineer surveying her X'd manuscript (she was a bad typist but soon could hire one).

While the Patient Slept continues the adventures of Nurse Sarah Keate, who became perhaps the most popular of the amateur women sleuths in that golden age. She is proud of her abundant red hair and thinks her high-bridged nose has character. "I have a somewhat snappish disposition," she admits. Many years later Mignon Eberhart expressed her fondness for Nurse Keate "because she had a good sharp tongue." Aided by strong nerves and good digestion, Sarah confronts dark shadows and unnatural death. Though claiming "little imagination," she is more than sensible to the chilling atmosphere that is Eberhart's trademark. Lance O'Leary, the dapper young detective with lake-grey eyes, relies on her.

No one, not even Sigmund Freud, could explain the cranny of Mignon Eberhart's mind that issued Sarah Keate in such assured style. A nephew claims that several stays in Lincoln's Bryan Memorial Hospital gave birth to *The Patient in Room 18* and *While the Patient Slept.* Beyond personal observation, Eberhart drew on her reading. Possibly she knew Mary Roberts Rinehart's few stories about a sleuthing nurse called Miss Pinkerton, circa 1914, and *Hilda Wade: A Woman with Great Tenacity of Purpose*, Grant Allen's 1900 novel about an English nurse whose photographic memory made her a "natural" detective. Remarkably, Sarah Keate stood almost alone as nurse and amateur crime investigator (to the detriment of duty) during the thirties.

But female fictional snoops who were *not* nurses dated back to the Victorian era. Mrs. Paschal in *The Experiences of a Lady Detective* by "Anonyma" had appeared in 1861, several decades before Sherlock Holmes. British readers followed the doings of women detectives (amateur and professional) with names like Doll Rainbow, Annie Cory, Loveday Brooke, Dora Myrl, Miss Van Snoop, and Lady Molly of Scotland Yard. American counterparts were Laura Keen, Constance Dunlap, Miss Frances Baird, and Miss Madelyn Mack. Nearly all of them were manufactured by men. By consensus, the first *woman* ever to *write* a detective novel was Anna Katherine Green of Buffalo, New York, whose *Leavenworth Case* was published in 1878. Green's later creation, Amelia Butterworth, a busybody who helps Detective Gryce, resembles Sarah Keate in her no-nonsense manner.

So the woman detective, official or not, was hardly a literary novelty by the time Mignon Eberhart wrote *The Patient in Room 18* and *While the Patient Slept.* To be sure, not many nurses had toted spyglasses. Historians of the mystery genre usually peg

Eberhart as the successor of Mary Roberts Rinehart, who invented the school dubbed Had-I-But-Known by Ogden Nash. Had I but known what waited in that room, behind that dusty curtain, Sarah thinks afterward—but Eberhart is too good a writer to use the phrase. Her heroines, like Rinehart's, are trapped in tight spaces—decaying mansions, uncongenial hospitals. The redoubtable Nurse Keate has the good sense to be scared. If Eberhart dealt in romance tinged with gothicism from the beginning, she also focused on the puzzle. She plays fair, eschewing tricks. "Her idea of a good mystery novel is one that the reader can almost figure out but not quite," wrote Norma Lee Browning in the *Chicago Tribune*. Detective buffs will recognize many classical conventions in *While the Patient Slept*. By the way, the treatment here of the Oriental cook Kema (and of the mulatto named Corole in *The Patient in Room 18*) may seem unpolitic today, but the old classics with Sherlock Holmes and Philo Vance often used "foreigners" to enhance mystery or dark ambiguity.

Eberhart scrupulously researched all details relating to the physical world, knowing that detective-novel readers are sophisticated and quick to spot mistakes (after writing about a new moon at midnight, she got letters). She drafted floor plans before moving her characters. The memorable Federie mansion in *While the Patient Slept* was inspired by an abandoned house in Lincoln. The third Nurse Keate book, *The Mystery of Hunting's End*, set in the Sand Hills of Nebraska, reconstructs a real hunting lodge whose antique pewter lanterns increased the spookiness. In the later novels Eberhart took special pride in her authentic locales, drawing on her experience as a world traveler.

In 1930 Mignon G. Eberhart could not have foreseen how far she would go—with translations in at least twenty languages, an honorary doctorate from her own Wesleyan University, prizes culminating in the Grand Masters Edgar from the Mystery Writers of America in 1970 and the Malice Domestic Lifetime Achievement Award in 1994. There were early clues in the critical and commercial success of *The Patient in Room 18* and *While the Patient Slept.* More than sixty years later, she recalled the excitement of being entertained in New York when the presses rolled off *While the Patient Slept.* Touring the Doubleday plant, the Eberharts were stunned to see her brainchild being duplicated thousands of times. When Alan's engineering jobs dried up during the Great Depression, Mignon was well established in her craft. Gertrude Stein declared her to be "one of the best mystifiers in America."

After the two *Patient* novels and *The Mystery of Hunting's End* (1930), Nurse Sarah Keate appeared in *From This Dark Stairway* (1931), *Murder by an Aristocrat* (1932), and *Wolf in Man's Clothing* (1942), the latter two without Lance O'Leary. She was brought back by popular demand in *Man Missing* (1954). During the thirties she was played in the movies by Aline MacMahon, Jane Darwell, and (incredibly) Ann Sheridan, the Oomph Girl.

Nursing types with detective tendencies are still around, witness Mary Kittredge's Edwina Crusoe. In other hands, medical mystery has devolved into the kind of terror that negates mystery. But gorycats be hanged—Nurse Sarah Keate still comes through. She belongs to detective fiction before it turned bright and brittle, before comedy-of-manners dialogue replaced atmosphere, before violence was confused with horror. Heightened and underscored by _____, the recognizable world of Sarah can be scarier than anyone supposed. There a shift in lighting can make a familiar room look ominous, and momentary blotting out of a night light can stop the breath.

ACKNOWLEDGMENTS

I am indebted to Mignon G. Eberhart, who corresponded and spoke with me on the telephone; to Jane Donovan, Mrs. Eberhart's friend and legal representative, who kindly interviewed her at home; to Professor William Vogelsang of the University of Wisconsin, Mrs. Eberhart's nephew, who reminisced at length about the Good family in an interview; and to Charles Schlessiger, Mrs. Eberhart's literary agent, who generously provided help.

SOURCES

Books: Earl F. Bargainnier, *Ten Women of Mystery* (Bowling Green, Ohio: Bowling Green State University, 1981); Jon L. Breen, *What about Murder? (1891–1991): A Guide to Books about Mystery and Detective Fiction* (Metuchen, N.J.: Scarecrow Press, 1993); Patricia Craig and Mary Cadogan, *The Lady Investigates: Women Detectives and Spies in Fiction* (New York: St. Martin's Press, 1981); Howard Haycraft, *Murder for Pleasure: The Life and Times of the Detective Story* (New York: Carroll & Graf Publishers, 1941); Linda Herman and Beth Stiel, *Corpus Delecti of Mystery Fiction: A Guide to the Body of the Case* (Metuchen, N.J.: Scarecrow Press, 1974); Michele B. Slung, ed., *Crime on Her Mind: Fifteen Stories of Female Sleuths from the Victorian Era to the Forties* (New York: Pantheon, 1975); Julian Symons, *Mortal Consequences: A History—From the Detective Story to the Crime Novel* (New York: Harper & Row, 1972).

Newspaper and Magazine Articles: Norma Lee Browning, "Murder Is Her Business," *Chicago Sunday Tribune Grafic Magazine*, 21 November 1948, and "New Mignon Eberhart Thriller Is Ready for Tribune Reader," *Chicago Tribune*, 16 March 1953; Fanny Butcher, review of *Fair Warning*, *Chicago Tribune*, 18 April 1936; Alice G. Harvey, "Nebraska Writers, VII—Mignon G. Eberhart," *Nebraska's Own Magazine* (September 1930); Pat Holecek, "Mignon G Eberhart: Sweet Old Lady Dotes on Murder," *Cleveland Plain Dealer*, 27 April 1975; "If Her Husband Is Bored with a Story, Mignon Good Eberhart Revises Plot," *Lincoln Journal*, 26 March 1930; Kenneth R. Keller, "Wesleyan Students to Dramatize Murder Mystery by Mignon Good Eberhart," *Sunday Lincoln Journal & Star*, 12 February 1933; "Mignon Eberhart," *Lincoln Journal*, 6 April 1930; "Mignon Eberhart Wanted a Book to Read—So She Wrote One,"

Lincoln Journal & Star, 6 April 1941; "Mignon Eberhart Wins $5000 Prize on Book," *Lincoln State Journal*, 26 January 1930; "Nebraska Woman Third among Whodunit Earners," *Omaha World-Herald*, 17 August 1941; Reprint from *Valentine Republican* in *Lincoln State Journal*, 12 January 1930.

Reference Books: Melvyn Barnes, "Eberhart, Mignon G(ood)," *Twentieth-Century Romance and Gothic Writers*, ed. James Vinson (Detroit: Gale Research Co., 1982); Susan L. Clark, "Mignon Good Eberhart," *American Women Writers from Colonial Times to the Present, Volume 1: A to E*, ed. Lina Mainiero (New York: Frederick Ungar Publishing Co., 1979); Jane Gottshalk, "Rinehart, Mary Roberts" in *Twentieth-Century Romance and Gothic Writers;* Joanne Harack Hayne, "Eberhart, Mignon G(ood), *Twentieth-Century Crime and Mystery Writers*, Third Edition, ed. Lesley Henderson (Chicago: St. James Press, 1991); Chris Steinbrunner and Otto Penzler, "Eberhart, Mignon G(ood), *Encyclopedia of Mystery and Detection* (New York: McGraw-Hill Book Co., 1976).

CONTENTS

WHILE THE PATIENT SLEPT

CHAPTER I

Twice, possibly, I had had occasion to travel the rather deserted and out-of-the-way road along which the old Federie house looms desolately magnificent amid the somber clusters of evergreens that surround it. At any rate, I recognized the place at my first glimpse of it through the fog, knowing that I had seen it at some previous time, though, until I arrived there that cold February day to nurse old Mr. Federie himself, I did not know even the name of the family that owned it.

It is a rambling place, built of worn red brick, with a long wing extending from the middle of the house back. The front of the house, which faces west, juts out at each corner in a three-sided tower; these two towers end in ugly cupolas above the second-floor windows and were probably the very height of architectural elegance when the house was built. The southwest tower is lined with windows on both floors, but the northwest tower has no windows at all. Add to this many chimneys bristling from the slate roof that needs repairing, narrow windows securely inclosed with shutters, rags of vines clinging to the old walls but not concealing the numerous places where the masonry is in need of mending, and you have Federie house.

The whole of it, rambling stables, evergreens, and all, is inclosed by a high brick wall, somewhat dilapidated, but remarkably solid nevertheless: entrance to a weed-grown walk leading to the massive balconied front door is provided by a grilled-iron gate.

It is not a cheerful place. There is a kind of morose secretiveness about the narrow shuttered windows and iron gate and rearing chimneys and blind tower wall that is not attractive. And its secluded location along that little-traveled road does not improve matters.

The affair at Federie house began for me one blustery day in early February. I had been off duty for several days, and when Dr. Jay telephoned, asking me to take a case for him, I promised with an alacrity that, looking back upon, seems the very essence of irony.

"It isn't a hard case," said the doctor reassuringly over the telephone. "The patient is old Mr. Federie. He has had a stroke and hasn't recovered his speech yet. You'll find the chart there and orders for the night, and I will call in the morning. Thank you, Miss Keate."

"Just a moment," I said hurriedly as he was about to ring off. "Did you say Federie? What is the address?"

He chuckled.

"A mile out Aufengartner Road from O Street corner. Then turn to the left. It's the first house after the turn." He clicked the receiver hastily upon that as if he were afraid I would change my mind. And it was not a propitious address: a nurse on private duty is supposed to have her four hours off in the afternoon, and cases that do not offer an easy and rapid means of transit into town are not looked upon with any favor on the part of the nurses. I was positive that there was no trolley line out Aufengartner Road and taxi fares are exorbitant in B——.

However, I called a taxi and by the time it had arrived I had packed my bag with fresh uniforms and other essentials, donned coat and hat, and was ready to go. The taxi driver's naturally truculent expression took on a happier aspect as I gave him the address. The robber!

It must have been close to five o'clock by that time, for it was rapidly growing dusk, and the wet pavements caught dismal gleams from the early lights of passing automobiles that loomed out of the heavy fog and passed us with a swishing of tires. We left the lights behind, however, as we took our way out Aufengartner Road, and nothing but cold and fog-drenched landscape met my eyes. It was a long mile before we swerved suddenly to the left, off the pavement and onto a muddy, little-used country road. The outlook for a pleasant case looked less and less favorable, especially as the taxi dropped into a mudhole and out again with a precipitancy that brought my head smartly into contact with the top of the car and then thrust me with some force into the seat again, with my umbrella athwart my ankles, my traveling bag in my lap, and my hat over one eye. In growing irritation I leaned forward, pushed aside the little glass window, and spoke to the taxi driver.

"Can't you drive more carefully?"

He did not appear to hear my inquiry, and I was obliged to poke him with my umbrella. Owing to the taxi giving a particularly frantic lurch just then I believe I poked him harder than I had intended. At any rate, he remarked "Urgh!" very distinctly and turned a startled face toward me. It was unfortunate that he turned from the wheel and, as I pointed out later, entirely his own fault. Left to itself the taxi swerved crosswise the narrow road, bounded lightly over the ditch, and I was never sure just what happened until I found myself crawling out from a mêlée of broken glass, leather seat cushions, and my own bags and umbrella, the taxi driver keeping up an exceedingly passionate monologue all the while. Neither of us was hurt, and standing in the muddy road I stared at the wheels of the taxi, gayly spinning in the air, and for a few sharp moments the taxi driver and I engaged in a somewhat lively dialogue. But mere words, no matter how vigorous, cannot force a recumbent taxi to its feet, so to speak, and I soon realized that I should have to walk the rest of the way to Federie house. Hoping that it might not be far, I took my traveling bag in one hand, my handbag and umbrella in the other, and started out.

It was hard going through the mud, and I soon began to search the country about with anxious eyes for a glimpse of the house that was my destination. Suddenly I saw it, a great bulk of a house, looming dimly through the fog about a quarter of a mile ahead.

This, then, was the Federie place!

I recall that I paused for a moment there in the road, my pulse quickening a little as I strained my eyes to follow its forbidding outlines, and the strangest feeling of—well, it was not entirely apprehension and not entirely depression, but a kind of vague mingling of both swept over me. But if I put any thought into definite words it was simply that dusk of a dismal February day was not the best time to penetrate the interior of that dreary-looking place.

The house was set some distance back from the road and was yet a long walk from the spot where I stood, and in spite of my heavy ulster I was chilled to the bone. I looked dubiously at the field that lay to my right. If I could cut across that field it would make a sort of hypotenuse to the triangle and shorten my walk considerably. And as if in answer to my wish I saw a stile over the fence inclosing the field, and beyond it a path that apparently wound through the field, down into a little valley, small but thickly wooded, and thence, I had no doubt, to some side gate of Federie house. Without hesitation I mounted the stile—and was to wish most fervently that I had remained in the road.

For it was just as I entered the small wooded strip and stepped upon a little bridge that crossed a stream that the thing happened which was to haunt me through weary days and fearful nights.

My bag had grown heavy and I set it down on the floor of the bridge to shift it to the other hand. In the very act of doing so a voice came clearly from somewhere near me:

"I *can't!* I *won't!* I'm *afraid to!*"

It was a woman's voice, young and vibrant now with a repugnance that approached terror.

I straightened up and looked about me. Just ahead of me the path curved sharply around a little thicket of cedars, and it was from there that the voice must have come.

"Don't be a little fool!" This was a man's voice, easy, lazy, yet carrying with it more than a tinge of arrogant demand. "You must do it, March. According to the doctor he may die at any moment. Afraid? Nonsense. A Federie afraid!" He laughed with a kind of easy scorn. "A Federie hand is born to fit the curve of a revolver."

"But—this——" faltered the woman's voice and broke.

"This is nothing if you look at it in the right way. If he were not so desperately sick—but he is! There's no time to be lost. It must be to-night. Everything's at stake." He ended on a note of urgency and there followed a short silence. I dare say I should have made my presence known, but I'll not deny that this extraordinary scrap of conversation caught my interest, and I am not a stickler for the niceties of convention at such a time.

"Very well, then," said the other voice suddenly and with indescribable reluctance. "I'll do it. But I think there could be some other way."

"This is the only way. You can arrange the whole thing, March, and no one will know anything about it. And you'll do it to-night?"

"Yes."

"Good girl! I knew you wouldn't fail me. To-night, then. Be careful no one sees you."

"Yes."

"Good girl," he repeated. There was a rustle, the

unmistakable sound of a kiss, and then the muffled sound of footsteps and twigs and branches brushing against each other as if the speakers were departing by way of the shrubbery. I picked up my bag, advanced a step or two along the bridge, rounded the little curve beyond it, and came upon a girl who turned a startled white face toward me.

Even in the twilight that filled the small hollow I saw that she was remarkably lovely. She was of slight figure, I thought, though I could tell little of that because of the heavy folds of a long blue cape that completely enveloped her. The cape had a scarlet-lined hood that fell back over her shoulders, capuchin-like, and her dark hair, close cropped and falling in soft little curls, was beaded with mist. She had an arrogant, straight little nose, a willful chin, and a rather sulky mouth that kept its soft crimson even though her face had apparently lost every shred of color at my unexpected advent. But her eyes were the most arresting feature of her face. They were blue, a very deep, sapphire blue that looked directly at you from between extravagant black lashes and from under brows that were very black and straightly penciled and rather heavy and at that moment wore a frown that intimated displeasure rather than anger.

"Can you tell me if this path leads to Federie house?" I asked somewhat hurriedly, feeling, in truth, a little bothered as I recalled the bit of conversation I had overheard, with its tender and abrupt conclusion.

She did not reply at once, studying me instead with those incredibly blue eyes.

"Yes," she replied finally. "It does. I am March Federie. Are you the nurse Dr. Jay was to send out?"

"Yes. My name is Sarah Keate. Is it your father who is ill?"

"My grandfather." She continued to survey me with a steady look that I found a trifle disconcerting.

"My taxi broke down," I found myself explaining. Instantly she was full of hostess-like concern.

"Why, you poor thing! Did you have a long walk? From Aufengartner Road? Come, we'll hurry to the house, and I'll make you a hot drink while you get into dry clothes." A pretty color flared into her cheeks as she spoke, but the momentary vivacity lapsed into a frowning and troubled silence as she walked along beside me, following the wet path. It was dusk by this time, and objects were growing blurred and indistinct before we emerged suddenly at a gate set in the brick wall that surrounded the house. I was much concerned with my wet feet and the pangs of neuralgia that were already beginning to shoot up my right elbow and paid little attention to the enormous dark bulk, with lights showing here and there in bright bars through the shutters that the opening of the gate disclosed. The girl led me through a desolate and uncared-for garden, where vines of the previous summer must have madly overrun the paths, around the southwest tower corner and toward the great old door. There was no porch, only steps, and above the door was a hideous arch of many-colored panes of glass through which a faint light streamed in eerie greens and reds and purples.

It was at the step that I dropped my umbrella, and

as I stooped to recover it there was a sudden rush of feet, a low growl, and then March Federie's voice, as sharp as a whiplash.

"Down, Konrad!"

I grasped the umbrella and turned. A German shepherd dog, looming enormously tall and lean through the dusk, stood as if checked in mid-charge, not six feet from me, his head low, his ears back, and a growl rumbling in his great throat.

"It is Eustace's dog," said the girl. "He is unchained at sunset. We are somewhat isolated here, you know," she concluded somewhat wearily, and then added as if at an afterthought: "Eustace is my cousin."

She turned to the door, fumbled for a second with a latchkey she must have had, and then the great door swung slowly back, a thin light streamed through the foggy shadows, and at her gesture I entered the wide hall. I blinked a little, although the light was not strong, and then my eyes fell upon a man at the far end of the room. It was not the man so much as his position that caught my eyes, for he was standing on a stepladder, engaged in the somewhat singular pastime of smoothing the walnut wainscoting with his bare hand.

"Grondal!" said March, in much the same tone she had used in speaking to the dog. He was either a little deaf or so much engrossed in his curious occupation that he was oblivious to our entrance until the girl spoke. And when he turned it seemed to me that the barest hint of consternation crossed his face. Then he got down from the stepladder quite deliberately and approached us.

"The walnut panels need waxing, Miss March," he said.

Now a man is to blame for his manner, but not for his face, and while Grondal's manner left nothing to be desired I am bound to admit that he had the most villainous cast of countenance I have ever seen in all my life. He was dark and swarthy, with thin iron-gray hair, small eyes of which you only caught the glitter under overhanging eyebrows, and heavy features that were not improved by a wide purple scar that ran slantwise across his face and made of his mouth a cruel and twisted line. If there was ever bandit and jailbird written in anyone's face it was in this man, Grondal's, and though I have about as lively and sprightly imagination as that of a cow I involuntarily took a firmer grip on my handbag as he drew near.

The girl at my side cast a fleeting glance toward the dully gleaming walnut panels that lined the hall. "I think it can wait," she said dryly. "Did you light a fire in the nurse's room?"

"Yes, Miss March."

"Then take her to her room, please," the girl directed crisply. "I shall send up something hot for you to drink presently," she added, addressing me.

Grondal advanced, grasped my bag, and took his way very sedately up a vast stairway that appeared at our right, and I followed, admiring as I went the walnut paneling, the slenderly carved newel post, and the broad, thickly carpeted steps. It was a little too shadowy, however, to suit my taste, as our sole illumination, once we got beyond the light cast by the hanging lamp in the hall, was from a candle thrust into a queer old wall bracket at the head of the stairs. The light from this flickered and wavered and cast elongated shadows from the figure of the man before me. Our footsteps were not audible on the heavily padded steps, and the stairway seemed interminable. But we did reach the top step, where Grondal turned to the left. Ahead of us and behind us stretched a long hall, papered and carpeted in a somber green that lost itself in shadows. Here and there were heavy doors of some dark wood, all closed, and over the whole place hung a thick silence and that chill, musty atmosphere that the walls of an old house seem to hold. I took a step forward and trod on something soft that galvanized itself into a squalling, yellow whirlwind and fled down into the shadows of the hall, shattering the silence as it yowled hoarsely at every bound. It was very disconcerting.

"What is it?" I cried.

"It is the cat," said Grondal with what, I think, passed for a smile. "It was the cat, Genevieve. You must have stepped on his tail, and he's very sensitive, if I may say so, as to his tail." There was a touch of satisfaction in his voice; whether at the cat's discomfiture or mine I did not know. He pushed open a door, beyond which a light appeared, and placed my bag on a chair. "A bathroom is the next door to the left. If there is anything further, please ring." He indicated a red plush rope that ended in a frayed tassel and hung beside the door, bowed briefly, and backed out, closing the door softly. Owing, I suppose, to the well-carpeted hall floor, I did not hear his footsteps departing and for a moment experienced the absurd feeling that he was lingering just outside my door.

The days of Federie prosperity must have predated electricity and centralized heating, for an old-fashioned, oil-fed lamp hung from the ceiling amid many bangles and gave a mellow but wavering light, and what heat there was came from a small, round-bellied heating stove whose fat sides were already growing red with its exertions. Back of the stove lurked a skimpy fireplace that looked as if it had not held a fire in thirty years. The room was high ceilinged, not too large, and was crowded with massive black-walnut furniture, dusty red curtains, and a padded carpet, and lugubrious steel engravings with tarnished gilt frames hung from the walls. I was to find that if Charles I and Mary Queen of Scots lost their heads once in that house they lost them a dozen times.

I had little time to consider my surroundings. In fifteen minutes I had got into dry clothes, figured out how the marvelously ancient plumbing in the bathroom worked, downed the hot and disagreeable drink that March Federie brought to me, and clad in a fresh white uniform, with my starched white cap concealing the gray streak in my abundant red hair, was descending the stairway.

No one was in the great hall and I paused irresolutely, looking at the numerous curtained doorways leading from the hall and wondering how and where I should find my patient.

Most of the doorways were dark, but from one under the stairs came the gleam of light and the sound of voices. As I started toward it, someone—a man— laughed loudly and unpleasantly, and through the dark green velvet curtain came a burst of furious music.

It was the first time I heard that particular composition; it was a wild, eerie tune that made little shivers start from inside my elbows, and it was curious that I immediately and definitely disliked the thing.

I crossed to the curtain, thrust it aside, getting a whiff of the stale smell that clung to its heavy folds as I did so, and entered a book-lined room at the opposite side of which an open fire snapped and crackled. At one end of the room a concert grand piano of the massive style of the 'nineties loomed out of the shadows and at its yellowed keyboard sat a young man, dark, slender, and meticulously groomed, whose nervous fingers lingered for a moment on the keys, even as his narrow dark eyes sought mine with interest, and his thin mouth curved in a smile that held a kind of cruel amusement.

Then he sprang lightly to his feet, bowed with an exaggerated courtesy, and advanced with quick, lithe footsteps.

"I am Eustace Federie," he volunteered, his quick eyes missing not a curve of my rather ample figure, nor a lace of my sturdy black oxfords. "I presume you are the nurse."

There was something familiar about his voice, and I hesitated in replying as I tried to recall where I had previously heard it. He did not wait for my assent, but turned with a panther-like grace toward a wing chair in front of the fireplace.

"Deke," he said with the little mocking overtone that I was to find his words always held. "Have you no manners?"

There was a movement, and another young man rose

somewhat reluctantly from the wing chair and turned to face me. He was a handsome young fellow in a clean-shaven, boyish way, with blond hair and nice blue-gray eyes, but his chief characteristic at the moment seemed to lie in a most remarkable sulkiness that completely enveloped him.

"Miss——" Eustace Federie paused, his brilliant dark eyes on mine.

"Keate," I supplied.

"May I present Deke Lonergan?"

Deke Lonergan bowed grudgingly and with a lack of interest that was not flattering. Eustace laughed.

"You find him at his worst, Miss Keate. He has been disappointed in a matter that lies near his heart. But he is a good friend. When the news of my grandfather's imminent demise brought me to this morgue of a house, Deke accompanied me. Volunteered, in fact, and insisted. Wouldn't take no for an answer."

"Oh, shut up!" growled the Lonergan man. His fists had doubled up and he thrust them viciously into the pockets of his brown tweed coat as if to hide this evidence of his feelings. Eustace's eyes glittered and he laughed again.

"Suppose you take me to your grandfather, young man," I suggested a trifle abruptly. Something very like a flicker of surprise crossed Eustace's face; I dare say he was accustomed to members of my sex addressing him with more deference. However, he murmured, "Assuredly," and swept the curtain backward for my passage. There was a shelf under the stairway that held matches, candles, and quantities of candlesticks, old and new. Several matches broke under his impa-

tient fingers, and when the candle he finally lighted
flickered feebly and went out he said something under
his breath that I made no doubt it was as well I did not
hear

The next time the flame held, and taking the candle-
stick in his hand he led me across the entrance hall
and thence through a succession of dreary rooms that
so far as I could see by the wavering candlelight were
exactly like my room upstairs, save that they were
drawing rooms instead of bedrooms and held a multitude of hideous sofas upholstered in shiny black haircloth or worn green plush, and numerous little cabinets
crowded with the curio claptrap of forty years back.
The candle cast a little circle of light around us, and it
was only the furniture that lay near our path that
was definitely visible. Somewhere along the way the cat,
Genevieve, picked us up. The first intimation I had of
his presence was when Eustace hesitated for a second
and then kicked violently into the shadows ahead.
There was a spit from the cat, a savage "Devil take
that cat!" from Eustace, and I craned my neck to see
beyond Eustace's shoulders. There ahead of us, just
within the circle of light, marched the cat with his great
orange tail hoisted triumphantly. There was mascu-
linity rampant in the majesty of his long-legged stride,
and I never knew why he had been given a name of such
feminine frivolity.

Then Eustace held back another curtain, Genevieve
and I passed through a doorway into a narrow and
very dark passage, whose dankly musty air struck me
unpleasantly, and thence around a curve where we
brought up before still another curtain. I was to grow

heartily to detest the many stifling curtains in Federie house, but at the moment I only gazed with interest into the room that the lifting of the heavy green velvet disclosed. It was a large room, as gloomy and dreary as any of its predecessors. Its northwest corner was a sort of alcove with three sides, along which climbed an angular, narrow stairway, with a banister that was thickly hung with tapestries and rugs. The stairway made two sharp turns at the angles of the tower, and from the steps to the floor below there was an elaborate paneling of some dark wood like that in the entrance hall. A wood fire smoldered under a mantel of dismal black marble, and near it was a great curtained bed. The old-fashioned curtains were pushed back, and my patient, an old man, was lying there, his face darkly flushed against the white pillows and his unseeing eyes half open. As I started toward the bed a man arose from somewhere in the shadows.

"Why, Uncle Adolph!" There was a faint jeer in Eustace's voice and his laugh grated on my nerves. "Still faithful? Such touching filial devotion!"

Adolph Federie advanced into the mellow circle of light from a shaded lamp that stood on a table in the middle of the room. He was dark like Eustace, but years of good living had given him a puffy bulkiness; his face was sallow, and there were great bags under the turgid whites of his eyes; his lips lacked Eustace's thinness, too; they were pale and hung loosely with an unlighted cigarette clinging to the lower one.

"That's enough from you, Eustace," he said in a tone

that held quite unconcealed animosity. "Is this the nurse?"

With much flourish Eustace gave us an elaborate introduction, during which Uncle Adolph's eyes studied me rather closely from under their drooping lids, and my fingers itched to come into smart contact with Eustace's ears.

"You can leave the patient with me now," I hinted, interrupting Eustace.

"Hear that, Uncle Adolph? Your loving attention is no longer needed. Come, let's leave the lady to her duties." With an airy gesture of farewell Eustace departed.

But Uncle Adolph lingered, his darkly opaque gaze not leaving me for an instant. Resolving to ignore the gentleman, I walked to the bedside table, picked up the chart, and began to study it. I was still conscious, however, of that still regard which lasted for a long moment or two before he spoke.

"I am deeply concerned about my father's condition," he said at last. "He has not spoken yet, Miss Keate. When he does speak—" the man paused while he walked over to stand beside me at the table—"when he does speak, have Grondal call me at once."

Well, that was a perfectly reasonable request, and it was only the man's ingratiating manner that affected me disagreeably. While I hesitated in replying he bent closer to me. My hand lay on the chart, and he pressed his own hand, clammy and soft, upon it. A large diamond of dubious color and set too elaborately winked at me.

"Beautiful hand," he murmured softly in my ear. His tone was very suave and smooth.

I jerked my hand away.

"A man in your condition of health had better look to his liver and forgo the study of hands," I said sharply.

"Coming, Uncle Adolph?" It was Eustace at the doorway smiling with a kind of malicious amusement into Adolph Federie's livid countenance.

For the space of possibly fifteen pulse beats Adolph Federie's eyes held mine. Then he, too, smiled.

"We'll meet again, Miss Keate," he said in a voice that held as much threat as promise, and the next moment the green curtain fell and I was alone with my patient, wiping on my skirt the back of my hand on which the touch of those clammy, soft fingers still clung, and wishing for the first but not the last time that I was safely out of Federie house.

The cat, Genevieve, with a flash of tawny tail, vaulted lightly to the mantel and sat down, curling his tail around his gaunt haunches and fixing me with an unwinking stare from his great topaz eyes that seemed to hold incalculable secrets. The fire below him sighed. The fog outside had turned to sleet, and I could hear it beating gustily against the shutters. A rug from the banister of the tower stairway slithered to the floor, and at the whisper of its fall I whirled, my heart leaping to my throat. Then I laughed a little nervously and turned resolutely to the charts. But I gazed at the red temperature line without seeing it, for all at once I knew why Eustace Federie's voice had seemed familiar to me.

It was the voice I had heard down by the little bridge, not an hour ago, wringing that reluctant promise from March Federie. What was it March had promised to do? What was it he had urged with such anxiety and determination? She had promised to do it "to-night."

I shivered suddenly, though I was not cold, and moved nearer the fire. There was that about the place that I definitely and positively did not like, and it was clear to me, even then, that it would not be a pleasant case.

And it was not.

CHAPTER II

I WENT about my duties somewhat mechanically, though at any other time my patient would have interested me. He was very old, with fine generous features, flushed now and full looking, vigorous white hair, and heavy eyebrows that were yet black and whose fine indomitable sweep reminded me of those of March Federie. Her face, for all it was so deliciously young and feminine, held much more of the strength and will that characterized the face of her grandfather than did either of the male members of his family.

At seven Grondal appeared, telling me in a hoarse whisper, presumably so as not to disturb my patient, that dinner was served, and he would show me the way to the dining room. I acquiesced, of course, and followed him. He carried a lamp in one hand and wore a faded and threadbare mulberry velvet livery that ended somewhat surprisingly in long wool golf socks and black brogues. This time we did not go through those ghostly drawing rooms, but followed the dark little passage around two corners and into the dining room itself.

March was already there, standing very straight at the head of the table quite as if it were her rightful place. She wore an amazing and very lovely dinner gown of crimson velvet, tight bodiced and long, with silver cloth lining its irregular hem line and a silver ornament holding her soft dark curls back from her forehead. She wore silver slippers, too—lamé, I think— and altogether the outfit must have cost an astonishing sum of money, which item was something at variance with the rather barren condition of the household. I thought it also a too magnificent costume for a simple dinner at home, but I was yet to learn of the remarkable state and dignity with which the simplest Federie act was invested.

Toward the other end of the table stood a tall, gracefully rounded woman, who I found was Mrs. Adolph Federie, although March addressed her as Isobel without the courtesy title, Aunt, and did not seem to be on terms of intimacy with the lady. Isobel Federie was an attractive woman, in a sense, although her hair was a little too obviously touched up in color until it was a peculiar crimson red that was swept very low above her eyes. Her eyes were a dreamy reddish brown with apparently no pupils and were heavily made up. Her somewhat sharp features, high cheek bones, and curving nose were disguised by the soft, fleshy curves of her face and hidden under cosmetics; her thin lips were thickly salved with red and her finger nails long and pointed and highly polished, which called attention to singularly broad and large-knuckled hands. She wore an elaborate yellow taffeta dress, with an enormous emerald, not very clear, hanging by a thin chain at her throat. She spoke to me in a studiously low voice and said not another word during the entire meal.

Eustace was standing beside March, speaking to her in a low voice to which she listened abstractedly.

Deke Lonergan and Uncle Adolph were there, too, and all of the men were clad in the most impeccable dinner jackets, which with the glitter of linen made a nice black and white contrast. From another doorway came a member of the household I had not previously seen and whom March, interrupting Eustace's remarks with the utmost composure, presented as one Mr. Elihu Dimuck.

He was a short little man of fifty or thereabouts, almost entirely bald, with a round, shiny face, benevolent eyeglasses with heavy gold rims, and a tidy little paunch that made him look not unlike a very spruce and decently clothed Cupid.

"So this is the nurse," he said in a high-pitched voice, rubbing his hands together happily and peering at me through the heavy lenses of his eyeglasses. "Now, perhaps, we shall see some improvement in your grandfather's condition, Miss March. I trust we may, indeed. I have already lingered past my time. Some improvement, yes. Yes, indeed. I trust we shall see some improvement now, dear Miss March."

"I hope so, I'm sure," agreed March dryly, giving him a rather cold blue look from under those level black eyebrows. She glanced about the room. "I wonder why Miss Frisling seems to find it impossible to come to meals on time. Did you ring the bell, Grondal?"

"Yes, madam," said Grondal impressively. I was to learn that whenever he wore that unspeakable mulberry livery March was "Madam."

March frowned and Eustace waited impassively, his eyes following the soft white curves of her bare arms with a gleam in them that was not cousinly.

"I see no reason why we should wait longer," said March, biting off her words with an imperious displeasure.

"At your pleasure, Cousin," said Eustace. He pulled out her chair with the air of personal compliment with which some men are able to invest their slightest courteous gesture.

"Ah——" March paused as a woman in faded blue fluttered hurriedly through the doorway, hesitated under March's cold regard, and then skittered nervously to a vacant place opposite me, the festoons and fringes of blue beads on her dress tinkling agitatedly. She was the type of person whom I dislike at first sight —pasty faced and fatter than a woman of her size should be, with colorless hair, light eyes, a vacuous mouth, and a fluttering, deprecating air that always irritates me.

Something to my discomposure I found I was to sit next to Uncle Adolph, and amid the rustle of chairs being pulled out and napkins unfolded I glanced toward him only to find that he was surveying me with what seemed to me at the time to be a peculiarly speculative look. He dropped his eyes at once when they encountered mine, but more than once during the meal I was conscious of his covert scrutiny. At the moment I attributed it to baffled vanity; there is no beau like an old beau, and possibly he felt that an old maid with a nose like mine ought to be more appreciative, so to speak, of his gallantries. Not that my nose does not suit me, for it does; it is large and high bridged, and while not pretty still I feel that it has character.

He and Isobel might have been the veriest strangers

for all the attention they gave one another, although once I caught her dreamy gaze upon him in a look that held in it something of scorn, something of malice, and nothing at all of affection.

It was a painfully quiet meal and not pleasant. Grondal served, looking more like a highwayman than ever in the flicker of the tall candles that lighted the long table. There was little conversation save from Mr Dimuck, and with the salad even his fluty voice piped out under the stern unsmiling eyes of his young hostess. Every so often Eustace bent forward to murmur something to which March never responded save with the coolest syllable, and her manner certainly held nothing of tenderness in it, despite the loving parting I had inadvertently overheard.

Somehow the dreary dinner dragged along. The young fellow, Deke Lonergan, was still sunk in the most extraordinary sulkiness and scarcely lifted his gaze from his plate. I believe he saw more than one would think, however, for once when Eustace leaned near to March, placed his hand for a second on her hand, and then ran his fingers lightly and smoothly along her bare arm to the shoulder before March could draw away, Deke Lonergan looked up suddenly, opened his mouth as if about to speak, closed it with a click, and returned, glowering, to his plate, with a white line around his tight lips.

Eustace caught the slight motion.

"What did you say, Deke?" he inquired solicitously. "Nothing? But I thought you were about to speak. Thought better of it? How nice it is to have Deke with us, eh, March?"

It was just at that moment before March could reply that from somewhere outside came the sudden sound of a deep and prolonged howl. It was an unearthly howl that made my skin prickle, and everyone at the table looked up sharply. Even Eustace appeared to be taken aback for an instant. Then he smiled.

"It's Konrad," he said. "Someone has passed along the road, too near the gate to suit his taste. He's a faithful brute, is Konrad. Police, judge, and jury rolled into one. He detects, judges, and executes, all in about ten seconds."

I believe I should not have remembered the incident had I not happened to glance at March. She was suddenly as white as the tablecloth and her slim hand gripped a fork until the knuckles stood out sharply white. Then she caught her breath a little and met Eustace's smile.

"We are well guarded," she observed, with the first touch of lightness I had yet seen her evidence. But her eyes remained darkly blue and troubled, and a moment later, when Uncle Adolph was moved from his abstraction to relate a tale that illustrated the sagacity of the so-called police dog, she listened with a frigid detachment that I'm sure wound up Uncle Adolph fully three minutes before the story was complete. Uncle Adolph shot her a glance of positive malevolence, and it was not difficult to see that he and his niece entertained no mutual fondness.

Conversation lapsed again, and several scanty courses came and went with much formality. Once Mittie Frisling sneezed, and March asked Grondal to place another log on the open fire, casting at the same time a coldly disapproving look at Mittie's bare, bulging shoulders that threatened to burst the loops of blue beads across them. And once something soft brushed my ankles, and on suppressing a cry and looking downward I saw Genevieve stalking from under the long tablecloth and bearing in his gaunt and ravenous jaws a chicken bone that someone—I suspected the Frisling woman —had surreptitiously passed him.

It was toward the end of the meal that a trivial but startling thing occurred. I was involved with a rather messy custard dessert when, impelled by that curious feeling of being under observation, I looked up suddenly toward the swinging door that led into the butler's pantry. The little slot in the middle of the door had been pushed aside, and I saw very distinctly a pair of yellowish eyes, which were fixed in a disquieting way upon me, and caught just a glimpse of a broad nose, a dangling gold earring, and a wisp of black, straight hair. Then the slot dropped into place.

"Your pardon, miss," said Grondal in my ear. "It is Kema, the cook."

Eustace, whose restless dark eyes saw everything, laughed acidly.

"Old family servants take a degree of interest in affairs of the household that is somewhat embarrassing." He spoke apparently to me, but his eyes went to Grondal's face.

"We'll have coffee in the library, please, Grondal," said March, rising before Eustace could get to his feet.

Having no desire for coffee and less desire for another strained half hour of their company, I did not accompany the others into the library. Instead I took a candle, found my way upstairs to my own room, secured my knitting, and returned through those darkened drawing rooms to my patient.

There was little I could do for him, so presently I pulled a chair up to the fireplace and sat down, letting my eyes roam around the large room. The narrow, angular stairway in the corner made it an unusual room. I reasoned that this three-sided alcove must be the northwest tower and that the presence of the stairway accounted for the tower's blank wall. Momentarily I wondered where the stairway led and even took a few steps up its length to the first turn, craning my neck in an effort to see around the second turn. However, it seemed only to provide a convenient approach to the second floor from the north end of the long house.

Having no wish to lose myself in the rambling upper story, I retreated to the chair again, knitting busily and casting occasional glances at an elaborate silver clock, tarnished but running, that stood on the mantel. Beside it were various objects of art—a Dresden bowl with dusty cigars stuck in it, a paper weight of varicolored glass, a couple of empty pottery vases, and a green elephant, not much larger than my hand, that looked to my inexperienced eyes as if it might be jade. It was a rather lovely piece, if you like that kind of thing. The slendering trunk, the large, fanlike ears, and the tiny sinister eyes were all carved very delicately and finely, and the small tusks were a shimmering crystal white that I thought might be white jade. The leathery folds of skin, the square, sedate legs, even the clumsy toes were artfully suggested, and the clear, cool green made the only pleasant spot of color in the whole room.

Along about nine o'clock Elihu Dimuck pulled back the curtain, peered cautiously about the room, and tiptoed toward me.

"How is Mr. Federie?" he asked in a whisper.

"About the same, I think," I said in my ordinary voice.

He looked a little shocked and made a silencing motion with his small, shiny hand.

"Not so loud, Nurse," he said reprovingly.

I lifted my eyebrows.

"Mr. Federie is quite insensible."

"You mean—he can't hear?"

"He is quite insensible. He can neither hear nor see."

"I hoped you would say that he is better," he continued with a sigh. "I am a busy man. But Mr. Federie is an old—client of mine, and one feels obligated. Yes, obligated." The firelight glinted cheerfully on his bald head and cast grotesque shadows about the shoulders of his old-fashioned dinner coat.

"Indeed," I said.

There was a short silence; then he sighed again and turned away.

"Well, I trust morning will see some improvement. By the way, Nurse, as soon as he is able to speak, will you call me, please? I am remaining here for the express purpose. He asked me to come to see him about a business matter; he must have written the day before he suffered this stroke. When I arrived I found him like this, and I've been waiting for three days."

"Certainly, Mr. Dimuck, if his family wish it. He

may not be strong enough to concern himself with business for some time yet."

He considered this thoughtfully, his head tipped to one side.

"Of course. Of course. We shall see. I really cannot delay my departure much longer, however, and from the tone of his letter I judged the matter to be urgent. But I should not like to retard his progress. No. No, indeed. Well, we shall see. Good-night." As he pulled back the curtain Genevieve marched composedly into the room, his eyes catching the light for a moment in an uncanny way. I think the cat's unexpected entrance startled Mr. Dimuck a little, for he said something under his breath and departed rather more hastily than was necessary.

The cat sat down near me, fastening a steady gaze upon my knitting needles. Not a sound from the library at the opposite end of the house drifted through those cold, intervening rooms, and I must say it was rather lonely. I knit rapidly for some time, went carefully over the charts and the orders for the night, and let my thoughts speculate widely as to the curious household in which I found myself.

About eleven I resolved to make myself comfortable for the night and arranged my chair with its back to the tower stairway so that the light from the table lamp would not fall in my eyes, found a footstool, and took one of the dusty tapestries from the stair rail to throw over me in case the fire went down. The night outside was increasing in violence; the shutters and window frames were rattling in the gusts of wind, and it seemed to me I could hear the somber evergreens tossing and moaning. When I went to adjust the window, however, I found that the shutters, rattle though they might, were yet remarkably solid and utilitarian in appearance and were fastened securely with old but heavy locks. They did not prevent the icy gusts of wind and sounds of the storm from filtering in through the spaces as I pushed the window up several inches. It was a wild night; the kind of night to spend, safe and warm, in one's own bed, not to spend sitting up with a sick man in an enormous old house that was so still that the sleet flying against the shutters, the sigh of the wind in the chimney, the creak of shutter hinges, and the moaning of trees were the only sounds to be heard. And assuredly these were not nice, cozy sounds.

I had barely lowered the flame in the lamp, removed my cap, and ensconced myself in the chair when there was a motion of the green curtain and March Federie entered, stood poised for a moment against the green curtain while she looked about the dimly lighted room, and then approached me. She still wore the crimson and silver gown which looked out of place in the dark old room, but had changed her silver slippers to small, black satin mules, with large crimson rosettes of ostrich feathers almost covering their toes.

She looked very tired and sank down on my footstool with a little sigh.

"Is Grandfather any better?" she asked quietly, and as I shook my head she turned to scrutinize that flushed face which showed dimly among the shadows of the bed curtains.

"Why—why does he hold his mouth like that?" She

turned back to me with a touch of horror in her half-whispered inquiry. "Half open like that with his tongue showing—is he in pain?"

"No, he's in no pain," I assured her. "They always hold their mouths like that."

"Oh. Can't he hear—or see——" She faltered.

"He is unconscious."

"Miss Keate, I wish—the moment he is able to speak, I wish you would call me. I believe he will want to see me."

"Very well," I promised readily, feeling, indeed, that if my patient would want to see anyone it would be this level-eyed, crisp-tongued granddaughter of his.

My ready acquiescence must have impressed her favorably, for she went on in a tone almost of confidence:

"You see, I think he felt that he wasn't in good health, for he sent for me—I was away visiting—asking me to come home. I arrived about four days ago, but——" She faltered, her voice died away into space for a moment, and then she continued: "Then he had this stroke. Uncle Adolph was here when I reached home, and Isobel, and Mr. Dimuck came the day Grandfather became ill, and we sent for Eustace right away. And Grandfather has been like this." She faltered again and stopped altogether, her eyes somberly on the fire.

"Who is Mr. Dimuck?" I asked conversationally.

"An old friend of Grandfather's."

Genevieve arose, stretched himself in a leisurely way, stalked over to the girl, and rubbed against her slim ankles.

"Go away, Genevieve." She pushed him away, but the cat returned and reluctantly she let him arch his gaunt back and rub against the toe of her slipper. He was very complacent, purring in a loud, grating voice and nibbling at the crimson rosette.

"I don't like cats," she said, turning her blue gaze to me. "Genevieve belongs to Kema as much as anybody. She feeds him unlimited liver and cream, but he is always thin. It must all go to bone and fur. Kema is the cook," she added in an explanatory tone. "Didn't she peek at you to-night at dinner?"

"She did," I said. "And a most unpleasant peek it was, too."

"She resents strangers in the house," apologized March. "But she is all right when you know her. She has been here ever since I can remember." She smiled. "When Eustace and I were children she used to threaten to cut off our ears if we didn't stay away from the cookie jar. We were meddlesome little monkeys."

"Eustace is your cousin?" I said idly as she paused. The smile lingering on her face vanished at once.

"Yes. He was left an orphan when very young and has always lived with us. I, too, was left on Grandfather's hands without parents. Poor Grandfather— how good he was. And how stern." She looked again toward the bed, her expression anxious and loving.

"And Mittie Frisling?" I said, perhaps inquisitively. "Who is she?"

The softer look in her face disappeared as if wiped out by a sponge and she rose, reassuming the air of distant coldness that she had displayed through dinner.

"Mittie Frisling?" she said quite distinctly. "I have not the least idea."

The curtain behind her wavered, and Eustace stepped across the threshold, his eyes going swiftly about the room. I fancied that he hesitated when he saw March, but if he did it was for only a fraction of a second. Then he advanced calmly into the room.

"You here, March? I thought you had gone to bed."

The girl, standing very straight and slim in her crimson velvet, swept him a frigid blue glance from under those indomitable eyebrows.

"I'm just leaving," she said. "Is there anything you want, Miss Keate?"

"Some boiling water, please. And an alcohol lamp, if you have one. I'm to give adrenalin hypodermics when necessary and I need the water to sterilize the syringe and needle."

She looked at me gravely.

"There is no alcohol lamp in the house, but I'll have a fire kept in the kitchen range all night with water on the stove. And I'll get you some boiling water now."

Eustace lifted the curtain for her and then approached me.

"What do you think of Grandfather's condition, Nurse?"

I do not like to be addressed as "Nurse."

"I'm sure I can't say," I replied coldly.

He raised his eyebrows; they were black like March's, but had a more suave lift.

"So? By the way, Nurse, do you think he will soon be able to speak?"

"Possibly. It's hard to say. Few cases are exactly alike."

There was a short pause, during which his brilliant dark eyes sought mine as if to wrest from me any secrets of medical knowledge I might possess.

"Will he be apt to say very much when he does speak? I mean, to hold long conversations?"

"Probably not." I disliked discussing the case and had to remind myself that he was my patient's grandson and had a right to make inquiry. "Probably he will say only a few words."

He considered this for a moment or two, his eyes never shifting from their intent scrutiny.

"Do you think he is going to die?" he asked then with rather callous definiteness.

"I really can't say," I evaded.

"Well, Nurse, in case he does try to speak, see that you call me. *At once.*" His voice was curtly arrogant, quite as if he were addressing a servant and none too courteously. "My room is directly above this one." He nodded toward the tower stairway. "At once, understand?"

"I shall do as I think best," I replied with some asperity.

His eyes flashed and narrowed and he took a step or two toward me. But I never knew what he was about to say, for just then March returned with a steaming saucepan, shot a quick look at us, placed the pan on the bedside table, and turned to leave.

"I hope you have a good night, Miss Keate," she said, politely impersonal, and added firmly: "Come with me, Eustace."

He stood for a moment without moving, then shrugged his shoulders impatiently and followed his cousin quite as if she had the right to order and he to obey.

While sterilizing my hypodermic syringe and inserting the tiny needle it occurred to me that there was rather more anxiety displayed on the part of the members of the family as to when old Mr. Feder would speak than as to his chance for recovery. And as I was measuring the adrenalin still another request came to me. It was from young Lonergan. He thrust his face between curtain and door casing, blinked a moment, saw me, and advanced hastily.

"See here, Miss Leet—Neat—whatever your name is. I've got to talk to him." He jerked his head toward the bed. "I've got to! As soon as he can speak. It's important. Will you call me the very minute he speaks? I'm bunking with Eustace in the room just above this one—and in daytime I'll be around close. Will you call me?" There was such urgency in his voice that I overlooked his rudeness.

"It's almost a matter of—life and death," he said as I hesitated. "How much longer will he be like this?"

"There's no way to tell," I said, feeling a little sorry for the boy.

He stared into my eyes for a moment; his own were quite black with excitement, his face was white, his blond hair furiously tousled as if he had been running worried fingers through it, and his breath came jerkily.

"If I wasn't such a *damn'* fool," he blurted all at once and his voice broke raggedly.

Knowing that, manlike, he would never forgive me

for hearing that break, I turned hurriedly away. But immediately he mastered himself.

"Thank you, Nurse. If you will call me—when he speaks—I shall be—very grateful." He spoke with labored formality, walked to the door, lingered there, his white face and lean jaw clear against the green curtain, said "Good-night" with painstaking politeness, and departed. But not before I had noted the set, ugly angle of that jaw and the blaze of something very like fury that suddenly replaced the desperation in his eyes.

Left to myself, I administered the stimulant, took a last pulse, and once more made myself comfortable in the big chair. But though I relaxed at once with the completeness of habit, gained by more years of nursing than I care to mention, it was a long time before I slept, and several times, when a shutter creaked or a log slipped in the grate, I roused hastily, looking with curious uneasiness into the shadowy corners of the old room.

I thought of all kinds of things, as one does when just about to sleep—March's lovely face and stern eyebrows, Eustace's laugh, and Uncle Adolph's clammy hand all merging fantastically together. I turned and twisted uneasily, opening my eyes to stare at the black, winking windowpanes, at my patient's still face, at the flames in the grate leaping and lowering spasmodically with the gusts of wind. Once my gaze fastened on the old-fashioned bell rope beside the door and I speculated idly as to how long it would take to summon Grondal in case my patient took a sudden turn for the worse.

And once I dozed and was dreaming when some sound aroused me and I sat up, blinking and searching the room with my eyes. The shadows in the corners, the storm outside, and the thick silence inside were not conducive to cheerfulness, and I was sharply conscious of being alone on the deserted first floor of the great house, with only a sick man for company, and that all the others were presumably sleeping at some distance. It is easy to imagine things under such circumstances, and for a moment I felt quite sure that eyes were watching me from some place near at hand. The impression was so strong that I even turned hastily and looked upward into the increasing shadows of the tower stairway. There was nothing there, of course.

Genevieve, I saw, had resumed his position on the mantel. Possibly he had disturbed some of the claptrap with which the mantel was laden and the slight sound had been the cause of my awaking. Convinced, if not entirely satisfied, with this explanation I leaned back in the chair again and pulled the musty tapestry over my shoulders. The cat had his enormous eyes fixed in the direction of the stairway in a steady, purposeful stare that never wavered, and every now and then his tail twitched slightly in a fashion that, I shall have to admit, was very disquieting.

But though I turned again and peered in that direction I saw nothing out of the way, and I leaned back once more, closing my eyes resolutely. It was then about one o'clock, I think, and the storm was, if anything, worse.

Eventually I must have gone to sleep, for the next thing I remember was dreaming that I was in the tumult of a summer storm, with lightning and then an enormous crash of thunder that brought me out of my dream with terrifying suddenness and sitting bolt upright in the chair. In the very second of opening my eyes my gaze fell on the velvet curtain over the door that I faced. It was falling slowly into place, the folds of green wavering gently as it settled into place and finally hung smoothly.

Then my bewilderment passed; I realized where I was and that some sudden crash of sound had awakened me. It couldn't have been thunder. There is no February thunder in our part of the country. What was it, then? A faint acrid smell—was it smoke?—drifted to my nostrils.

I sprang out of my chair and stared about me.

My eyes fell on Genevieve. And at the sight my heart leaped to my throat.

He was standing at the foot of the tower stairway, his gaunt outlines but half revealed in the dim light. He was staring at something upward on the steps out of my range of vision. His ears were laid back, his eyes glaring horribly; his tail was lashing furiously from side to side and his lips were drawn back from his teeth in a soundless snarl.

Somehow I reached the table, snatched the lamp, turned up the wick with a quick motion that sent wisps of black smoke up the lamp chimney, and holding the lamp high in my hand I advanced to the stairway. The cat drew back, still snarling. I held the lamp forward and took a few steps up that narrow stairway.

A dark shape lay just beyond the first angle. It was a man sprawled grotesquely on his face.

The lamp flared and smoked and flared again.

Then I forced myself to take another step or two and bent and turned the distorted body so its face was turned to the flaring light.

It was Adolph Federie.

He had been shot through the heart.

CHAPTER III

LANCE O'LEARY COMES TO FEDERIE
HOUSE

I HAVE never known how long I stared, horror drugged, at the fearful sight.

But all at once the cat gave one long raucous yowl and fled into the shadows of the room below. The ugly sound roused me from a paralysis of terror and I let the inert body drop heavily on its face again. And at that second the light in the lamp flared wildly again and went out, leaving me in gibbering blackness with a man who had been violently done to death within reach of my hand, and someone—it must have been I— screaming madly through a stiffened throat.

My knees were shaking and I felt dizzy and sick, and I think it was the quick dread of falling on that sprawled body at my feet that frightened me to a vestige of rationalism.

I must do something—call someone—arouse the house. I recalled the bell rope across that dark room below and with the thought started down the narrow steps, felt for the banister, edged past the body, felt cautiously for the floor beyond the last step, and crossed the room. By this time my eyes were adjusting themselves to the blackness and I found that the faint glow from the dying fire vaguely outlined the shadows of furniture. But still it was dark, and I had to grope my way across the room, feeling that grisly hands were clutching at me from every shadow. At last I found the post of the bed, guided myself past it, stretched my hands out before me, and advanced a few steps before my fingers touched velvet that billowed and gave under them, groped for the side of the door, found a plush tassel, gripped the bell rope, and pulled it up and down in a very frenzy of released energy.

And at that instant there was a sound of running feet from over my head, and a man's voice called from the head of the tower stairs.

"What is it, Nurse? Was it you screaming? What is the matter? What——"

The voice broke oddly. I think the speaker must have started down the stairs, stumbled, and stooped to feel in the darkness of the stairway with his bare hands, for there was a sharp silence, a quick-drawn breath, and then a hoarse whisper that hissed across the black void between us: *"What's this!"*

''Miss Keate! What is it? What's happened?" Voices now from the passage, the glimmer of candles, hurried footsteps, and March, closely followed by Eustace, burst into the room.

I remember Eustace lighting a lamp and how the bosom of the dress shirt he still wore glimmered whitely between the dark satin lapels of his lounge coat while his dark gaze flashed about the room. I remember Deke Lonergan, in light pajamas, leaning from the shadows of the banister above and crying in horrified, curiously hoarse tones: "Eustace, look here! Look here! Look here!" And I remember how I clutched at March's silk negligée, feeling dimly that she should not look at what lay on the stairway, and how she jerked away from me and followed Eustace, stopping only to snatch the lamp.

Wave after wave of nausea was sweeping over me by that time, but I, too, followed. Near the stairway, just about at its foot, I stumbled over something. It was the little green elephant, and I stooped, picked up the thing, and automatically replaced it on the mantel.

Then Elihu Dimuck brushed past me, a strange figure in a bright yellow dressing gown, and paused abruptly to stare at the group on the stairway. The body lay as I had left it; Eustace was kneeling beside it but not touching it; Deke was standing above, leaning over; and March, crouched down below Eustace on the stairs, was holding the lamp high so that its light threw into relief those grotesquely huddled shoulders and contorted limbs. All three were looking downward, immovably intent, as if held by some evil spell.

"What is it?" cried Dimuck, his voice rising to a terrified squeal. "What happened? Who shot him?"

And with the fearful question, Grondal thrust aside the curtain and ran into the room; he was barefooted and still wore a nightshirt, but had hastily donned trousers whose suspenders were all twisted over his shoulders.

"What's the matter?" he cried, and at the sound of his voice Eustace rose slowly and turned to look over the banister. The eyes of the two met in a long look before Eustace said deliberately:

"It's—Adolph. He's been shot."

Through the hubbub of excited questions that seemed to have no answers, of finding more lights until the whole room flared garishly, of all of us crowding around the narrow stairway, but few things stand out distinctly in my mind. I recall assuring them over and over again that I had heard nothing and had seen nothing until I was aroused from sleep by what must have been the shot that killed Adolph Federie. I recall March's paper-white face and how it seemed to me she was forcing herself to stand there, the toe of her slipper all but touching the dead man while she held the light for Eustace. And I recall how Eustace looked up at me presently and said:

"How about it, Nurse? Shall we call a doctor?"

"You might," I replied dubiously. "But it is too late. I think he was killed instantly. It seems to me——" I hesitated—"it seems to me that you had better—call the police. At once."

"The police!" cried March in a tight voice.

"We have found no revolver," said Deke Lonergan soberly. "It—cannot be suicide if there's no revolver."

"Do you mean—do you mean—— *Is this murder?*" screamed Elihu Dimuck.

There was a moment of silence while the word rang in our ears and was taken up in muted echo among the shadows and muffling curtains and garish, flickering candles and the heavy walls themselves, and repeated by the very wind outside in whispering sighs: "Murder! —murder!—murder!"

Our terrified eyes, staring from death-white faces, met each other's. Then Eustace, with the barest hint of a shrug, rose to his feet.

"It looks that way," he said coolly. There was a touch of fatalism in his manner; a kind of "so be it then, and devil take the hindmost."

There was another silence packed with unnamable fears.

"You'd better carry him to a bed," said Elihu Dimuck suddenly. "Try to do something for him. You can't just—leave him there on the stairs. It is not—decent." His thin voice shook a little and he kept darting anxious, troubled glances about him.

"Very well," agreed Eustace briefly. "Can you take his arms there, Deke? We can put him on my bed."

"No, no," I interposed hurriedly. "You must not move him. I'm sure you must not. The police must find him just as we found him."

Eustace darted a strange look at me, but acquiesced at once—so promptly, indeed, that it occurred to me that he had not been acting in ignorance.

"Miss Keate is right," he said. "We must leave him just as he is. The only thing we can do is call the police."

I left the group on the stairway and crossed hastily to the bed. But old Mr. Federie was apparently as he had been, no worse and no better for the tragedy that had taken place almost at his bedside, and after assuring myself of his condition I returned again to the others. They had followed me away from the stairway with its dreadful burden and were standing in a cluster near the fireplace, talking spasmodically in low voices. As I reached them Dimuck was saying worriedly:

"—if we could find the revolver. He might have taken his own life. It's terrible. Terrible! Never happened

before to any of my clients. Never! Never!" He probably would have kept on chattering in high-pitched
syllables had I not interrupted. As I spoke he turned
to me peevishly, pulling his amazing bathrobe tighter
about his rounded front.

"Nonsense! That man there did not die by his own
hand. It was murder. And someone—someone shot him,
right here in this house."

"Telephone to the police, Grondal," said Eustace
crisply.

"Mister Eustace, you'd better wait. Wait till morning." Grondal's low words carried an oddly warning
note.

"It's a clear case of murder, as Miss Keate says,"
said Eustace coolly. "Someone certainly shot him and
we'll have to give the police all the help we can. Have
them come at once so they can search the place."

It just happened that my eyes fell on March as he
spoke. She was standing a little back of the others,
and at Eustace's words she started violently, her face
set itself into a grim white mask of terror, and one
hand flung itself across her mouth, palm outward, as
if to hold back a scream. Then, as I watched, she appeared to recall herself, dropped the hand, set her
mouth in ugly straight lines, and—well, it was not
pleasant to see her eyes narrowing furtively as they
darted about the room.

"Isobel!" she cried suddenly. "Isobel doesn't know!
Someone must tell her. I'll go!" Without waiting for
another to offer to take that difficult duty she hurried
from the room. And it was just then that, bursting
upon my consciousness like a thunderclap, the memory

of the conversation between March and Eustace which I had overheard down by the little bridge came upon me—a conversation that in the light of the night's horror took on a new and sinister meaning. I have never known why I so immediately resolved to keep my knowledge of her strangely reluctant promise a secret—unless it was because of that white, helpless terror in the girl's young face.

"Telephone at once, Grondal," said Eustace sharply, and as the green curtain dropped after the butler's figure Eustace laid another log on the fire, pulled up a chair, and sat down. Elihu Dimuck was teetering gingerly on the edge of a straight chair, and Deke Lonergan dropped into the easy chair where I had rested, his silk pajamas looking chilly and himself plunged in gloomy thought.

"We may as well make ourselves comfortable while we wait for the police," said Eustace calmly. "Cigarette, Deke? Dimuck?" He selected a cigarette for himself from the case he held open, returned the case to the pocket of his lounge coat, and lighted the cigarette with a steady hand. Save for the lounge coat in place of the dinner jacket, he was dressed exactly as he had been the evening before, and a question went through my mind that concerned the reasons for his being up and dressed at an hour when respectable people are in peaceful slumber.

There was a stir as a shapeless figure in voluminous gray padded softly from some corner of the room, and I caught my breath sharply before I had a glimpse of black hair and broad, dark face and the glint of a gold earring, and knew that it was the old cook. Had not March called her Kema?

She padded toward the tower stairway and up a few steps. We could see her stoop and survey what lay there without a flicker of expression on her dark face. After a long moment she drew a rug from the banister, which, slowly but without tenderness, she adjusted over the body and without a backward glance descended the steps and squatted easily on the hearth rug, where she sat like a brazen image in absolute quiet.

"The police are on the way," said Grondal, lifting the curtain.

Eustace looked at the silver clock on the mantel.

"They'll be here in about a quarter of an hour." He flicked a dark glance from one to the other of us, and added with gruesome impudence: "Have we our stories ready to tell them?"

No one replied.

It was a ghastly vigil. Through the banister left bare where Kema had taken the rug from it we could see the huddled dark outlines of the body on the stairway and from under the rug protruded a patch of white that looked like starkly clenched fingers.

At last through the storm outside and the heavy silence within the great house came the sound of a siren and the furious barking of a dog. My patient's pulse had seemed to weaken a little, and I touched Kema's shoulder.

"I need some boiling water."

"In the kitchen." She surged lightly to her feet. "Come with me!"

And at that second Isobel Federie entered the room, stood for a moment looking at us, her flowered negligée brilliant in its gay orange and green and purple, and her face sharply haggard without its make-up, and then approached us.

"Did he die?" she asked with a curious glance toward the bed.

Eustace rose to meet her.

"Didn't March tell you?"

She met his eyes blankly.

"March? Why, no. I haven't seen March since last night. I heard someone scream—oh, quite a while ago. I knew what it was, of course. I didn't see how I could help, so I didn't come down right away." Her eyes went to the bed again. "Did he die?"

"Isobel." Eustace reached for her hands and held them tightly. "You don't understand. Someone died. But it wasn't Grandfather."

"But—we've been expecting him to——"

"Yes, yes!" interrupted Eustace. "But—Adolph died. Adolph—was shot to death."

For a ghastly moment she just stood there staring at Eustace. Her face grew suddenly hard and yellow like cold wax and her eyes were sunken. Then she pulled her large hands from Eustace's grasp, drew the silken folds of her negligee more closely about her so the somewhat exaggerated curves of hip and bosom and very slender waist showed through the gleaming silk, and looked slowly about the room. It was strange that her eyes went almost directly to the tower stairway.

"Here, Isobel. Sit down. Get her something to drink, Kema."

But Isobel brushed away Eustace's arm.

"Is he there?—I see him."

"Stay here, Isobel."

"The police, sir," said Grondal from the doorway, pulling the curtain aside with an impressive air as he ushered tall, blue-coated figures into the room.

"I'll get you the hot water," said Kema to me.

I snatched a lighted candle from the table and followed Kema past the crowding policemen through the little passage, across the great shadowy dining room, between the cupboards that lined the butler's pantry, and so into the kitchen. Apparently Kema could see in the dark, for she padded on soft feet ahead of me. I might say that I always suspected Kema of going barefoot, although, owing to the concealing folds of gray gingham, I never actually saw her feet. But there was a soft thud and beat in her tread that suggested bare, broad heels and led me to what, so far as I know, was an entirely baseless and unjust suspicion.

The fire was low in the great range, but under Kema's skillful manipulation it burned furiously, and the water in the kettle began to bubble. I was pouring the steaming water into a pan when all at once there was a click back of me. A current of cold air struck my shoulders and I turned in time to see March Federie, wrapped in her blue cape, closing the door that led apparently to the back entry and thence outdoors. Her hood shaded her face as she bent to listen at the door, her hand still on the knob. Then she turned. She was breathing heavily as if she had been running, her cape looked wet, a brown leaf shred clung to the rim of her hood, her bedroom slippers were muddy and sodden, one crimson rosette gone and the other wet and draggled, and her slim bare ankles were pink with cold. I think she had not expected to see me, for she drew back when she met my astonished gaze, and her eyes sought Kema's swiftly as if conveying some message that I could not understand. It was the clearest of impressions, caught during the moment that she stood there, her hand clutching the folds of cape about her, and her face, white and fear ridden, looking out from the scarlet-lined hood.

There was a sudden scuffling of feet outside the door, and at the sound March darted another meaning look at Kema and without a word ran on light feet toward the pantry. The swinging door into the pantry was still moving when two policemen burst into the kitchen from the back entry. I don't know what felonious impulse led me to step quietly to that door and steady it with one hand, while the policemen were blinking in the light and reaching politely for their caps when they saw me.

"Where is she? Where did she go?" they cried almost together, one adding: "Didn't someone just come through this door?"

The boiling water in the pan splashed onto my hand just then, and somewhat abstracted me while Kema assured them blandly that there had been no one besides the two of us in the room, that no one had just entered through the door, and would they please close it behind them.

"She must have dodged around the house, then," said one.

"Or into some of the other doors in that back entry."

The speaker pulled the back door wide, and I could see beyond him a back hall, bare and cold looking, with a closed door or two leading into what I supposed were store closets, and at the end of the hall a shabby flight of stairs starting upward around a turn. At once the policemen departed as hastily as they had arrived, and as the door closed Kema turned unconcernedly to me.

"Here is more boiling water, miss."

Once having connived at deception there is no use re penting it. I held the pan of water steadily this time, and with the candle again in my other hand I took my way back through the dining room.

It was just at the end of the long table that a small object, lying at my feet within the little circle of light, caught my eyes and I stopped and bent to examine it. It was a small, sodden, black satin slipper. March must have dropped it in her flight. And as I identified the thing there was a sudden stir from somewhere close at hand.

"*Sarah Keate!*" said a man's voice out of the darkness. "*Sarah Keate!* Look out—you are going to drop that thing!"

With an effort I righted the pan of water.

"Who——"

"I did not intend to startle you like this," continued the voice good-naturedly. "But—you startled me, so accounts are even. Now what in the name of common sense are you doing here?"

As he spoke he moved toward me, so that gradually his face loomed up out of the darkness into the light from my candle. The light was wavering and flickering, but at once I recognized the young, rather delicately cut features, the thoughtful forehead, and the clear, penetrating gray eyes, almost black now in the faint light.

"Lance O'Leary!" I cried. And at once: "Did you come with the police?"

"I did," he said gravely. "And I suppose you are the nurse they told me of?"

I nodded, my eyes taking in every feature and expression of a face that I remembered well.

"I'm glad to see you again, Miss Keate," he said. "It's been a long time."

"Are you going to have charge of this——" I paused, at a loss for a word.

"Investigation? So it seems."

"Thank heaven!" I said devoutly, and remembered the slipper that lay at my feet. "Thank heaven," I repeated, a shade less devoutly, as almost without conscious volition on my part my foot began to grope about on the floor.

"Your faith is very flattering," O'Leary was saying as my foot found the slipper and began to edge it toward the long tablecloth. "I only hope you'll give me the assistance you gave me the first time we met. I remember that your help was invaluable."

"Oh, yes, indeed," I said earnestly, wishing I dared look down to be sure the cloth hid the slipper. Not that it meant anything, but still, with this slender, clear-eyed young man opposite me, it was not safe to take a chance. He was looking at me somewhat curiously and I added with haste: "I have been here only since last night. I have not seen much of the household."

He smiled.

"You being you," he said with doubtful compliment, "you probably know more of the household after one night than another woman would in a month. Your patient is old Mr. Federie?"

"Good gracious, I must get back to him!"

Lance O'Leary nodded.

"I'll see you again, Miss Keate."

It was with mingled feelings of relief and apprehension that I hurried on through that dark little passage, along whose walls my starched skirts rattled nervously, and so into the tower room. The lights were still blazing furiously, and a policeman was on his knees on the first turn of the tower stairway, his broad blue back visible through the banister. Another policeman was wandering about in the room. He gave me a questioning look, but I proceeded at once to my patient and he said nothing.

My patient's condition was unchanged and the matter at hand took only a few moments. As soon as possible I returned to the dining room, intending to retrieve the slipper and hide it somewhere, at least until I knew where my duty lay concerning it.

But at the door into the dining room I stopped, blew out my candle which was dripping hot wax on my hand, and peered through a crack of the curtains. Lance O'Leary, a flashlight in his hand, his face clear and pale in the reflection of light cast by the white tablecloth, was standing there, gazing quietly at something he held in one hand, directly in the glow of the light. I made no doubt it was the slipper.

Well, the thing meant nothing, anyway, I told my-

self sensibly. All it could possibly indicate was that
March Federie had some errand that took her out of
the house, and had not wanted—as who would want?—
to be caught by the police. The only thing that troubled
me was the thought that it must have been a singularly
pressing errand that took her outdoors in the middle
of the night, into a storm and with murder at large,
in such haste that she had not even put on her stockings. And, moreover, she had offered an excuse to get
away. "Isobel!—I'll go." But apparently she had not
gone near Isobel.

And again I recalled the sinister conversation I had
overheard—and again resolved to protect the girl.

"Oh, Miss Keate," said O'Leary quietly. "Come
here, will you, please?"

I had forgotten the man's exasperating way of having eyes in the back of his head and ears all around. I
advanced, feeling like a child caught in mischief.

"Why did you kick this slipper out of sight?" he
asked pleasantly. "My experience with you leads me
to think there was some reason for it."

I hesitated.

"Come on," he persisted, still with the utmost good
humor. "Out with it. You know I'm not going to pin
guilt upon anybody without complete proof. So don't
be afraid of implicating anyone."

Well, of course, that was perfectly true. Besides,
having once found the slipper he would get at the truth
of the matter by hook or crook, so I might as well tell
him the little I knew.

I told him simply that it was March Federie's slipper, that an errand had taken her outside, where she

was pursued by two policemen whom she had naturally endeavored to escape, and had succeeded. But I added nothing to that, although the words "A Federie hand is born *to fit the curve of a revolver*" rang guiltily in my memory.

As I talked Lance O'Leary studied the small, muddy slipper with a most peculiar look on his face.

"How did you know it was her slipper?" he asked when I had finished my very brief statement.

"I recognized it. I saw her wearing it last night—that is, to-night—about eleven o'clock. And also a few moments ago when she came into the kitchen."

"Was it always plain like this over the toe? It looks as if something had been stitched there and had pulled loose."

"There was a rosette, but she must have lost it."

"Rosette?"

"A feather ornament."

"Blue?"

"No, red."

"I see. Thank you, Miss Keate." He stuffed the slipper into his pocket. "You were in the room when the shooting occurred, were you?"

"Yes. The sound awakened me. But I had seen nothing and heard nothing that would throw any light on the matter."

"Don't be too sure of that, Miss Keate. By the way, is your patient entirely unconscious?"

"Yes."

"There's no chance of a witness there, then?"

"Not the least in the world," I said decisively, and O'Leary sighed.

"Well—I'll see you later in the morning. There are some things I want to know. And—er—Miss Keate!"

"Yes."

"I shall be very grateful if you give me any information that comes your way. You know, you do have the most extraordinary way of—er—being around when things are happening." He smiled. I had forgotten, too, his remarkably winning smile. It changed and lightened his whole face. And while his words were just a polite way of calling me a busybody, still I couldn't be angry. It's true that while I hope I'm not snoopy, you understand, nor meddlesome, still there's no use denying the fact that I do have a lively and inquiring mind.

So, before I knew it, I found myself pledged to help him if it lay in my power to do so.

Once again in the tower room I took my cap, crushed and wrinkled, from the chair where I had been so fearfully aroused, and sat down to fill in my neglected chart. The two policemen were still in the room, and while you may say what you like as to the blundering methods of the police, still and all I never saw anything like the thorough way in which they examined that great, cluttered old room and narrow stairway. They finally ascended the stairway, stepping lightly past the body that still lay there, and I surmised that they were going through the room at the head of the stairway. Some other men came into the room presently, too, with cameras, and besides taking pictures of the body on the stairway, and filling the room with smoke from their flashlight affairs, they also blew a kind of yellowish powder over things and appeared to take pictures of that also. I watched them with interest, but did not know enough of such matters to understand exactly what they were doing, though I knew in a general way, of course; and I did not like to ask. They, too, went up the stairs after a while. They had barely gone when O'Leary himself came into the room, and without so much as a glance at me he, too, ascended the stairway and vanished beyond the second turn. But after a few moments he came down again, a heap of men's clothing from which dangled some very gay silk suspenders, freshly laundered shirt cuffs, and knife-edged trouser legs on each arm. I guessed that the clothes belonged to Eustace or young Lonergan or both, but could not even hazard a guess as to what O'Leary was doing with them.

It was only a few moments later that Grondal lifted the green curtain and ushered in two orderlies, carrying a stretcher.

"It's on the stairway," said Grondal, leading the way across the room. The orderlies followed, their white duck coats gleaming, and their eyes darting curiously about, and I left the room somewhat hastily. I have nursed for too many years to be squeamish, but I simply could not stay there and watch them lift that rug.

Lights in the library led me there. A little group was huddled desolately near the cold ashes in the fireplace. Isobel, still in her thin silk negligee, was sitting with Eustace on the old red plush sofa; she looked rather horrible, her dyed hair disarranged, her yellowish pallor accentuating her sharp features, and her eyes small and sunken in dark rings. She was composed, however, and was smoking very deliberately. March had managed to get into a little crimson wool frock that made her look about fourteen, and some stockings and slippers, and was sitting very straight and still opposite Isobel. Elihu Dimuck, too, had dressed, but the Lonergan man was draped modestly in a tapestry rug, which he pulled closer about him as I approached, though, goodness knows, white silk pajamas with blue polka dots on them are no treat for anybody's eyes, let alone those of an elderly nurse.

Mittie Frisling was nowhere to be seen.

No one spoke. There lay over them all a tense, determined quiet that seemed to restrain hysteria. I lingered for only a few moments. Gray daylight was beginning to filter in pallid streaks through the shutters.

At the muffled sound of the hall door closing I started back to the tower room. From the window in the hall, beyond the wet path and dreary iron gate, I caught a glimpse of an ambulance. It loomed coldly white through the dismal, gray dawn. The sleet was turning again to heavy fog. The shrubbery, bare and brown and dripping, mingled indistinctly with the shadows of the fog. Toward the north of the house the dense thickets of evergreens made black blotches. And all about the place reared that solid wall, hemming in the evergreens and the shadows and the lifeless garden and the grim old house in which I stood, where murder had walked that night.

It was a world of its own. And I, Sarah Keate, hitherto a respectable and respected spinster, was involved in that dreadful world and, by virtue of my profession, forced to stay there!

It was not a pleasant thought. The only modicum of comfort I had as I took my way back through those ghostly drawing rooms to the more ghostly tower room was that Lance O'Leary was in that house, too.

CHAPTER IV

LANCE O'LEARY was, as I have indicated, a detective, although I have never heard him give himself that somewhat bombastic title. I had had some acquaintance with him several years back, during that unpleasant affair at St. Ann's hospital, which, if you live in the Middle West and read the newspapers, you will at once remember. I had heard of him from time to time since then—not much, for his was the force behind force that does not always get reportorial credit, but enough to assure me that he was progressing in his profession. He was no magician; he did not turn criminals out of his pockets as a conjurer does rabbits. Neither did he possess that quite marvelous faculty of distinguishing at a glance between things that were clues and things that were not, as do certain fictional detectives. But he did manage to solve some of the most important criminal cases that arose in our part of the country.

He was a slender young fellow, not very tall, his features clear and finely cut, his head well shaped and thoughtful, and his eyes a clear cool gray that saw everything. His light brown hair always shone smoothly; he was immaculately groomed and must have spent more money on his clothes, quiet though they were in style and color, than any man should spend. He had a partiality for gray and liked a thin scarlet stripe in socks and tie, drove a long gray roadster of a make that I did not recognize, kept a manservant with the most discreet and secretive voice I have ever heard, and—well, beyond these few facts I knew little of him.

But if, as I went about my duties in the tower room, I felt that with Lance O'Leary in the house the fearful thing the night had held was at an end, I may as well admit here and now that I was never more mistaken in my life.

The rest of the night, or rather early morning, was like a singularly depressing dream. About six o'clock Grondal brought me a tray laden with coffee and an uninteresting breakfast consisting of a small orange, burned toast, and a soft-boiled egg that was cold and unprepossessing. I remember that as I sat down to drink the coffee I turned my chair so that I faced the tower stairway; it was the first of many times that I was to do so.

The coffee cheered me a little, though I still had a twitchy feeling up the small of my back. It was not pleasant to be alone in the room with only the sick man on the bed for company, and I worked feverishly in an effort to keep my thoughts occupied.

Grondal brought me fresh linen for the bed and hot water and towels for my patient's bath. It was faintly surprising to find that Grondal combined the peaceful duty of housemaid with his other occupations. He lifted my patient easily and gently and mitered the corner of the sheet which he helped me to adjust with as deft a precision as that of any nurse. He straightened the room, too, having, as he assured me, the permission of "the policeman in the gray suit" to do so. He ran an antiquated carpet sweeper over the thick carpet, which looked as if it had never been taken up properly, and dusted, unlocked, and opened the heavy shutters, and as cold gray daylight crept reluctantly into the room he blew out the many lamps and candles that had been stuck hurriedly here and there. He dusted, too, with the casual attention that a man always gives to the rounds of chairs and loose articles.

"I'll put matches here on the mantel, miss," he said as he finished. He moved the little green elephant to make room for a box of matches.

"That's a pretty thing," I said, referring to the elephant. "Is it jade?"

"I don't know, I'm sure. Mr. Federie is very fond of it; he likes it to be here on the mantel where he can always see it. Very fond of art, is Mr. Federie, as perhaps you've noticed." Grondal's eyes went proudly to an enormous atrocity in oils that hung on the opposite wall.

"The cat knocked it off last night," I said, turning my gaze hastily from the picture and going back to the elephant. "It's lucky it didn't break."

"The cat knocked it off?" said Grondal musingly, taking the small green thing in his hand and scrutinizing it.

"Yes. Somehow it rolled almost to the stairway. I stepped on it when I—" I cleared my throat as my voice quavered a little—"when I—that is, after the —shooting occurred. I hope it wasn't damaged."

"No, it wasn't damaged," said Grondal slowly, turning the thing in his hand. I caught myself staring at that hand—long, yellow, corded, with patches of hair along the back, and on the spaces between the bony knuckles it was not nice to look at.

"Miss Keate," said O'Leary from the doorway. I turned at once. He was standing on the threshold, holding the green curtain aside. "Can you leave your patient for a little while? There are a few questions I should like to ask you all," he added, as I hesitated. "The others are waiting in the library. Will you come, too, please?" he concluded, addressing Grondal.

"Certainly, sir," said Grondal. "I'll just put a fresh log on the fire first."

I followed O'Leary through the cold drawing rooms, where the desolate haircloth of the furniture and the glass doors of curio cabinets caught dismal highlights, through the wide entrance hall, where Grondal caught up with us, and into the library. As I approached the little group sitting there I had a strange feeling that they had not moved during the few hours intervening since I had found them there earlier in the morning, even though I knew that they must have had breakfast, had presumably gone to their rooms and rested, and had certainly got themselves into less disheveled clothing. But that indefinable air of tense restraint still held them, one and all, in a silence so brittle that I felt that any sudden sound would shatter their tense rigidity and release a very panic of terror.

Mittie Frisling was not among them, and while I was too much engaged with the matter at hand to give her more than a passing thought, still it did occur to me that she was the only member of the household who had not made her appearance during the night.

Several blue-coated figures were scattered here and there, among them the chief of police himself, and I was interested to see the deference with which the chief greeted Lance O'Leary.

It was an extraordinary scene: the vast old library with its book-lined walls, its massive chairs and tables and lounges, its ornate hanging lamps whose crystal bangles glittered coldly in the gray daylight that made its way between faded red curtains which hung at the narrow windows. The tower alcove was set off from the rest of the room by curtains, too. The piano loomed, dully gleaming, in one corner; a sullen fire smoldered below the elaborate, low mantel, and above the mantel hung a gilt-framed mirror that reflected our white faces. And our feet made no sound on the heavy carpet as we approached the still group waiting us.

March, sitting very straight on the divan, moved over with a gesture like an invitation, and I sat down beside her. Her soft, dark hair clustered over her head in little curls, like a rebellious baby's, but her eyebrows were implacable and her young mouth stern.

Lance O'Leary remained standing, leaning a little on the high back of a tapestried armchair, while his thoughtful gray eyes went from Eustace and Isobel on the sofa opposite me to Elihu Dimuck, sitting in a great mahogany rocker that when he leaned back took his feet entirely off the floor but did not lessen his dignity, on to Deke Lonergan, standing just before the fireplace with his hands thrust in the pockets of a coat that did not match the trousers he wore, and included Kema, standing at ease in the background,

Grondal and March and me, all in one swift glance. It was a glance that, I thought likely, identified the brand of cigarette that Isobel was smoking, the size of shoe I wore, and the grade of linen in the handkerchief which Mr. Dimuck was passing across his shining head.

"I was given only a summary of the situation about three o'clock this morning when I arrived," began Lance O'Leary. "There are a few questions I should like to ask, and it will facilitate matters all around if you will answer promptly and—directly. It is a matter of routine, so please don't be afraid of implicating yourselves or anyone else. Just tell me the truth as simply as you can."

He paused, looked swiftly around the group again and began with me.

"Miss Keate, will you tell me, please, how and when and under what circumstances you found the dead man?" O'Leary spoke in a quietly conversational manner and seemed considerably more interested in a stubby red pencil he drew from his pocket than in hearing what I had to say. But I knew that quiet manner and told as briefly and concisely as possible of the tragic discovery I had made.

"Now let me see if I have this right," said O'Leary when I had finished. "To the best of your knowledge, you went to sleep about one o'clock. You were awakened by the sound of the shot. You roused yourself, walked over to the stairway, and found Adolph Federie dead. Why did you go at once to the stairway?"

"It—it was the cat!" The shock of that discovery was still so close upon me that I had to force myself to speak through a suddenly stiff throat. "The cat was standing there, staring at something. I took the lamp and went to the stairway. And there—he was."

"Did you examine the body? How was it lying?"

"He was on his face. I turned him over, saw it was Adolph Federie. Then—I had turned the wick in the lamp too high and the light went out. I—crossed the room, found the bell rope and pulled it. I must have screamed, too, for Mr. Lonergan came down the tower stairs, and Miss Federie and Eustace Federie came with lights from the passage that leads from the tower room to the other rooms on this floor."

"And then?"

"Then the others—Mr. Dimuck and the butler and later the cook came. We looked at the body, found there was nothing we could do, and called the police."

"In your opinion what caused the death of Adolph Federie?"

"A revolver shot, I think, entering his heart."

Lance O'Leary studied his pencil for a long moment. I had forgotten that this was one of his gestures and it exasperated me; there was nothing of any interest in a shabby stub of pencil and there was considerable of interest in the pallid faces surrounding him.

"Such is the first report of our medical examiner," said O'Leary.

A policeman came to the door and hesitated.

"What is it?" asked the chief.

"That female in that bedroom upstairs," said the policeman. "She has still got the door locked and still refuses to come out. We can't search the room, sir, till she gets out."

March started.

"Why, it's Mittie Frisling!"

"Who is Mittie Frisling?" inquired O'Leary.

March did not reply and Grondal stepped suddenly forward.

"Miss Frisling is—an old friend of the family's," he said deferentially. "She came to see old Mr. Federie about a business matter and has been forced to remain until Mr. Federie will be in a condition to—talk with her."

"How long has she been here, then?" asked O'Leary, his bland gray eyes on the butler's face.

Grondal did not blink, but the scar on his face grew dark purple.

"A few days, sir. Several."

"Shall I have her out?" inquired the policeman vigorously.

O'Leary shot the chief an amused look.

"Gently, gently," he said, turning to the policeman. "Tell the lady that the others are waiting for her in the library and ask her to be so good as to join us."

He turned briskly to us again.

"In the meantime—Mr. Lonergan, I believe you were the next to enter the room after Miss Keate found the body. Will you tell me just what your impressions were? Had you been asleep? What wakened you?"

"I was awakened by what must have been the sound of the shot," said Deke Lonergan, meeting O'Leary's eyes with an open and candid look. "I lay there for a moment or two, trying to figure out what sound had aroused me and from where it came. Then it seemed to me that someone was moving about in the room below me, and after a moment I heard—screams. I jumped out of bed and felt my way through the darkness to the tower stairway, there beyond Eustace's room. I started down the stairway and—and it was dark—and I—well, I stumbled over something. It was —a man's body." He stopped abruptly.

"You had no difficulty in finding your way through the bedroom and into the little room beyond it and down the stairway—*in the dark?*"

"No," said Lonergan simply. "I knew the general direction. I bumped against a table, but that was all."

"The two of you—Eustace Federie and yourself— shared the bedroom directly above the tower room?"

"Certainly," said Lonergan a bit sulkily. "We told you that when we asked for our clothes."

"Were you both in the bedroom when the shot was fired?"

"No," replied Lonergan. "I was alone."

"No," said Eustace in the same breath. "I was reading in the library. I had not gone to bed yet."

O'Leary's clear gray eyes rested for a moment upon Eustace; his gaze was speculative, but he turned back to Lonergan again as if to finish the business at hand before he went on to further inquiry.

"So you found your way from the bedroom, into the little room beyond it, started down the stairway and stumbled over—the body of Adolph Federie——" O'Leary glanced somewhat apologetically toward Isobel, but she was engaged in selecting a fresh cigarette from the case Eustace was holding toward her and did not appear to be particularly affected by the gruesome suggestion. "Go on, please. What happened, then?"

"Well, then March, that is Miss Federie, and Eustace came running into the room from the passage. Into the tower room, I mean. Eustace brought a light, and I called him to come and look. They came to the stairway and we found it was Adolph Federie. Then the rest of them came. We talked some and looked for the revolver, but didn't find it. I guess we were—sort of upset, maybe. The nurse said he was dead and we must leave him alone, just as we found him, and call the police. And we did." He concluded with an air of giving all the facts at his command, and O'Leary gave me a fleeting glance of approval.

"Let me see, now," said O'Leary with a quietly musing air that made me regard him with suddenly quickened interest. "The tower stairway leads up into the small room adjoining the bedroom that you and Eustace Federie were sharing. The only door from that room is the one leading into your bedroom. Thus anyone going from the tower stairway into the corridor of the second floor—as the murderer would have to do to escape—would of necessity pass through the bedroom, and so from the bedroom door into the corridor. Is that right?"

Deke Lonergan grew rather white but answered at once:

"I—believe so."

"Yes," said Eustace definitely. Lonergan gave him an unfriendly look, and Eustace, with a fine disregard for tidiness, airily flicked the ashes from his perpetual cigarette onto the carpet.

"Then," went on O'Leary very gently, "in the pause after the sound of the shot awakened you, did you hear no one pass through the bedroom? The room in which you lay *wide awake?*"

There was a ring of steel in the last words. My heart began to pound faster, and March at my side was twisting her hands together.

"No one," said Deke Lonergan very deliberately. "Of course, when I awoke I did not leap immediately to the conclusion that I had heard a revolver shot. I am a fairly heavy sleeper, and it always takes a moment or two to orient one's self when aroused suddenly out of a sound sleep."

"Then you think it possible that the person who fired that shot could have retreated through your bedroom before you were thoroughly aroused without your knowing it?"

Deke Lonergan hesitated for just a fraction of a second. It seemed to me that his eyes, which up to now had been open and ingenuous, took on a wary, guarded look.

"I think it possible," he said flatly. "At any rate I heard nothing. Personally I—am convinced that no one passed through the room." There was a slow deliberation about his words that gave them significance. And though I couldn't account for it, the moment he spoke I was sure that he was not telling the truth.

"So you heard nothing? No footsteps? No sound of a door closing?" O'Leary's voice was very bland and easy.

"Nothing," said Deke Lonergan. "Nothing save the sound in the room below of someone moving about. That was the nurse, I suppose."

"You couldn't have been confused as to the location of that sound? It couldn't have been in your bedroom instead of the room below?" O'Leary was harping on the point with a nagging persistence that was not usual with him.

"No," said Deke Lonergan with certainty.

"You expected Mr. Eustace Federie to come to bed later?"

"Why—yes."

"Did you leave the bedroom door open—the one into the corridor, I mean—when you retired?"

"Why—yes, I believe I did."

"That being true, of course, you didn't lock the door into the corridor."

"Of course not."

"Do you have the key to that door?"

"No!"

There was a brief silence. Lance O'Leary rolled and twisted the pencil, his thoughts apparently engrossed with it and nothing else. A gust of wind blew against a window near at hand and it rattled uneasily. A policeman in the corner shifted his weight restlessly, the chair creaked, and he subsided at once. March, at my side, took a long, tremulous breath. Isobel crossed her silken ankles, squashed the end of her cigarette on an ash tray, and linked her fingers across her knees, her dreamy gaze upon O'Leary. The jewels on her curiously broad hands caught lights from a suddenly leaping flame in the fireplace and winked knowingly at me.

"Miss Keate, you say you were asleep when the shot was fired. Does that mean that you were soundly sleeping? Sound·y enough so that anyone could have entered the tower room from the passage without you knowing it?"

"No," I said positively. "My chair was near the bed, with its back to the stairway. Someone might have come down that stairway without arousing me, as it is some distance from where I sat. But the least stir from my patient would have awakened me. When I say I slept, I mean that I—slept as a nurse does—with one eye open."

"Then could anyone have entered the tower room —from the passage?" asked O'Leary again. "So quietly that you did not hear him?"

"No," I repeated. "I'm sure I should have roused at once. You see to enter by that door and cross the room to the stairway, anyone would have had to pass quite near me."

"And yet at least two people did enter the tower room—Adolph Federie and—his murderer. And you are sure no one entered by way of the door into the passage, and Mr. Lonergan here is equally sure he did not hear anyone passing through the bedroom above, and so by way of the tower stairway into old Mr. Federie's sick room."

"I tell you I was asleep," growled Deke Lonergan.

"Then," went on O'Leary, paying no attention to Lonergan's remark, "one of those two people escaped *after the shot was fired*, which presents an even more interesting problem, for that shot awoke both Miss Keate and Mr. Lonergan. The shot was fired presumably from the top of the stairway. In order to escape the murderer had to do one of two things: He had to descend the tower stairway, cross the tower room, passing close to Miss Keate after the shot had awakened her, and escape through the little passage. O* he had to pass through the bedroom above without attracting Mr. Lonergan's attention, and thus into the second-floor corridor. You, Mr. Lonergan, are sure that no one passed through the bedroom above and also that you would have heard anyone doing so. Miss Keate, could anyone have passed you without your knowledge after the shot was fired?"

"Not without wings!"

"You saw nothing to indicate——"

"Wait!" A memory was trying to thrust itself into my weary mind. I closed my eyes trying to recall the moment of my waking. "Wait," I continued slowly, groping for that memory. "I was dreaming that it was a summer storm and there was thunder. A loud roll of thunder roused me, and as I opened my eyes I saw——" I had it now! "I saw the folds of the green velvet curtain there in the doorway wavering, and then the curtain fell into place as if it had just been dropped. That is all I saw. Then I realized that I had been dreaming, and that it was not thunder that awakened me, and I stood up and looked around the room."

"And saw nothing?" asked O'Leary very quietly.

"Nothing. Only the cat. And in the shock of my discovery I forgot the curtain moving until just now."

"Thank you, Miss Keate," said O'Leary. "Do you think that the person who dropped that curtain could have had time to descend the stairway and cross the room after the shot was fired and before you opened your eyes and saw the curtain falling into place?"

"No," I replied with decision.

"Then our problem is still a problem. Especially since——" O'Leary was studying the pencil in his fingers very carefully—"since the door from Mr. Lonergan's bedroom into the second-floor corridor is locked. And the key is gone. And the fingerprints on the glass door-knob have been carefully rubbed away."

"*What!*" It was Deke Lonergan who cried out. The rest of us sat in a stupefied silence under the impact of O'Leary's quiet words.

"Have you nothing more to say, Mr. Lonergan? You are sure you have—forgotten nothing?"

"I've not another thing to say!" Deke Lonergan's blond eyebrows had drawn together and his face was sullen and ugly looking.

"I'm sorry," said O'Leary gently. "Because you see, Mr. Lonergan, if you were, as you claim, awakened by the sound of the shot, while someone might have slipped through the bedroom without your knowl-edge—mind, I say *might*—you couldn't have helped hearing the door into the corridor close and the key rasp in the lock. It would be better for you, you know, if you *had* heard something of the kind."

Deke Lonergan stared at the imperturbable features of the young detective for a long moment. Then his face darkened furiously and he sprang forward.

"What do you mean by that?"

"Nothing more than I have said." Lance O'Leary's good humor was unshaken.

"Look here, you can't accuse me of murder on such a slim excuse as this!"

"No one has accused you," said O'Leary, adding mildly, "yet."

There was a short silence while Deke Lonergan stared angrily into O'Leary's clear gray eyes. Then all at once he dropped into a chair, gripped his hands around its arms, the fury in his face gave place to a kind of sullen and defiant reserve, and his eyes, wary and guarded again, met O'Leary's fully.

"You are trying to get me to talk. And I have nothing to say. Nothing to tell."

Lance O'Leary's eyebrows lifted a little and Eustace spoke lazily:

"By the way, Mr. O'Leary, have you got that door unlocked yet? It was good of you to bring us some of our clothes but—" he glanced at Lonergan's mismated coat and trousers—"but it is a little inconvenient to be locked out of one's own room like this."

"In fact, the whole thing is inconvenient, is it not? But I'm afraid you'll have to put up with it until— until we find who locked that door." O'Leary's face was as quiet as ever, but there was an undercurrent in his voice that was neither bland nor easy. Eustace's dark eyes gleamed unpleasantly as he examined a match he drew from his pocket case with unnecessary care and struck it viciously along the polished arm of the sofa. The tiny flame sputtered, breaking the little silence and simultaneously a subdued commotion arose suddenly in the hall that, growing louder, drew our eyes that way. And at that second Mittie Frisling, propelled on either arm by a policeman, entered the room. The fringes of her bunchy, pale-green kimono fluttered, her eyes were nearly popping out of their sockets, her sticky-looking hair was in untidy strings about her ears, and her face a sickly yellow green.

Her terrified eyes went from one to another of us, lighted on the chief of police, and she at once began:

"I know nothing of this! Nothing at all! I tell you I know nothing of it! These policemen have been knocking at my door all morning. Since early this morning! Of course, I wouldn't let them in. Why should I! It's an outrage! I know nothing of it. Nothing! *Nothing!*"

By this time she had reached us, walking hurriedly and awkwardly on the high heels of the shabby pumps into which she had thrust her pudgy feet and above which her fat ankles bulged unpleasantly.

"Nothing of what, Miss Frisling?" inquired O'Leary.

She turned her pale eyes toward him, recognizing authority in that quiet voice.

"Of Adolph's death, of course!" she cried shrilly. "Of Adolph Federie's murder!"

"You knew, then, that he had been poisoned?" asked O'Leary gently.

"Not poisoned!" she cried. "He was shot. I know nothing of it!"

O'Leary glanced at her escort.

"Did either of you tell her?" he asked.

"No, sir."

"How did you know that Adolph Federie was— shot?" asked O'Leary, turning again to Mittie Frisling.

Her eyes darted desperately from me to March and on to Eustace. She ran a quick tongue over her ashen lips.

"I didn't know it," she denied wildly. "I—I heard people talking. In the hall, outside my room. I didn't want to come out. I wanted to stay there."

Isobel leaned forward and spoke for the first time. Her voice was studiously low but had a harsh note of strain in its husky depth. She had taken time before coming to the library to put on her make-up, and two orange-red spots of rouge showed on her whitened cheek bones and her lips were stiff with paste. "Mittie—Mittie!" she said in a voice that was half rebuking and half amusedly tolerant. "Don't let yourself become so excited. What is done is done and we can't help it. No one is trying to accuse you. You need not deny things so vigorously. Try to control yourself."

Mittie's colorless eyes flickered once and fastened hatefully on Isobel. Her face lost some of its terror and became spiteful.

"That's all very well for you," she cried, spitting out the words like an enraged cat. "You never cared for him. You quarreled all the time. You quarreled last night. *I heard you!* You hated him. You were glad to get rid of him." She turned to O'Leary, flinging out a plump, clammy-looking hand that shook rather horribly. "Search among her things for the revolver that shot Adolph!" She screamed, quite beside herself with rage and terror.

It seemed to me that the spots of color on Isobel's cheek bones stood out more distinctly and her mouth was a sharp red line. But she laughed and leaned back against the sofa. It was a tight, strained laugh, so bitter, so indefinably ugly, that little shivers started inside my elbows, and I stared at Isobel as if seeing her for the first time.

"Still suffering from jealousy, are you, Mittie?" she said, her voice still very low and harsh and dreadfully amused. "You always loved Adolph, didn't you? And hated me."

She paused, and in the dreadful hush the smile on her painted mouth vanished, and she sighed a sigh of pure weariness.

"Good Lord," she said unexpectedly. "I wish you had had him!"

CHAPTER V

NO ALIBI

"ISOBEL!" cried March sharply, breaking the shocked silence. "He was your husband. And he's dead."

Isobel lifted her beautifully curved shoulders in a shrug.

"Yes. He was my husband. And he's dead. Give me another cigarette, Eustace, please." She lighted the cigarette with steady fingers, the jewels on them glittering maliciously. She took a deliberate puff or two, then looked straight at Mittie Frisling. "He's dead," she repeated, her voice lower than ever and somehow cruel and deadly in its soft cadences. "He's dead, and I only hope he suffered what he deserved to suffer."

"Isobel!" cried March again.

"Isobel! Stop that!" said Eustace in a curiously tight voice, laying a hand over one of Isobel's and pressing it until the rings must have cut into her flesh, although Isobel did not wince.

"Hear her! Hear her!" squealed Mittie. "I told you so! She did it! She shot him! Why don't you arrest her? Put handcuffs on her?" Her voice was rising with every word and her fat hands shaking, and all at once she began to sob—horrible high-pitched sobs that rang through the room, echoing from every corner in queer spasmodic gasps.

Well, I simply couldn't stand it. It made gooseflesh

come out on my arms and my knees began to shake and a quaky feeling came into the pit of my stomach.

In one motion I reached her, seized her bulging shoulders in my hands, and shook. In my agitation I may have shaken a little harder than I intended, for her teeth clicked together furiously, and I think she bit her tongue. At any rate, she suddenly gave a short, sharp yelp, almost strangled on a sob, and an expression of acute pain came into her face.

"Let me alone," she cried indistinctly, clutching at one side of her jaw. "You've nearly killed me."

Her voice wavered upward again, and I gave a last shake for good measure.

"Don't be a fool," I said. "Can't you see that we are all just on the verge of hysterics? We've had a harrowing experience. We are worn and tired and holding onto decent self-control with all our might. It's all we can do to keep from screaming and yelling and carrying on as you are doing. But we've got to be quiet. Why, we'd all be gibbering idiots by night if we would let ourselves go!"

In involuntary emphasis I strengthened my grip on her shoulders, and she must have thought I was about to shake again, for she turned an agonized countenance toward O'Leary.

"Take her off!" she cried, holding her jaw. "I've bitten my tongue in two already."

"She'll be all right now, Miss Keate," said Lance O'Leary to me, and as I resumed my seat he gave me a look in which there was just a spark of laughter and a good measure of respect. And I don't mind saying that when I do anything I do it thoroughly.

"Now, Mr. Eustace Federie," went on O'Leary quietly. "Let's hear your account of the night's tragedy. You say you were in the library reading when you heard the sound of the shot?"

It was strange how O'Leary's tranquil voice put a period to the tumult of ugly emotions that had been surging about us. I took a long breath and adjusted my cap, which had fallen over one ear, and March leaned back against the divan with a little sigh. But her hands kept twisting themselves in her lap.

"Yes," replied Eustace.

"You had not gone to bed at all?"

"No," said Eustace easily. "I am a poor sleeper and often read late."

"When did you last see Adolph Federie—alive?"

Eustace paused, frowning a little as if to recall exactly all the events of the night.

"About eleven o'clock, I think. After dinner we all, save the nurse and Grandfather, of course—sat here in the library until ten o'clock or so. One by one we drifted upstairs. Isobel was the first to go. Close to eleven I went into Grandfather's room. Miss Keate was there, of course, and my cousin March. March and I walked upstairs together, and she went to her room. I took off my dinner jacket and put on a lounge coat, got my pipe, and returned to the library. As I was coming downstairs I met Uncle Adolph. He said good-night and went on upstairs. And that is the last time I saw him—alive."

"You went at once to the library?"

"Yes. And settled down with a book. I read on and on and did not realize that it was getting late—for

Federie house. I was thinking of going to bed, though, and was just finishing a chapter when I heard a sound —a sort of reverberating crash. It seemed to come from the other end of the house. I did not at once identify it as being a revolver shot. But as I listened I heard screams. I dropped my book and hurried out of the library into the hall. My cousin"—his suave glance indicated March—"was just running down the stairs. I lighted candles and we hurried to the tower room."

He stopped and folded his arms composedly.

"Were you surprised to find that your uncle had been shot?" inquired O'Leary in an abstracted manner.

"Murder must always be a surprise," said Eustace smoothly. "A surprise—at least."

"About how long a time elapsed between the sound of the shot and your entrance into the hall?"

It had seemed to me that Eustace's recital of events had been a little too pat, a little circumstantial, and I listened with some interest for his reply.

"Not long," he said calmly. "It is hard to say, though. Possibly two minutes after I heard the shot Miss Keate screamed. I went directly into the hall, then. Oh, it might have been three minutes. It is hard to say exactly."

"And you say that you did not identify the sound you heard as being a revolver shot?"

"Not at once. No. Of course, I was not expecting anything like that."

Lance O'Leary glanced about the large room with its heavily padded carpets and its doorway muffled in heavy velvet.

"About where were you sitting, Mr. Federie?"

Eustace's quick dark gaze went swiftly about the chairs and massive divans. One chair stood not far from us, with a book, opened face downward, across one upholstered arm. I may have imagined that a glimmer of satisfaction lighted his eyes as, without a word, he motioned toward that chair.

"There?" said O'Leary. He rose, approached the chair, and appeared to measure with his eyes the distance from the chair to the doorway. Eustace watched him narrowly through the cloud of cigarette smoke that almost obscured his gleaming dark eyes.

But at once O'Leary returned to his former position, and without another word he turned to March.

"Miss Federie, will you be so good as to tell me just when you last saw your uncle? I know that you have been through a trying ordeal," he added. "But if you will make the effort——"

"Thank you," said March steadily. "I am quite all right. I last saw my uncle alive at about eleven o'clock last night. At that time I went upstairs to my own room, came down again and went to Grandfather's room to see if the nurse wanted anything. Uncle Adolph was in this room when I left it and I did not see him again until—until—" her voice broke abruptly but she went on—"until after he was shot."

"Did you hear the sound of the shot distinctly?"

She hesitated.

"Y-yes. That is I heard the sound but didn't know what it was. I was in the lower hall just at the foot of the stairs——"

Eustace broke in.

"You mean that you were in the upper hall at the

head of the stairs, March. You must have been there when you heard the shot. You were just running downstairs when I came into the hall and met you." He spoke with the utmost ease, rather lazily, in fac), but his eyes were very intent on March's face.

Her black eyebrows drew themselves together and she bent a slow regard upon her cousin that was in no way friendly. Then she met O'Leary's clear gray gaze directly and spoke with just a tinge of defiance.

"I was just at the bottom of the stairway out there in the hall when I heard the shot. It—frightened me a little, and I just stood there listening for—possibly two minutes. Then I heard someone screaming. Then Eustace was in the hall. He gave me a candle and we ran to Grandfather's room."

"Did you see your cousin come into the hall?"

"Why—no. That is, the light was dim, you know— the night light that is left burning there in the hall— and I was listening, thinking of nothing else but those screams. I supposed he came from the library."

"But you didn't actually see him enter the hall?" persisted O'Leary.

"No," said March flatly and without any visible compunction.

"What do you mean, O'Leary?" asked Eustace unpleasantly. "Do you mean to doubt my word?"

"This is my business, Mr. Federie. I have to pursue it in my own fashion. You had been on the first floor, then, Miss March?"

A flare of crimson came into March's soft white cheeks and at once subsided.

"I had," she admitted, and added as though against

her will: "I was—troubled about something. I couldn't sleep. I came downstairs to—to get a glass of milk. But at the dining-room door I—changed my mind and decided to go back to my room and go to sleep. You know the rest."

"Why were you—troubled?" asked O'Leary gently.

I felt the child's muscles stiffen and even her lips were white.

"I don't—" the words were only a hoarse whisper, and she pressed her hand to her slim white throat and tried again—"I don't know. That is—I was troubled about—about Grandfather."

Lance O'Leary looked at her thoughtfully, and even to me it was obvious that her incoherent reply held a terror that the question had not warranted. Perhaps he decided the matter would keep until he could talk to her alone; perhaps from very humanity he forbore to harry the child further. At any rate, he went on coolly.

"About what time was that?"

"When I heard the shot? It must have been after two—about half-past two, I believe."

"What is your opinion as to that?" O'Leary turned to Eustace.

"It was probably about two-thirty," agreed Eustace lightly. He seemed in no way disturbed by March's direct repudiation of the one item in his own story. "I can't be sure, however."

"And you, Mr. Lonergan? What time would you say it was?"

"I haven't the least idea," growled young Lonergan. "I tell you I was asleep."

"Miss Keate?"

"It must have been close to two-thirty," I said. "At least, after we had talked a little and sent for the police, I looked at my watch and it was not quite three o'clock. I think that finding the body and rousing the house and all must have taken about half an hour."

He nodded, and having given March a breathing space returned to her.

"Just one more thing, Miss March; within half an hour after you discovered that Adolph Federie was dead, some errand took you out of the house. What was that errand?" He spoke in a voice that was even milder than usual, but March's eyes widened and grew dark, and I felt Kema looking at me reproachfully.

"Why, yes," replied March in a small, stifled tone. "Yes. I—I remembered that Konrad—that's the dog—was unchained. The policemen were on the way and Konrad is savage with strangers. I went to—to chain him."

"I see," said O'Leary gently. "And did you succeed in—chaining up the dog?"

"No," said March. She looked hunted. "No. He—I couldn't—make him come to me."

"You were wearing black satin bedroom slippers?"

"Yes."

"Were there red feather ornaments on the toes of those slippers?"

"Why—y-yes. Yes, there were."

"You lost one of the ornaments. *Do you know where you lost it?*" The last words were unwontedly sharp.

A quick wave of fear stilled the girl's face and gave a
pinched, blue look to her mouth and nostrils.

"No—no. I don't know," she said in a half whisper.

Lance O'Leary said nothing for a long moment or
two, letting his eyes rest contemplatively on the girl's
white face in the meanwhile. Then he seemed to de-
cide whatever question he had been silently considering.

"Thank you, Miss March," he said briskly. "Mrs.
Federie, if you don't feel equal to the strain of answer-
ing a few questions I can wait, but it will oblige me
immensely if——"

Isobel brushed away O'Leary's cool gesture of courtesy. She was leaning indolently against the red plush
back of the sofa, apparently quite relaxed and at
ease, but her hands lay at her sides in what seemed to
me a too deliberate repose.

"I understand perfectly," she said in that throaty,
low voice that was somehow unmusical and colorless.
"Ask me anything you like. You want to know at what
time I last saw Adolph? About twelve, I think. We
have been sharing his rooms in the back wing of the
house—he has three rooms up there, bedroom, sitting
room, and bath." She motioned toward the back of the
house. "I had gone to bed early and was reading myself
to sleep. He came in and we talked for about half an
hour. Then he went back to the sitting room. I blew
out the lamp and went to sleep. I supposed he had
gone to sleep on the daybed in the sitting room. I did
not awaken until I heard someone screaming. I supposed old Mr. Federie had died. I knew I could do
nothing, so I did not go down to the tower room for

about half an hour. Then—when I did go down, Eustace told me." Her voice was marvelously steady; clearly Isobel had capacities that would bear investigation.

"You did not hear the sound of the shot, then?" Isobel considered the question gravely, and her reply, when it came, sounded truthful.

"No. I was already awake. Had been for a moment or two when I heard Miss Keate scream, so the sound may have awakened me, although I was not conscious of it. A scream would have a piercing quality, while a heavier, duller sound would not penetrate far through these thick old walls and heavy doors."

O'Leary nodded, and I felt a queer respect for Isobel growing within me. While there was nothing about the woman that attracted me, still she was no fool. The quiet, grave way in which she was speaking would go a long way with a jury.

A jury! I caught myself up quickly, resolving to keep a tighter hold on my suspicions, and turned my attention back to O'Leary.

"You will pardon the inquiry, Mrs. Federie, but— were you and your husband on the best of terms?"

"No," said Isobel calmly. She must have expected some such question.

"Were there any particular matters of dissension?" Isobel did hesitate here and took a quick breath. But:

"No. We were simply mismated. And Adolph never had enough money."

"Was he cruel to you?" said O'Leary softly, but with a fine edge to his quietly uttered words.

Isobel's reddish-brown eyes narrowed between her blackened lashes.

"It depends upon what you mean by cruelty," she said evenly. "If you mean did he thwart every desire I had, did he deny me any pleasures or interests of activities such as normal women have, did he drag me from one gambling rendezvous to another, did he humiliate me in every possible way—if you mean that, yes, he was cruel. Wickedly cruel. But if you mean did he beat me —abuse me—no." She paused and added in a measured deliberation: "He was afraid to touch me."

It was not nice to sit there and hear her saying such things in that calm, unmoved way, of her husband so recently and dreadfully dead. I think if her voice had trembled or broken or given any evidence of emotion it might not have sounded so ugly. But, as it was, her even, low tones going on and on so deliberately made my flesh crawl.

March at my side was whispering, "Isobel, Isobel," but no one heard her save myself, and I think she did not know she was speaking. Eustace stretched out a hand to Isobel and withdrew it without touching her. Grondal coughed, and Mittie Frisling sprang suddenly to her feet, and I was never sure just what happened in the space of a few seconds, during which Mittie's and Isobel's voices rose suddenly. There was a sound of tearing silk, a smart slap, a shriek from Mittie, and then Eustace was thrusting Mittie back into her chair, and Isobel was leaning forward, her eyes like smoldering red coals and her lips drawn back from her teeth. The thin sleeve of the frock she wore had been torn from shoulder to wrist, exposing what might have been a lovely arm, but was now disfigured with purplish bruises between the elbow and shoulder.

"Look at that!" shrieked Mittie Frisling. A red blotch on her sallow cheek showed where Isobel's fingers had struck, but Mittie seemed unconscious of it. "Look! They fought last night. She wouldn't tell you. But I heard them. He struck her, and she said she'd be even with him."

"And I shan't forget what I owe you, Mittie," said Isobel, her low voice deliberately venomous.

"Ladies—ladies——" said the chief helplessly; he had advanced to O'Leary's side.

"Isobel—careful," said Eustace in a warning way. With a gentler manner than I had credited him with he drew the torn edges of thin silk together so that the ugly-looking arm was covered, though now that I knew the bruises were there I could trace their dark outline through the flimsy material.

Dimuck from his chair was muttering, "Never in my life! Never in my life!" Deke Lonergan was staring distastefully at Mittie, and March, her horrified eyes fixed on Isobel, was gripping my hand.

Lance O'Leary alone was unmoved.

"You have all been under a great nervous strain," he said briefly, and as if Mittie's actions were quite customary under such circumstances. "Just a few more questions, please. Mr. Dimuck, will you tell me your story of the night?"

"Certainly. Certainly. I was awakened by the sound of the shot. I rose at once, put on my bathrobe, and came downstairs. I was delayed, owing to having to light a candle in my room, before venturing down the stairs. In the meantime I heard screams coming from the tower room. When I reached that room Eustace and Miss March, the nurse and Mr. Lonergan were all clustered about Adolph on the little tower stairway. It is dreadful—dreadful! Never in all my——"

"I believe you told me you were an old friend of Mr. Federie's?"

"Yes, yes. And in a sense, his business adviser. That is, he occasionally makes use of my advice as to market conditions. Yes, we are old friends."

"How is it that you are here now?"

"Mr. Federie asked me to come, just before his illness. When I arrived he was unable to talk to me. I have been waiting until he could speak. I don't know what he wished to see me about in particular, of course. Now that this highly unfortunate——"

"He wrote to you? May I see the letter, please?"

"Certainly. Certainly. It's upstairs, I think, in my bag. Or——" he was feeling with nimble precision into his pockets. "No, here it is. Just a brief message, you see."

O'Leary took the letter, glanced through it, and read it aloud as if to himself: "Dear Dimuck: Will you come down here within the next few days? Adolph is here. Yours, Jonas Federie."

"'Adolph is here,'" he repeated slowly. "Thank you, Mr. Dimuck." He returned the letter. "Can you tell us something of Adolph Federie? What was his—er—business?"

"He—" Mr. Dimuck cast a deprecating look toward

Isobel—"he had no business or profession. None that I know of, at least. I'm afraid I can tell you very little about him. He has not been here much in the last few years. However, I may say that it was my impression that he came home this time because—well, because he wanted money."

"He did," broke in Isobel coolly. "He always wanted money. This time he hoped to get some from his father. He was very much annoyed by his father's being ill."

Annoyed! Was it cleverness on Isobel's part, or was it honesty that was making Adolph Federie more despicable with every word she uttered?

Elihu Dimuck cleared his throat importantly; the big chair in which he was sitting combined with his heavy eyeglasses and faintly shocked manner to give him a magisterial air.

"Yes," he went on, quite as if Isobel had not spoken. "It was my impression that Adolph wanted money. Needed it rather desperately, perhaps. Poor fellow! Never happened before in all my——"

"Why was that your impression?"

The abrupt question seemed to discompose Mr. Dimuck. He rubbed his nose agitatedly and gave O'Leary a peevish look through the thick lenses of his eyeglasses.

"One thing and another. One thing and another."

"I've already told you——" began Isobel.

"Such as what?" prodded O'Leary, paying no attention to Isobel.

"Well, it is hard to say. His father's letter to me gave that impression. And I'm afraid Adolph seldom came home unless he did need money." Elihu Dimuck glanced at Isobel, who nodded in a horribly matter-of-fact way. "I—it is not becoming to speak ill of the dead, but I—I fear Adolph did not lead the life he should have led." He looked at Isobel again as if in apology.

"Don't mind me," she said. "The things he did were not—becoming, either." There was a cruel little sneer in her tone as she used Dimuck's word.

"Mr. Dimuck is quite right," said March suddenly to O'Leary in a frozen little voice. "Uncle Adolph did not lead quite 'the life he should have led.'" She appeared to quote Dimuck's phrase with a kind of delicate distaste. "Also Uncle Adolph always wanted money. He tried to borrow of me no longer ago than—last night," she concluded with a cold scorn that was not pleasant, coming right on the heels of the man's terrible death.

"Did he say anything of the reasons for his need?" inquired O'Leary.

"No. I refused him as I have—at other times."

Eustace tossed his cigarette violently toward the fireplace; it fell on the hearth and Deke Lonergan pushed it into the fire with his foot.

"Don't you think we have aired the family's dirty linen enough now, March?" said Eustace cuttingly.

March's face flared into anger at once, and Elihu Dimuck held up a pink hand.

"These things are deplorable—deplorable, but this is not the time to conceal any matters that should be brought before this gentleman. This is a terrible thing, yes, a terrible thing——"

March interrupted him.

"Adolph Federie was not a member of the family to be proud of," she said distinctly, her stormy blue eyes going from Eustace to O'Leary and back again. "He was weak, easily led, drank too much—gambled too much—" she paused as if to add significance to her last words, as she repeated them—"gambled too much. But he was his own worst enemy. I know of no one who could wish to—to kill——" She stopped suddenly as if at an unpleasant recollection and left her sentence hanging unfinished in the air.

"What is your theory—your explanation of his murder, then?" asked O'Leary.

Her air of stormy defiance had inexplicably collapsed.

"I don't know," she said. "I don't know."

"So you and Adolph Federie were not on good terms?"

"No!" she cried very distinctly. "I—hated him!" And as Eustace sprang to his feet at that with a violent gesture and, reaching her, stretched out his slender hand to grasp her shoulder, she twisted away from him, crying: "And so did you, Eustace! You know you did! You hated him, too!"

And in the curious hush that followed Isobel laughed!

It was a laugh of malicious, insolent, indecent amusement that, coming from the woman who had been Adolph's wife, actually made me shiver. Then Kema padded softly from the background and placed a wide, dark hand on Eustace's arm. His face, dark and furiously flushed, turned toward her and his hand dropped to his side.

"You quarrel," said Kema. "And there is death in the house." She was unexcited, rather detached and stolid. "Let him rest."

Eustace drew away from her and laughed gratingly.

"All right, Kema. Anything more, Mr.—Detective?"

O'Leary removed his clear gaze from the pencil stub that had apparently held it during the strange little contretemps.

"Why, yes—a number of things. You were surprised, of course, to find that Adolph Federie had been killed, Mr. Dimuck?"

Elihu Dimuck brought his fat pink hands together sharply.

"I was horrified! Horrified! Shocked beyond measure!"

"And you, Grondal." O'Leary turned briskly to the man. "What awakened you?"

"The bell, sir. I thought it might be that Mr. Federie had died." The man's face was as unprepossessing as ever, but his manner left nothing to be desired.

"Where do you sleep?"

"In the back of the L, sir, upstairs."

"That room in the southeast corner?"

"Yes, sir."

"Did you come down by way of the front stairs?"

"No, sir. There's a flight of stairs for the servants' use that leads to the back entry, there back of the kitchen—but doubtless you know where it is. I came down by that stairway."

"And you saw or heard nothing unusual on the way?"

"No, sir, nothing," said Grondal, very positively and promptly. A shade too promptly. I had an extraordinary feeling that he had expected the question and had prepared his very definite answer. But, of course, every one of us must have expected detailed inquiry.

"Then you went directly to the sick room?"

"Yes, sir. I only stopped in the kitchen to light a lamp."

"Then you found your way along the back hall, upstairs, and down the back stairway without a light?"

"Why, yes, sir. I know this house like the palm of my own hand. But I thought an extra light might be needed in the sick room. You may have noticed that we do not have electrics."

"Yes," agreed O'Leary somewhat grimly. "I have noticed that."

"Yes, sir," said Grondal imperturbably. "While I was lighting the lamp Kema came into the kitchen. The bell connects in her room, too."

"I see." O'Leary's eyes went to Kema. She was standing at March's side, the folds of gray gingham hanging meekly, her wide hands on her hips—or where I supposed her hips to be—and her incurious yellow eyes on O'Leary.

"Did the bell arouse you?" he asked her.

"Yes. I was asleep. I heard the bell. I thought Mr. Federie was worse. I went downstairs and to the tower room. By the time I got there they were all standing around Mr. Adolph. He was on the stairway. I stayed there and watched them." The gold hoops at her ears caught light for a second. She spoke in an emotionless way that was almost unconcern.

"Were you shocked to find that murder had been done?"

She moved her vast shoulders in a kind of shrug.

"Yes. But death comes. What matter how?" Her

hands moved in a slight upward gesture that oddly con-
veyed a hint of the serene fatalism of the old, those
whose eyes have seen much coming for the brief little
space of man's life and much going into that immeasur-
able, incalculable realm of infinity.

Impressed in spite of myself, I twisted uneasily, and
the little crisp rustle of my starched uniform brought
me back to practicality. A man's life *was* important;
it was at the very height of our finite scale of values.
And at the other end of that silent house a man's life
had been taken.

"Then you know nothing of it?" came O'Leary's
voice with a sharper edge than was its custom.

"I? No," replied Kema impassively.

O'Leary studied the dark, secretive face for a long
moment, then he took out a slim platinum watch,
glanced at it, replaced it in his pocket, and looked
about as if mentally checking up the members of the
household.

"Now, Miss Frisling, may we have your story?"

"My *story!*" gulped Mittie Frisling. She had been
extraordinarily quiet since her last bout with Isobel.
The red streaks on her cheek still showed and her colorless eyes had taken on a brooding look, but with
O'Leary's request terror licked once more across her
face.

"You are a guest here?"

"Why, I—not exactly. That is, yes."

"You mean you are a guest, or are not?"

"I—I am." She brought out the reply hurriedly, with
an uncertain side glance toward March, whose eyes
were severe.

"Miss Federie's guest, are you?" inquired O'Leary with bland persistence.

"No," fluttered Mittie. "No. I——" She stuck momentarily, and O'Leary waited with an air of politeness that did not disguise to my mind his interest in knowing just why the question of Mittie Frisling's status in the house should agitate her so markedly.

"I was here when she came home," said Mittie, who, I was to discover, always found silence unendurable. "I was already here." She stuck again, twisting her pudgy hands in the bedraggled fringes of her kimono. Grondal coughed suddenly; the scar on his face was a dull red and he was staring fixedly at Mittie. She moistened her pale lips, shot him a helpless look, smoothed her kimono over her fat knees, swept us all with those light eyes, and burst into hurried, breathless words.

"I came on business. I came to see old Mr. Federie. He can't talk. He is sick. They've been telling me he can't talk for days. I am waiting for him to be better. I haven't done anything. Why do you question me? I know nothing of this. I was asleep when they knocked at the door of my bedroom. Before daylight, it was." She paused to take a panting breath. "I wouldn't answer."

"Why would you not answer, Miss Frisling?"

"Because I——" her eyes darted quick glances like the eyes of a hunted animal—"because I—was afraid."

"Why should you be afraid? You say you knew nothing of the trouble. Did you know Adolph Federie had been murdered?" His easy voice changed suddenly, becoming crisp and cold.

She flung both hands before her face and pressed her whole body backward against the chair. Her face was a sickly yellow and her lips like dead ashes.

"No. No. But I—I heard them talking outside the door."

"Did you hear the sound of the shot?"

"*No!*"

"Did you hear Miss Keate scream?"

"*No!*"

"How did you know Adolph Federie was shot?"

"I—I tell you, I heard them talking in the hall."

"What time did you retire to your room?"

"About—eleven, I think."

"You said that you overheard Adolph Federie and his—wife—quarreling. Was that true?"

"Yes. Yes. That is—I——"

"Where were you at the time?"

"I was going down to the kitchen to get some hot water for my hot-water bag—my room is as cold as a barn," she interpolated with another side glance at March. "I passed their door. I heard them; their voices were loud and angry. I—couldn't help hearing them."

"Did you hear what they said?"

Isobel leaned forward suddenly, fixing her hazy eyes upon Mittie.

"Yes, Mittie," she said silkily. "Do tell us what you heard."

"I heard you cry out when he struck you," said Mittie vindictively.

Isobel's features sharpened, but she smiled.

"But *words*, Mittie. Words that will interest the police. Can't you think up something more lurid? If you didn't hear anything, why, make up something! Didn't you have your ear at the keyhole?"

"Isobel!" said Eustace again in a warning tone.

"I—well—I knew from the sound of the voices that they were quarreling. And I heard Isobel cry out when he struck her, and Adolph laughed. And then—" Mittie ceased to mumble and her light eyes fastened themselves in ugly triumph upon Isobel—"and then I *did* hear words. I heard Isobel say—" she paused and leaned forward, her voice sinking to an ugly, strained whisper— "'*I'll kill you for this!*' And she did."

There was a strange silence. Then Isobel laughed again, though her wide hands had gripped together as if she thought they were on Mittie's fat throat.

"Oh, Mittie, Mittie, can't you do better than that! That is too apt. You must be subtle, my dear. Subtle!" But the dabs of rouge on the woman's cheek bones stood out with hideous clearness.

"I did hear it. I can swear to it. That's what she said." She stopped to catch her breath, spent with the vehemence of her jerky sentences, and lifted both shaking hands to push the strings of hair from her face.

For a long moment no one spoke. The room had grown cold while we sat there. The fire had smoldered itself out, and the damp, mildewy smell that hung over the whole place, penetrating even the layers of dust that clung to the heavy curtains and carpets, seemed to rise more distinctly, permeating the very air we breathed. The dreary daylight came in reluctant gray streaks through the narrow windows. Our faces were without exception drawn and haggard and fearfully tired looking.

It seemed to me that I had lived in that house for years; that I was an intimate of the thick old walls and strange, yet curiously familiar, household.

Lance O'Leary's voice, when it came, had an edge of cold mercilessness; it was one of the rare occasions when he cast aside his mask of easy good humor, and one caught a glimpse of the relentless spirit that lay below it.

"Some one of you is lying," he said quite deliberately. "One of you shot Adolph Federie. This house was locked up like a vault. There was a man-killing dog guarding the place. I can see no possibility of an outsider making his way into the place, undetected, shooting a man—with apparently no purpose—and getting away without being seen. It lies among you." He paused. The faces before me look ghastlier. Mittie Frisling clutched at the arms of her chair and her lower jaw fell, but no one else moved. I knew what they felt, for even I, who knew myself to be innocent, felt exactly as if a hand had gripped my heart and was slowly and relentlessly pressing upon it. And if I felt that, what did that one feel who had a terrible secret hidden in his heart?

"You understand, of course, that this is only the beginning of the inquiry. I must ask you all to remain in the house until I permit you to leave. Unless, of course, you prefer to have warrants sworn out against you. Can we do that, chief, if necessary?"

I think the chief had not expected the abrupt question, for he started and had to shift an enormous mouthful of chewing gum before he could stammer:

"S-sure!"

"The inquest will be held to-morrow morning," went on O'Leary crisply. "We shall leave a small police guard about the place to attend to certain duties, so you need not be ill at ease." He placed the shabby little pencil in his pocket very carefully and turned away. I was one of the first to rise and start toward the hall. As I reached the door I turned for a glance backward. Deke Lonergan was leaning over March, talking to her. Isobel sat without moving, staring at the carpet, a cigarette poised in her hand. Mittie had risen and was following me, taking short, hasty steps. Elihu Dimuck was getting fussily out of the large chair and kicking his feet a little to shake down his wrinkled trousers. Grondal was stirring the fire, and Kema had not moved. Then Eustace approached March; he was frowning and interrupted Lonergan, and I turned again and crossed the hall. Lance O'Leary was talking in a low voice to the chief of police, and as I passed he called to me:

"Miss Keate, I'll want to see you sometime to-day. You'll be here, of course?"

"Yes. I'll rest during the afternoon. Mr. O'Leary, if that murder was done by one of the people right here in the house and going to stay here, I—well, I want to leave. Why, there are only eight of them, nine including me—and I can't believe that one of them would—*murder !*"

"You've forgotten your patient," said O'Leary gravely. "He makes ten. And as for you, Miss Keate—" a faint smile flickered in his gray eyes—"as for you, wild horses couldn't drag you away, and you know it! By the way," he added as if at an afterthought; "did you notice a peculiar thing about this affair? Usually the people implicated in murder all have alibis—or at least some of them. And in this business there is not a single alibi. No alibis," he repeated soberlv. "It should be an interesting case."

And he was perfectly right; it was interesting enough, in all conscience, but not the kind of entertainment I like. Indeed, there were moments in the dark days, upon which Adolph Federie's death launched us, when I had serious doubts as to the chance of ever again being in a position to be entertained by anything in the world!

CHAPTER VI

THE rest of the day passed quietly enough but very slowly, and the horror that had come upon Federie house during the night still lingered about the hushed old walls. If I had had my way I should have yanked down every curtain in the house and thrown the whole batch of them outdoors, for every time I passed a window or a curtained doorway I had an absurd but hideous feeling that hands might reach out from those heavy drapes. And once when a draft from somewhere billowed the green curtain over the tower-room doorway I caught myself on the verge of screaming.

The whole household showed a tendency to linger about the library, but so far as I knew they spoke little, picked up books and laid them down, looked out the windows, moved from one chair to another, and all the time eyed each other covertly. March wrote a few notes, Eustace sent a telegram or two to distant members of the family, Mittie worked on a beaded bag, raising her eyes every little while to send Isobel quick, furtive glances like a cat with a mouse, and Isobel brooded gracefully and did nothing. I should have thought that after a night that had drained us all of vitality they would have rested and tried to sleep. But no one did. Probably they felt the same need for company that I felt.

Somewhat to my dismay Genevieve appeared to have taken a liking to me and he followed me closely all day, sitting on the mantel in the tower room while I worked over my patient, watching me with inscrutable eyes whenever I picked up my knitting, and following on my heels every time an errand took me to another part of the house. I have never mistreated an animal and never shall, but I don't mind admitting that Genevieve's continual presence aroused brutal thoughts within me. Once, indeed, as he was sitting at my feet, following the progress of my long needles interestedly, the thought occurred to me that a quick and well-placed thrust with the toe of my shoe would be a pleasant diversion. But the thought had no sooner entered my head than Genevieve got up on his four gaunt legs, moved about three feet away, just out of reach, and sat down again, eying me reproachfully.

Considering the number of kittens that are placed in sacks and drowned, it seemed to me, then, and does yet, somewhat unnecessary that Genevieve had escaped an early fate.

Several times the doorbell jingled, and I think the callers were reporters, for no one got into the house, and once I entered the hall just as Grondal was closing the door. Through the window I saw a gentleman with a camera over his shoulder retreating toward the gate and even his back had a look of discomfiture. But somehow they got together a story, probably with the help of the police, for when the doctor came, shortly after a strained and silent lunch (during which the only words uttered constituted a timid request on the part of Mr. Dimuck for someone to please pass the salt) he carried an extra in his pocket, that B——'s more enterprising newspaper had got out, with the ink still blurry on it. The doctor was inclined to be a little pettish as to my failure to telephone to him and explain matters.

"But my patient was all right," I said. "There was no need to call you."

"Patient all right! Good Lord! A murder committed right in the sick room, and the woman tells me that there was no need to call me. Besides, it must have been exciting."

"It was not," I said decidedly with an involuntary glance toward the tower stairway. He followed my eyes.

"Was that the place?" he asked with the liveliest interest, and was starting toward it when March pulled the curtain aside and paused in the doorway. She still wore the straight little frock of crimson wool; it had soft white silk cuffs and collar. Her hair lay in dark, misty waves over her head, with short little curls here and there; there were faint purple shadows under her eyes, but her chin was steady and firm and her gaze darkly blue.

"Good-morning, Doctor," she said gravely. "Grondal told me you had come. I am March Federie. Is Grandfather better?"

The young doctor gave her one long look.

"He will be better," he assured her. "We are doing our best for him."

"Thank you, Doctor. I—I am very anxious."

Her voice shook a little and Dr. Jay took her slim wrist for a moment in his practised hand, released it, and turned to his bag.

"Give her these two capsules in warm water, Miss Keate, and send her to bed."

"Oh, no! Not upstairs! Alone!" cried March, off the guard that she had so carefully maintained.

"Of course not," agreed the doctor soothingly. "Right over there on that couch. Miss Keate will be here in the room." He nodded toward the roomy old couch in the corner of the room, caught my eye, and flushed a little. "You can take your hours off just the same, Miss Keate. Can't you sleep right here in this fine big chair?"

Which only goes to show what blue eyes and youth do to an otherwise sensible man. Hours off, indeed! Right in the sick room!

"Very well," said March. "I'll just speak to Kema and be back."

As the curtain fell into place the doctor sighed.

"So that is March Federie," he said. "Well," he added somewhat wistfully, "I'm a married man, myself. Good-afternoon, Miss Keate. If anything more happens be sure to telephone to me."

"If anything more happens I shan't be here," I said firmly. "Good-afternoon, Doctor."

Thus it was that I spent the entire afternoon in the sick room, dozing occasionally, but for the most part lying back in the big chair, staring at the moisture that dripped down the windowpanes and trying to keep my thoughts from going over and over every detail of the ugly situation in which I found myself. I had pulled the old couch out from its corner, and March lay on it, quietly asleep, her slim figure childishly relaxed on the humpy green plush. The couch looked to be rather comfortable, and I resolved to try it myself later on. But I did not. In fact, I never did lie on that couch, and there was a good and sufficient reason for it. Grondal hovered about the tower room almost all the afternoon. I don't know whether it was devotion to our welfare or curiosity that kept him so constantly about, but, whatever his motive, hardly a quarter of an hour passed without his tiptoeing into the room, peering anxiously about, and stirring the fire or adjusting the window. Twice he awakened me out of a cat's nap and he looked shamefaced, and rightly, both times.

There was not a sound from the other rooms until about six o'clock. An early dusk had fallen, dark and cold and desolate. The shadows in the corners and around the bed curtains and up and down the tower stairway had gradually lengthened and darkened, and Grondal had just come into the room again, bearing, this time, two lighted lamps, when from the other end of the house, crashing through the dead silence, came suddenly a ripple of notes and then the eerie strains of music that I had heard Eustace playing the night before on the old piano.

March stirred at the sound, opened her eyes, and I reached for my cap and sat upright, yawning.

"For mercy's sake," I said. "What is that tune?"

March took a long breath.

"I've been asleep," she said drowsily. "Why, it's night."

"Six o'clock," I told her, and repeated my question: "What is that tune that Eustace is always playing?"

"I think it's called 'La Furiante'—I'm not sure. It's from some Bohemian composer. Eustace likes it."

"He has poor taste," I remarked with some acerbity. The thing was full of swift minors and shivering crescendos that made little chills run up and down my backbone. I like music, but I like a tune that *is* a tune, so to speak, and gets somewhere, and have never been much for these haunting moodish things that in their very perversity irritate me. Besides, there was something about the music coming from the other end of the house that, to my strained nerves, savored of menace and of evil triumphant.

"Don't be a fool," I said to myself, and did not know I had spoken aloud until March turned a startled face toward me. "Did you have a good sleep?" I inquired hurriedly.

She sat up slowly, swinging her slender knees around and passing a hand across her eyes.

"Y-yes," she said slowly, adding with a little shiver, "only I dreamed. Dreamed horribly." She stared down at the green plush of the couch. "Something about this couch."

I eyed the couch rather warily, but said in my most professionally cheerful voice:

"One usually feels uncomfortable under just a slight opiate. It's nearly dinner time, isn't it? I should like to get into a fresh uniform. Are you——" I hesitated, and she guessed my thought.

"Thanks for staying with me all afternoon," she said at once. "Go on to your room now, I'm perfectly all right. I'll stay here with Grandfather until you return. Don't hurry."

Eustace's playing grew louder as I approached the hall, but broke off suddenly, and I heard low voices from the library. I met no one on the stairs, and as I climbed their dim length I was struck with the fact that it had been only some twenty-four hours since I had entered Federie house. I seemed to have known the place all my life.

It took only a few moments to freshen myself and don a clean uniform and cap. As I left the bedroom I looked up and down the long green corridor. The longest portion of it stretched to my left, and I took a few steps along it, walking more briskly as I advanced. Here and there candles were placed along the wall, shielded by old-fashioned reflectors, and their tiny flames wavered feebly. About midway the corridor was bisected by another passage which led apparently along the back wing of the house. Its floor was the only uncarpeted floor, save that of the kitchen, in the whole house, so far as I knew, and stretched coldly narrow between a wall of dormer windows on the north and several closed doors on the south. I passed it by, however, and remained in the main corridor, for I wished to find the room that lay directly over the tower room. And I brought up suddenly before a wide door that extended clear across the corridor. It was a heavy old door made of some dark wood that gleamed dully in the faint light.

I studied it for a moment or two before I reached out and gingerly tried the knob. It turned, but the door was locked.

Had not O'Leary said that the key was gone? Perhaps it had simply dropped from the lock to the floor. It was an idle chance, but I bent over. Owing to the dimness of the light, I was obliged to get down on my knees and I was groping over the dusty carpet when a voice spoke suddenly over my shoulder.

"Lost something?"

It gave me a start, having heard no one approach; I twisted about on my knees.

"Y-yes," I said quite at random. "That is, I was looking for—for the back stairway."

"Well, you won't find it there." The figure turned so that the light fell on his face, and in the same instant I recognized O'Leary's voice. I rose, ignoring his offered hand, and brushed the dust from my white skirt.

"I suppose you were actually trying to get in that bedroom," he said severely; his voice was sober enough, but his eyes held just a flicker of amusement. "Well, it is still locked. And I wish I knew where the key is! By the way, Miss Keate, there is something on which I should like your opinion. Come this way."

A few steps back along the corridor and he flung open a door into a dark bedroom. At first I could see only a dim shape or two looming up in the little avenue of light that the opening of the door stretched through the room. Then there was a tiny click as O'Leary snapped the button of an electric torch he carried and the rays of light darted here and there under guidance from his hand. I saw a vast bed with a candlewick counterpane that was stiff with dust, an enormously tall wardrobe of a dark, varnished wood in the corner, a wide dresser with a marble top, a chair or two, an old washstand, faded red curtains, and heavy green carpet.

Lance O'Leary was bending over.

"Look here, Miss Keate." He turned the light at differing angles. "Have I got the light so you can see it?"

"See what?" I was bending, too, following his gaze along the carpet.

"The dust on the carpet. There's a perceptible layer of it and——"

"*Oh ! I see.*"

Quite distinct on the film of dust were small footprints. The heels had made sharp indentations at short intervals, and the rounded impression of the ball of the foot was fairly distinct, too. Beside the small footprints were other blurs, larger.

"The big ones are mine," said O'Leary explanatorily. "The point is, Miss Keate, the footprints lead to the corner behind the big wardrobe, turn, and come back to the door. And in the corner I found—this."

"This" was a small but very efficient-looking revolver, which he held just at the edge of his pocket so I could catch the wicked blue gleam of the thing, and then let slip back again out of sight.

"It looked as if it had just been tossed there and left. But whoever left it there, took pains to wipe the fingerprints from it before leaving it."

I returned in fascination to those small footprints, so faint, so perishable, traced there in dust—and yet so dreadfully permanent and lasting.

"They are——" I began, and stopped. If he had not noticed it, there was no need in calling it to his attention. But being neither blind nor a fool he had noticed it, of course.

"Yes," he said. "They are a woman's footprints."

My thoughts flew back to those slim satin mules March had worn.

"The trouble is, however," said Lance O'Leary very slowly, "two women in this house wear the size shoe that fits these marks. Mittie Frisling crowds her foot into a high-heeled slipper that exactly fits over these impressions. And Mrs. Isobel Federie wears the same size; her foot isn't crowded, but I can't tell from these faint impressions whether they were made by the crowded slippers or those that are not."

"You are sure it is one of the two?"

"Oh, no. I'm sure of nothing—right now. But I've matched these footprints exactly with some rather shabby black satin slippers from Miss Frisling's room, and also, worse luck, with a pair of black velvet pumps— with, by the way, quite gorgeous rhinestone buckles— from Madam Isobel's room. And there you are. Now, then, do you credit either of the two women with the psychology to—shoot straight?"

I had expected him to say "murder," and the ending of the question came as a little shock to me and put the problem in a different light. I could well believe, after the ugly little scene of the morning, that either of them might shoot, but as for shooting straight——

"No," I said. "I should be more inclined to believe it of Isobel than of Mittie. Isobel is more secretive; she suggests concealed depths. And yet—her behavior this morning when she came into the tower room and Eustace told her of Adolph's death was that of an innocent person. She appeared to be profoundly shocked—not grieved, perhaps, but sincerely shocked."

"That was your impression, was it?" O'Leary's gray

eyes, dark now in the dusk of the green corridor, were fastened on mine as if to penetrate and absorb every fleeting thought and impression I had experienced during the previous night. "You may be right. But—the stage lost an actress in Madam Isobel. Did you notice how she discounted Mittie's story of her threat to kill Adolph before Mittie had told it? And as to Mittie— well, a woman capable of shameless desperation is capable of almost anything."

"H'mm!" I said brusquely. "If Mittie ever made up her mind to shoot she would shoot six times without stopping and not a single bullet would hit it— mark."

"Still," said O'Leary dubiously, "there's a kind of feline craftiness and cunning about the woman. Well— I'll just close this door. The room is not in use; if it had been in use neither footprints nor revolver would have been there. Which strengthens my conviction that the murderer was one of the household, for who else would know that the room was unoccupied." He had closed the door, and we were walking slowly along the muffled corridor. "As to the revolver—one shot was fired from it and the bullet extracted from the body is of the same caliber. It's a small caliber, but deadly enough with careful aiming. It's possible that this revolver in my pocket is the one used to kill Adolph, you see—indeed, it is probable. And while, when I questioned them regarding it, both Mittie and Madam Isobel insisted that they were not near the bedroom back there, and knew nothing of any revolver—still—there are the foot- prints," he concluded enigmatically.

We had reached the uncarpeted passage that led

along the back wing of the house and I looked specu-
latively down it.

"Where are Adolph's rooms?" I asked.

"That door about midway down the hall leads into
his sitting room. The next door beyond it leads to a
small bedroom that adjoins the sitting room. A bathroom leads off the bedroom. It is one of those ridiculous,
stuffy suites that were considered very fine some fifty
years ago. Miss March's room is straight on down the
main corridor, past the stairway and in the southwest
corner of the house; it includes the second-story portion
of the southwest tower. Dimuck's room is directly
opposite Miss March's room. Miss Frisling's room is
next to Dimuck's, this way. Then comes the trunk room,
with a ladder and a trapdoor leading to the attic. Your
room is there to the right, of course, just opposite the
trunk-room door. Next to it is a bathroom and next
to that"—he motioned to a door about six feet back of
us—"is the room Eustace and Lonergan are using until
—until we find the key to their original bedroom."

"Find the key," I repeated. "Do you think the—the
murderer has that key? Why do you think the door was
locked at all?"

"To throw dust in our eyes, I suppose," said O'Leary.
"Or else because the murderer wanted to provide a
means of approach to the tower room. There—there—
don't be alarmed, Miss Keate. Let's go downstairs.
You are shivering, These old houses are like cold, damp
barns. And this business of candles and lamps is enough
to give anybody the creeps. Why on earth didn't they
install electricity? Look out for the steps. This candle is
about as illuminating as—as the footprints in the dust."

A figure in clinging dark lace rounded the corner by the newel post below us and started upward. It was Isobel, her hair catching pale red gleams and her face haggard and sallow in the dim light. She shot us a veiled look from those curiously clouded eyes and moved a little aside as we met and passed.

She said nothing, but I felt that she was intensely aware of our presence and of our being together. As I turned at the foot of the stairway I looked upward. Her figure, suave and graciously curved, was outlined against the small circle of light cast by the candle above. She was mounting the steps with the lovely erectness of shoulders and deliberate, smooth swaying of hips and back and arms that is a lost art in this young generation.

The same thought, or something like it, must have entered Lance O'Leary's mind, for he said in a musing way as we crossed the hall toward the drawing rooms: "She can't be more than—thirty-five, would you say? But she has the deliberate, studied charm of an older time. You feel that she would know how to manipulate a fan, for instance, or show off the most beautiful curves of her shoulders at a harp. It's just an atmosphere she carries, of course. As a matter of fact, she is likely an adept at poker, driving a motor car, and mixing a cocktail. Wonder why they didn't build more real doors downstairs! This is a queer old place; nothing but curtains over these doors—shutters—no decent lights—here we are."

I preceded him into the tower room.

March was still sitting there; I think her reverie had fallen into the events of the night past, for she turned too quickly as we entered, her face white and rigid and her fingers widespread and taut upon the arms of the chair. She murmered something, rose, and crossed swiftly to the door. It had the effect of an escape.

"She doesn't like my looks," said Lance O'Leary.

"Or possibly my conversation."

"Possibly your conversation," I agreed, going to the sickbed.

"Is Mr. Federie better?" asked O'Leary, watching me as I shook my thermometer vigorously before placing it between those distorted lips.

"I think there is some improvement."

"By the way, Miss Keate, did Adolph Federie wear a ring? From the mark left on his finger I should say it was a large ring with a heavy setting. Do you remember any such ring?"

Again the dubiously colored diamond winked at me from a soft clammy hand laid over mine.

"Yes. It was a diamond. Not a good stone, I think."

"It was not on his hand when I first viewed the body. Do you remember seeing it after he—was dead?"

I shivered. I would always be able to see again that huddled figure and clutching, outstretched fingers, but I could not recall the diamond's being on his hand.

"I can't be sure."

I began wringing out hot and cold packs, and Lance O'Leary watched me idly, talking in the meantime in a lightly conversational manner, as if he had just dropped in for tea.

"Well, so far as I can discover the people in this house are what they seem to be. Eustace and Deke Lonergan came down from O——, where Eustace maintains a law office of sorts, and Lonergan has some connection with the Dekesmith and Lonergan Construction Company, which is largely owned by his father, who lives here in B——; it is a small concern, but still it handles some good-sized contracts. Eustace, by all accounts, does more dabbling in music than business and spends quite a lot of money. March Federie has been visiting a connection of the family in the South— an elderly cousin who wired somewhat perfunctory condolences this morning and has offered March a home in case old Mr. Federie dies. Adolph and his wife were apparently wanderers from city to city, enjoyed life when they got hold of some money, and came home when they had none. He had none too savory a reputation, but there's nothing definite that I can unearth against him—at least nothing that would present a motive for his death."

"It looks to me as though there were motives enough right here in the house," I interjected.

He gave me an unseeing look and went on. I felt as if he was not talking to me so much as he was thinking aloud. I took dry towels from the stack on the shelf of the bedside table, shook them out, arranged them carefully to protect the sheets and pillows from the wet packs, pulled the covers straight, glanced at my watch, and took a seat near O'Leary.

"Then Mittie Frisling," he was saying. "She has been living for years in a rather stuffy apartment in the city with her father, of whom I can discover nothing save that his name was Matthew Frisling, that he was at one time a notary public, and for the last ten or fifteen years of his life he did nothing. They lived a very quiet, retired life. The father died recently, and Mittie picked up bag and baggage and moved out. Apparently she came here. Certainly she has been here for a number of weeks and had plenty of time to interview old Mr. Federie to her heart's content before he fell ill. Why she hangs around only she and, I suspect, Grondal can explain. Possibly Isobel knows; she seems to have known Mittie for some time. At any rate, here she is, and what claim she has on the Federies and what she hopes to accomplish I don't know—yet."

As he talked he had found a chair and settled himself in it, crossing his knees and leaning back rather wearily. The light from the table lamp in the center of the room fell mellowly upon him, casting his nose and fine mouth and well-cut chin into sharp relief, while the shade of the lamp made a shadow over the rest of his face so that I could see nothing of his eyes. I had not realized before how completely his gray eyes dominated his whole aspect. Seeing now just his mouth and chin and nose, and hearing his voice, gave me the most extraordinary feeling of listening to the voice of a kind of reasoning machine to which both Lance O'Leary and I were listening as audience.

In the little silence a log dropped suddenly in the ashes with a hissing sigh, and at the slight sound every nerve within me jumped. At once O'Leary turned, alert and keen.

"Have you had any rest this afternoon, Miss Keate?" he asked abruptly.

"Some. That is——" Briefly I explained the situation. I am not accustomed to people caring for my comfort, and it gave me the strangest little feeling of warmth to see his face darken angrily.

"You go to bed to-night and sleep," he said. "I'll make them get another nurse to help you. You need rest. You've had a severe shock. Anyone but you would have been in hysterics long ago."

I wouldn't let him get another nurse, of course. Did he think I wanted someone else bothering around and further complicating matters! She'd very likely be the fluffy-haired type with whom Eustace could flirt! And, anyway, the case was mine, and I proposed that it should remain in my hands. Time was to come when I had reason to regret my decision, but there it was.

"Then there is Elihu Dimuck," resumed Lance O'Leary finally, leaning back again in his chair. I saw that his slender, well-kept hands were fumbling around in his pockets and expected that a stubby red pencil would be forthcoming, as sure enough it was, smooth and shining as any well-told rosary. With it rolling between his fingers he became brisker and less ruminative.

"He is an old acquaintance of Mr. Federie's and comes to visit him quite frequently. He owns some fine farming land about fifty miles south of here—quite a lot of it—keeps a large cash deposit at the bank upon which he draws every so often, but, according to his banker, does not spend it in riotous living. He is considered fairly wealthy in Stockville, where he lives, and is rated as being worth seven or eight hundred thousand. He lives quietly, is and always has been a bachelor, and the only scandal I could dig up about him had to do with his determined repulsing of a matrimonially inclined widow some years ago. His dealings with Mr. Federie appear to have been purely in an advisory capacity, for I could find no record of any money changing hands. Yes, he seems to be just a fussy old maid of a fellow who hates trouble like a cat hates water."

"Why, I never thought of suspecting him!"

"Suspect everyone, Miss Keate, if you would discover guilt. Suspect the very walls themselves. Well— that leaves the servants, neither of whom seems guilty. They are not a handsome pair, it's true, but—" he stopped abruptly, cleared his throat, and went on in a smooth voice—"the inquest will be just a formal affair, I think. The coroner was out last night—I don't believe you saw him."

Grondal was crossing the room on such silent feet that it was only when he came within arm's reach of my chair that I understood why O'Leary had changed his subject so suddenly.

"Oh, Grondal," said O'Leary quietly.

"Yes, sir." Grondal was carrying a bunch of keys in his hand. Again he wore the threadbare livery, and O'Leary's gaze was puzzled as it rested on the faded mulberry velvet, almost bare of nap, and went on to the woolen socks and heavy brogues.

"I'll just lock the shutters, sir," went on Grondal respectfully, suiting the action to the word.

"Lock them every night, do you?" asked O'Leary without shifting his easy, relaxed position.

"Yes, sir. It is a custom with us."

"A rather wearisome job, isn't it?"

"No, sir. There are only a few, you see, that we open during the day. Many of the rooms are not in use now."

"You have quite heavy bolts on those shutters."

"Yes, sir. They are the same bolts that were put in

place when the house was built. They've served us well." He replaced the bunch of keys in his pocket and lowered the second window softly. "Did you want something, sir?"

"Have you been with the Federie family long?"

"A matter of some forty years. I started working for old Mr. Federie when I was a boy."

"You know a good deal about the family, then?"

"It is a family I'm proud to work for, sir," said Grondal quickly.

"No doubt," said O'Leary. "The tragedy last night must have affected you deeply."

"It did, sir. Though as to that, Mr. Adolph had not been much at home during recent years."

"He was not the only child?"

"Oh, no, sir. Old Mr. Federie had four sons. There was Mr. James, the oldest—he was Miss March's father —died when she was a child. And Mr. Charles—he came next. He—was a lot like Mr. Adolph if you understand what I mean, sir." He shook his head in a deprecating way. "He—er—disappeared some years ago. It was owing to a quarrel over cards, to tell the truth. Mr. Federie considered that he had disgraced the name and would not permit him to be buried in the family lot. Very sensitive to wrongdoing is Mr. Federie. Then there was Mr. Adolph, and the youngest was Mr. Eustace— our Mr. Eustace's father; he died of—well, he died of drink in this very house nearly thirty years ago and his wife followed him within the hour. It was the time of our Mr. Eustace's birth. They were—a bad lot. But old Mr. Federie has high hopes of Mr. Eustace, though, if I may say so, I believe Miss March is his favorite.

Dinner will be served at seven, Miss Keate. If you are in the house, Mr. O'Leary, Miss March hopes you will join the family at dinner."

The curtain had fallen into place behind Grondal and was quite still before O'Leary turned to me.

"'A bad lot,'" he quoted softly. "And 'Miss March is her grandfather's favorite.' Look here, Miss Keate."

He extended his hand, palm uppermost in the circle of light. In it lay a crushed, soft rosette of crimson ostrich feathers.

"I need not ask if you recognize it," he went on quietly.

"Where—did you find it?" I whispered.

"It was clutched in the dead man's hand. How it got there is a matter for conjecture."

CHAPTER VII

FOOTSTEPS AT NIGHT

THE crimson rosette from March's slipper found in the murdered man's hand!

With appalling swiftness I fitted the thing into the events of the previous night, and phrases of that sinister conversation returned to my memory with frightful clarity: "A Federie hand is born to fit the curve of a revolver"—"I still think there is some other way"— "It must be to-night."

"What is it, Miss Keate?"

"N-nothing," I replied jerkily, and repeated it. "Nothing. Nothing at all."

"I suppose you'll tell me in your own good time," commented O'Leary lazily. "But in the meantime I should like to have your assurance that, at least, I— have a clue to the knowledge you appear to be withholding."

I had forgotten that his clear eyes were hidden in the shadow above that straight mouth and that my own face was entirely in the light.

"You have that assurance," I said crisply.

"It is lucky that I know you, Miss Keate. Otherwise I should certainly suspect you of harboring guilty knowledge. The chief of police, by the way, suggested that you shot Adolph Federie, since you were right here in the room, you know. When pressed for a motive he—

suggested a love quarrel. There, there, now! Control yourself, dear lady! I made him see the error of his reasoning. In fact, I vouched for you. You may have shot Adolph Federie and successfully concealed both your motive and the revolver, but I can't believe it." His mouth was quite sober, and I longed to see his eyes. There was a note of humor in his voice, yet it was sober, too. Sober enough to make a cold little chill start up from the small of my back.

"Now, then, Miss Keate," went on O'Leary briskly, "I want you to tell me *every single thing* that has happened since your arrival at Federie house. What has been said and done and particularly your impressions of personalities. And tell me, too, in the most minute detail, of last night—where you sat, how the room looked, how the lamps were adjusted—of the shot, how it sounded, what you did, where you stood, how you looked at the body, how you got to the bell rope, what people said when they came into the room—*everything*. I know that you are a keen observer and I want those observations." He smiled in that engaging way he had.

"My impressions," I replied slowly, "are not the kind that make for pleasant thoughts and comfortable sleep. That is, I have a feeling of forces pulling against each other—of personalities struggling and clashing together. This whole, terrible house seems to be—" I hesitated and my voice dropped—"a sort of shell full of conflicting desires."

"I did not credit you with so much imagination," said O'Leary dryly. "Go on, please."

"It is intangible but very real, too," I said, fumbling a little for words. "Don't you understand?"

"I—well, yes. I do feel something of the kind. But I have to stick to material facts. It is one of the restrictions of my profession. No matter how many people wanted to kill Adolph Federie, still only one bullet reached its mark. And it is my duty to find the hand that aimed that revolver. There's a lot of scoffing at material evidence just now; a lot of laughing at fingerprints. But so long as we live in a material world we will have material clues. Of course, I'm not saying that a material clue always proves anything. I've got several—clues—on this case, but just now I'm more interested in the psychology of the crime. When we learn to govern the laws of psychology we will be able to govern crime and make of the criminal a decent——"

"Psychology, fiddlesticks," I interrupted crisply. "When we hear less talk of releasing repressed desires, and more talk of exercising decent self-control, then only will we have less crime. Psychology, indeed! A man sins because the devil is in him!"

O'Leary smiled faintly.

"And in the meantime, Miss Keate——" he hinted.

So discarding theories and turning to facts, I told him all that had happened since my arrival at Federie house, and since I have a good memory I think I omitted very little. The only thing I failed to tell him actually happened before my arrival at Federie house and was, of course, that incriminating conversation between March and Eustace, and I had the full approval of my conscience in omitting that. I even told him of stumbling over the little green elephant, of hunting for the bell rope, of Adolph's clammy hand laid over mine, of Dimuck's yellow bathrobe and his horrified cry!

"Who shot him!", of March's holding the lamp while
Eustace examined the body—in short, of every smallest
occurrence, trivial though it might seem.

O'Leary interrupted me rather sharply as I came to
the examination we had made of the body.

"You say Eustace and Lonergan were bending over
the body?"

"Yes."

"Then either of them could have placed the rosette
in the dead man's hand if he wished to do so. Oh, I'm
not saying that either of them did! But still if he had
wanted to—that's why I say clues are treacherous
things. Well, go on."

"Where is the toy elephant you spoke of?" asked
O'Leary when I had finished my rather lengthy recital.

"There on the mantel."

He rose; the mantel was in the shadow, and after a
moment's prowling through the clutter that crowded it
O'Leary returned to the lamp, removed the shade, and
as the light leaped to the mantel he surveyed it carefully.

"Everything else in the world is here," he said.
"Junk galore, but—I don't see any elephant."

"It's green," I said without much interest. "Looks
as if it might be jade. It's about four inches high." I
glanced at my wrist watch—nearly seven o'clock.
Another night would soon be upon me. "Mr. O'Leary,
will there be any police in the house to-night? I—don't
care to stay alone in this room all night." I glanced involuntarily over my shoulder; the tower stairway
twisted out of sight in the shadows.

"Yes," said O'Leary briefly. "Grondal might sleep

there on the couch if you are nervous. I may be blind, but I don't see anything remotely resembling an elephant."

"Well, it is there. It is—" I rose, approached the mantel, and stared at the pieces loading it—"it's gone! Why, that's queer! It is only a little curio. Grondal said this noon that old Mr. Federie is attached to it. But it is just a toy."

"Just what did Grondal say?"

I told him the few sentences we had exchanged, while my eyes went fruitlessly about the mantel and the floor below it, seeking that little spot of vivid green.

"I came into the room, then, while you were talking," said O'Leary. "And both you and Grondal followed me to the library at once. No—Grondal waited to put fresh wood on the fire."

"Yes. And either I or March Federie has been in this room ever since you questioned us this morning, there in the library. And every soul in the house was in the library, and I was the first one to leave. And since then, as I say, either March or myself has been in this room ever since."

"But you were asleep this afternoon."

"Not soundly."

"H'm. Well, the important thing is that someone has thought enough of the thing to remove it. Did it look to be valuable?"

"It might be, for all I know," I replied uncertainly.

"Couldn't you tell by looking at the thing?" he said in a peevish way.

"My interests lie along pulses and thermometers," I

replied with some dignity. "I don't know a thing about little green elephants. Perhaps the Federies used it to cut their teeth on."

He gave me an annoyed look and turned away. "It may mean nothing at all," he said. "I'm going into town. Is there a telephone in this house?"

"I believe so," I said, adding rather hurriedly: "You don't think anything will—will happen to-night, do you?"

"I'm leaving a couple of policemen," he said blandly. "And lightning seldom strikes twice in the same place, you know. Let Grondal sleep over there on the couch. Are you afraid?"

I have not Revolutionary ancestors for nothing. I stiffened.

"Certainly not," I lied, and wished he were not so easily convinced.

"I've some work to do in town," he went on. "I want to scare up some family history about these Federies, for one thing."

"Dinner is served," said Grondal sedately from the doorway.

O'Leary had not more than gone when I came upon the first of the blue beads. It happened this way.

Grondal had retired on the heels of his announcement and I changed the cold pack on my patient's head before I took a candle, lighted it at the fire, and followed. As I stepped through the doorway, pulling aside the green velvet curtain and letting it fall behind me in long, wavering lines, I recalled the falling of that curtain immediately after the sound of the shot that killed

Adolph Federie. I lifted the curtain again experimentally while the candle in my other hand cast a dim light over the small passage, reflecting against its faded green walls. Yes, the curtain had certainly been lifted and let fall by a hand, for no draft could move that heavy curtain in exactly that fashion. But by whose hand?

My gaze fell on a small nail that projected from the door casing and caught a glimpse of a wisp of blue thread, and I looked closer.

Depending on the thread and hidden by the casing was a dejected little cluster of blue beads!

There must have been five or six of the things, and the thread was broken at both ends, looking very much as if the nail had caught on the thread and pulled it loose from—*from Mittie Frisling's dress, of course!* The previous night she had worn a dress heavily decorated with blue beads exactly like these.

I stood there, looking at the telltale little cluster of blue beads for several moments before I recalled that dinner was waiting. Then I detached the thread, slipped beads and all into my pocket, and went on to the dining room.

The others were waiting, and I slipped hurriedly into my chair. Glancing around the long table, I experienced a distinct sense of shock. The men were again clothed in the most meticulous fashion, their shirt fronts gleaming white, their coats black and smooth. March wore again the crimson velvet gown with its extravagant silver ornaments. Isobel appeared again in the shining yellow taffeta, the emerald suspended at her soft throat and the bruises on her arm showing darkly through a heavy coating of liquid powder. And the blue beads on

Mittie Frisling's gown tinkled stealthily with every spoonful of soup she lifted to her lips.

Everything was the same, save for the place beside me. Grondal, with a complete lack of forethought, had left the chair in that vacant place. It was rather grisly, sitting beside that chair, with only a gleaming expanse of white linen where the night before there had been silver and china. All through the meal I caught furtive glances in that direction.

Through the soup I busied myself with trying to discover the place where one of the dangling festoons on Mittie's gown had been broken, and as Grondal removed the plates I found it, quite near the shoulder. The thread had evidently been snapped about the middle of the loop, for the remainder of the thread, denuded of beads, hung desolately among the other beaded loops. There had been about fifteen beads on it, I thought. I had only five or six in my pocket. The others had fallen somewhere; the woman must have left a trail of blue beads.

It was about this time that Mittie began to bridle and twist and cast me resentful looks, and I withdrew my gaze.

I don't believe a word was spoken during the whole meal, and I have never sat through a more unpleasant dinner. It was interminably long, in the first place, with Grondal putting on and removing rather sparse but very formal courses, Kema peering though the slot in the door of the pantry every now and then, in a way to freeze the blood in your veins, and Isobel glancing occasionally at the vacant place beside me in a natural and undisturbed way, quite as if Adolph were still sitting there. This effect was so convincing that once I turned sharply to follow her gaze, expecting I don't know what. Of course, the chair was empty.

As the meal progressed the dead silence became more and more oppressive. Along toward dessert Konrad, somewhere outside, barked suddenly and loudly and Mittie gave a stifled little cry, March went white as a sheet, and Dimuck dropped his fork on the floor. And after a curiously still interval of about four or five seconds Grondal brought Dimuck another fork, his face expressionless, and March withdrew her eyes from the vacant place beside me. I suppose everyone at the table was thinking of the dog's bark during the dinner of the previous night, when Adolph had endeavored to tell his dog story.

After that the meal was even more unpleasant. The little, subdued clatter of silver grew louder and louder as the breathless, waiting hush deepened. It seemed to me that everyone around that table was clinging determinedly to the rôle he had chosen for himself. building up walls of silence and nonadmissions. Even their choosing, one and all, to dress exactly as they had dressed the night before, seemed to me to strengthen this effect. Their faces, secretive and fear ridden, were brought into sharp relief by the wavering lights of the tall candles on the table, and behind them, in the shadows, Grondal crossed and recrossed.

It was just as we were finishing the somewhat languid dessert of stewed prunes that the rather horrible thing happened.

All at once, from somewhere above our heads, breaking dully through the smothered silence, came the sound of footsteps! One after another they fell, slow and deliberate, on the floor above our heads.

Every head jerked.

March gripped the table edge, her tense fingers wrinkling up the cloth, her face rigid. And all at once no one was eating and everyone was looking upward with strained, fearful eyes, and then darting swift looks all about the table. But the only vacant chair was Adolph's!

Still no one spoke. I think no one breathed for the long moment during which those footsteps went on slowly and with dreadful deliberation. They seemed to be falling on the bare floor of the corridor of the back wing, and the sound came from directly above us. Then, just as Isobel's hand went to her mouth and pressed frantically against her teeth, the footsteps broke into a quick, light run and fell suddenly into silence.

We were all standing; Eustace was thrusting back his chair with a swift motion and running from the room, followed by Deke Lonergan and then Elihu Dimuck, whose napkin, still clutched in his pink hand, floated back of him and disappeared into the drawing room. And simultaneously Grondal ran heavily along the carpet, past the table and out of the room in the wake of the other men.

And Mittie Frisling, leaning over the table, one hand planted in a plate of cake and the other spread wide on the tablecloth, her face a sickly green in the glow of the candles and her opaque eyes fixed on Adolph's chair, suddenly and dreadfully began to scream.

The screams cut in a high, thin thread of horror into the shadows and corners of the great old room before Isobel reached Mittie's side, thrust her ringed fingers over Mittie's mouth, and held them there, while Mittie, her eyes never wavering from their fixed glare, twisted and pulled, but could not escape.

I stirred from the lethargy of terror that had held me, seized my goblet, and flung its contents full into Mittie's face.

It had the desired effect.

She caught her breath under the icy water, gasped, choked, and as Isobel released her groped for her napkin and dabbed futilely at the water that dripped from her hair and face.

"Shall we go into the library?" asked March in a question that was a command. Her face and lips were drained of color, but her voice was very tight and careful.

She turned and led the way, but instead of going toward the library she turned into the little passage and went to the tower room. Mittie, seeming rather dazed and still mopping at her face, followed March, and Isobel and I brought up the rear. I had the presence of mind to take a candle from the table and it cast a flickering light on the musty, green walls of the narrow passage and on Isobel's massed, reddish hair and her creamy back and arms.

Once in the tower room March poked at the fire until it blazed and then stood, slim and straight, before it; the folds of her gown touched to a bright glow under the light from the flames, her face still white, but her black eyebrows drawn sternly together. Isobel sank gracefully into an easy chair, the yellow taffeta whispering with every movement, her eyes veiled and one tense hand gripping the emerald at her throat. Mittie sat on the couch, digging at her reddened eyes with the damp napkin and darting furtive glances above it, and I moved to the bed, my starched white uniform rattling a little as I bent over my patient. We must have made a strange picture.

It was a good fifteen minutes before the men came in, Eustace lifting the curtain as they filed into the room. A policeman, his badge shining against his blue coat, was the last one to enter.

"It was nothing," said Eustace, smiling easily as if to reassure us, but with an unfathomable look in his dark eyes. "There was a policeman upstairs in the main corridor all the time. He saw nothing at all."

"Did you search the house?" asked March.

"The whole place," Eustace assured her, his tone still light. "We even crawled up the ladder from the trunk room and had a look around the attic."

"I think that cook of yours was prowling around up there," said the policeman. "She likely saw me and dodged back down the kitchen stairs and is afraid to say so. At any rate, there's nothing to be alarmed about."

Kema? I accepted the explanation simply because it seemed the only rational one to accept, but I felt in my heart a kind of instinctive repudiation of it. And yet— the house was locked, the policeman had searched it— it must have been Kema.

Grondal brought coffee into the tower room and served it in small demi-tasse cups that looked like silver. The policeman accepted one, looked in a puzzled way at its delicate lines, lifted it suspiciously to his nose, and finally swallowed the coffee at one gulp. Shortly after that he disappeared.

The others remained in the tower room that entire evening. Whatever were their feelings toward each other, still a common terror bound them together, and a kind of fear-drugged inertia appeared to hold them in that room, above which twisted the darkening shadows of the tower stairway. And one of them knew the secret of that stairway. One pair of those furtively meeting eyes masked that secret.

It was not a nice thing to contemplate.

Little was said; a thing that marks my memory of those grisly days and nights in Federie house is the recollection of the strained, distrustful silences that fell whenever we were all together.

Eustace was the only restless one; he smoked innumerable cigarettes, fussed with the fire, walked over several times to stare at his grandfather's face, picked up my chart, and scanned it as carefully as if he understood any of it, and finally, in wandering about the room, he came upon an old violin case that lay on a cabinet across the room, blew a cloud of dust from the plush-covered case, opened it, and took out the violin.

The thing must have lain idle for an indefinite time, but there were still strings in it, and he played with it for some time, tightening the strings, tuning it, and finally drawing out the bow, tightening it also, and drawing it across the strings. At the first wail Genevieve, who had stalked into the room a few moments before, got up with a look of outrage and stalked out again, and March put up a protesting hand which Eustace did not see—or possibly saw and did not heed, for it seemed to me that very little escaped his narrow eyes. He persisted, dragging from the old violin a slurred tune that gradually began to bear a grotesque resemblance to "La Furiante."

At one chromatic in a minor scale that fairly set my teeth on edge, Isobel tossed her cigarette into the fire, rose in one long sinuous motion, and stood for a moment facing us, her gleaming yellow taffeta falling gracefully about her body and the faulty emerald at her throat glittering hatefully.

"Stop that, Eustace!" she said, her voice sharp and shrill and her face a painted mask.

Elihu Dimuck, startled out of his reverie, struggled to his feet and Deke Lonergan took his eyes from March's profile and rose, too.

"I'm going to bed," announced Isobel abruptly, her voice resuming its customary smoothness. "Good-night."

Mittie Frisling rose also, looked about her in a hazy way like a sleepwalker, and followed Isobel, and one by one the others departed. It was quite as if a chord of fear and suspicion held them all together. Elihu Dimuck and Deke Lonergan both paused to ask whether Mr. Federie showed any improvement, and March stopped to ask if there were anything I needed. Eustace approached her as she stood beside me and passed his arm lightly around her waist, his fingers lingering caressingly on her bare wrist. She freed herself at once, said, "Good-night, Miss Keate," and walked toward the doorway where young Lonergan, his face dark and his mouth tight, was apparently waiting to light her through the dark passage.

"Do you think Grandfather will be better soon?" asked Eustace.

"I can't tell, I'm sure."

He surveyed his grandfather's face thoughtfully for 'a moment and then he, too, was gone, and I was alone with the scent of Isobel's cigarettes, the flickering light from the old lamps, the sick man, deaf and dumb and helpless on the bed, and in the three-sided corner of the room a narrow angular stairway that lost itself in ascending shadows.

And the green elephant was gone and the blue beads were in my pocket and the red rosette had been in the murdered man's hand. A colorful crime, I thought crazily, laughed shrilly, and at the sound pulled myself up short and went about my business.

But those slow, deliberate footsteps kept echoing in my thoughts.

Grondal came in after a little carrying more hot water and a blanket.

He put the water where it would keep fairly warm and dropped the blanket on the couch.

"Shall I just lie down over here, miss?"

"Yes. Go to sleep if you like. If I need you I'll call."

"Very well, miss."

Without any ado the man settled himself comfortably and, so far as I could see, went immediately to sleep. At least he closed his eyes, looking more villainous than ever, and began to breathe heavily.

To tell the truth, feeling as I did toward Grondal, it seemed to me that his presence offered a somewhat dubious protection. But, at the same time, the mere fact of another person being in the room did in a slight measure relieve the tension of nameless apprehension that possessed me.

Genevieve came into the room as I was taking a last pulse and mounted noiselessly to the mantel, contriving in his usual deft way not to disarrange any of the claptrap around him. I took off my cap, wound my watch, and sat down in a big chair, first turning it so that it faced the stairway. I had not lowered the flames in the two lamps, one on the bedside table and one on the table in the center of the room, and I studied the bright red roses on the large bowls of the lamps, their ornate brass standards, tarnished and greasy looking, and the tall glass chimneys that reared thinly above the shades which were decorated, too, in painted roses and finished around the bottoms with fringes of glass bangles that every now and then shivered faintly under some draft that managed, despite heavy curtains and shutters, to sift through the room.

Every time I roused to look around the room I found the same picture until I knew every detail familiarly: the lamps with their gaudy roses, the fire burning fitfully, Grondal's hawk nose emerging from the blanket against the background of dark panels that lined the tower stairway, and the gaunt cat hunched on the mantel, with his great tail sweeping around his toes and his shoulders and hips making tawny points of light.

In spite of the indefinable apprehensions that kept me restless and uneasy, the night passed quietly.

About midnight, I think, I fell into a cat's nap, but I am a light sleeper and roused at once when Grondal got up with his customary noiselessness and approached the fireplace. I had the strangest impression that he was moving very softly as if not to attract my attention, though he said nothing, arranged more wood on the fire in a methodical way, and returned to the couch. I was still restless and a victim of the uncanny feeling of being under close but secret observation, and I would catch myself clutching the arms of my chair and leaning forward to peer, every nerve a-tingle, into the shadows lurking about the corners of the room and shrouding the tower stairway. And, indeed, later events proved that we were under surveillance most of that long night.

By three o'clock the fire had died down again and the water Grondal had brought was only lukewarm. Kema had promised to leave a fire in the kitchen range and a kettle of water on, so, overcoming a feeling of reluctance at the thought of traversing the silent, black rooms between the tower room and the kitchen, I took a candle and started out.

I accomplished the errand without mishap—if not without an exceedingly quaky feeling about my knees. Encumbered with the candle in one hand and steaming water in a pan in the other hand, I paused at the door of the tower room in order to negotiate the curtain without catastrophe.

My approach through the little passage must have been very quiet, for through the crack of the curtain I caught a glimpse of Grondal crouched on his knees before the wood box. I could only see his shoulders and bent head, but it seemed to me that he was examining something he held in his hands, turning and twisting it, and entirely absorbed in the thing, whatever it was.

Had I thought twice, I should have lingered there for a moment or two, but I was concerned only with the possibility of the water cooling before I could use it, and I pushed the curtain aside with my elbow and entered the room.

And at my hurried entrance there was a shimmering flash of green from under Grondal's great yellow hands and he suddenly jerked out some wood, let it drop on the hearth, and was all at once busily engaged in building up the fire. Well, it needed it and I said nothing. But I watched him carefully as he returned to the couch and apparently fell again into a sound sleep.

And as I sterilized my needle, measured the adrenalin, swabbed a spot on my patient's resistless arm with alcohol, thrust the needle in, and pressed the tiny piston with my thumb, my thoughts were busy. I was sure that the small green elephant was in that wood box and I was equally sure that Grondal had taken the thing from its place on the mantel.

I revolved a number of possibilities in my mind, but could come to no satisfactory conclusion. The only thing I could be sure of was that the green elephant must have some kind of meaning. Mr. Federie had an attachment to the thing, so Grondal had said, and that reflection, in conjunction with my own statement as to finding the toy at the foot of the tower stairway immediately following the murder, must have inspired Grondal to at least a surmise as to its significance.

It certainly began to look as if the jade elephant had some bearing on the case. I did not know, of course, whether the thing had an intrinsic value or in some inconceivable fashion held a clue to the mystery, but in any case I was sure that I wanted that elephant.

And within fifteen minutes I had manufactured a

plausible excuse that took Grondal to the kitchen, had watched through the crack in the curtain until the gleam of his candle disappeared beyond the turn in the passage, had crossed the room swiftly and knelt at the wood box, felt a thrill of exultation when my groping fingers encountered that smooth, cold surface, and had extracted and hidden the green elephant, in what I fallaciously considered an inspired moment, in the case for the old violin. Eustace had let the case fall shut and had carelessly laid the violin across it; I lifted the violin, opened the case, deposited the tiny elephant within, and closed the case so that not a gleam of its translucent, shimmering green was visible. Then I replaced the violin at the careless angle at which Eustace had left it.

It was just as I returned to the bedside that I experienced again that strange and disturbing feeling of a presence near at hand. But the velvet curtains over the doorway hung straight and undisturbed and the tower stairway loomed, so far as I could see, emptily black.

Then Grondal was back, carrying the freshly filled hot-water bag as if it had been a tray and eying me and the wood box with a covertly suspicious air.

It was not long after that until streaks of dawn, gray and cold, began to filter into the room through the bolted shutters, the lamps began to pale, their flames garish amid the flat, silly roses, and Genevieve dropped lightly to the floor, stretched his front legs and then his back legs in a leisurely manner, yawned cavernously, and sauntered from the room, intent on some secret expedition of his own.

Presently Grondal roused himself, bundled his blanket over his arm, and went to the wood box. I watched him closely. I think he had intended to replenish the fire and in so doing withdraw the elephant from the wood box and conceal it under the folds of blanket. As his hand went into the wood box and found no elephant I saw his back stiffen and he hesitated for just a second or two. Then without further indication of inward disturbance he stacked some wood on the fire, rose, and left the room.

Half an hour later he brought me a breakfast tray. I met his eyes openly as I took it, but his were shadowed by those overhanging eyebrows and told me nothing.

But as I sat drinking the welcome, if somewhat thinly creamed, coffee, I came to two decisions. One was to guard that green elephant, willy-nilly, until I could give it to O'Leary.

And the other was that if, as I had told O'Leary, a man sinned because the devil was in him, then Grondal might well be that man, for it seemed to me that the marks of the cloven hoof were plain upon him.

CHAPTER VIII

A TRAIL OF BLUE BEADS

MARCH FEDERIE came into the room as I finished my breakfast. She looked white and weary, as if the night had held little peace for her. She bade me a languid good-morning and inquired immediately as to her grandfather's condition. I remember that I asked her to stay with him while I made a hurried trip to my room to don a clean uniform and freshen myself after the trying night. I hope it is no reflection upon my charity of mind to say that March was the only member of the household in whom I felt any degree of trust. And I felt that she might bear watching!

I made my errand to my room very brief. On the stairs I met Mittie Frisling. She looked haggard and afraid; her sallow face was colorless, and her eyes circled in great brownish rings. She would have detained me, but I replied briefly to her hasty inquiry as to old Mr. Federie's state and brushed past her.

Once back in the tower room, March having gone to breakfast, I went to the violin case and opened it. The jade elephant was still there, and I picked it up and examined the toy carefully. Even to my inexperienced eyes it was a lovely thing, with exquisite carving and color, but though I stared for some time at the delicate, shimmering green, the knowingly slanted eyes, the fanlike ears, the tiny, ferocious trunk, it told me nothing, of course, and at the sound of someone approaching through the passage I returned it hurriedly to its hiding place.

It was only Kema, however, wanting to know if I had finished with my breakfast tray.

"Yes," I replied. "There it is. By the way, Kema, where were you during dinner last night?"

"In the kitchen," she answered at once, taking the tray between her broad, dark hands.

"All of the time?"

"Yes."

I think she did not relish my questions, for there was a look of veiled distrust on her stolid face and she began to edge toward the doorway. But I persisted.

"You were not upstairs during dinner?"

"No, miss. I was in the kitchen doing my work." She glanced rather suggestively toward the bed, as if I might do better to follow her example, and in another moment her enormous bulk had vanished.

If it had not been Kema whose footsteps we had heard, who, then, was it? Or—what?

I am a practical, matter-of-fact woman, but I don't mind admitting that my thoughts flew to Adolph's vacant chair with gruesome speed. And my hair prickled and gooseflesh came out on my arms and I cast a nervous glance toward the tower stairway.

Then I shrugged my shoulders impatiently and set to work with feverish zeal.

Half an hour later Grondal, his arms full of clean linen, came into the room again. As before, he assisted me in lifting my patient and changing the bed linen,

and there was a touch of grim irony in our joining in
that peaceful task. But I recall that my hand shrunk
back from any contact with his long, yellow fingers.
He gave the room only a cursory cleaning and did
not even approach the violin, explaining as he worked
that the detective in the gray suit had somehow arranged for the coroner's inquest to be held in the library, there in Federie house, and that he, Grondal,
would have to hurry to get the library in order.

And about nine o'clock he came to the tower room
to summon me.

"They are about to begin, miss, and Mr. O'Leary
sent me for you."

"Is everyone else already there, Grondal? I don't
want to leave my patient until the last minute."

"Yes, miss. Everyone but you."

Well, it seemed to me that since everyone in the house
was in the library it would be safe enough to leave the
elephant in its hiding place until the inquest was over.
As I passed through the doorway, Grondal stepped aside
and murmuring something unintelligible about adjusting the window, he entered the tower room. But if he
meant to make a swift search for the elephant I fore-
stalled his plan, for I simply stood there in the doorway and watched him putter around the windows and
fireplace doing nothing in particular, until, giving me
a black look, he joined me. And I saw to it that we
walked together toward the library.

As Grondal had said, everyone was there. I was disappointed in not having seen Lance O'Leary previous
to the inquest in order to tell him of the various things
that had come before my attention since the evening

before. But, as I reflected, it would doubtless be as well to tell him after the inquest, for, after all, the inquest was more a matter of form than anything else and did not pretend to fix guilt.

An effort had been made to give the room a kind of official appearance, I suppose, for chairs were ranged in neat rows and the coroner, with O'Leary seated near him, sat facing the rest of us. A small table had been placed before him and he leaned on it rather wearily, surveying us coldly from pouched eyes that looked as if they had seen too much of human frailties. There was a sprinkling of spruce young gentlemen whom I took to be reporters and who, one and all, seemed to have more eyes for March and Isobel than for anything else in the room—a few others not so spruce whom I thought might be attached to police headquarters and who viewed proceedings with a sort of detached nonchalance, as if it was all in a day's work—a few blue-coated policemen, and the jury, a motley collection of gentlemen, who showed a very lively curiosity as to the matter at hand.

The rest of us sat in a group, and I wondered if my own face were as sharply apprehensive as those others.

The coroner's voice, thin and cold, caught my attention at once, and I listened with much interest to the testimony of one Dr. Hiller, the medical examiner. It was given rapidly and weighted down with technical terms which I, very likely, alone of the entire audience understood. He spoke so rapidly that more than half of it was not intelligible even to me, but there was a sentence that struck me as holding significance.

"—and thus owing to the angle at which the bullet

entered the heart," he continued rapidly, "it seems likely that the bullet was projected from a position slightly above the murdered man." At this point the coroner interrupted to ask at what distance the shot was fired. The medical examiner's reply was wordy but, in spite of much reference to powder burns and velocity and explosive quantities, rather vague, and I received the impression that notwithstanding the accuracies of modern science there might be some doubt regarding the point.

And just then it occurred to me that if Adolph had been bending over the stair rail, for instance, a shot *from the doorway* of the tower room might have struck him at the same angle. And I was positive that Mittie Frisling had stood there, and the curtain had wavered into place again *after* the shot was fired.

Of course, Mittie's visit to the door of the tower room might have taken place hours or even days before Adolph's murder. And, too, there was the locked door of the bedroom above and the effect Deke Lonergan certainly gave of having some knowledge of that locked door.

There followed a discussion as to how the body lay when it was found, but I was inclined to think that that meant nothing. Much is made, in what little I have seen of crime detection, of the position of the body, but my experience as a nurse leads me to think that this matter may be overemphasized, owing to the involuntary muscular contractions that nearly always take place. However, the coroner asked me about it rather particularly during my testimony which followed that of the medical examiner. I had attended an inquest once or twice before and had some idea of what was expected of me, and I flatter myself that I gave what evidence I had to give, merely a story of how and when and under what circumstances I had found the body of Adolph Federie, in a brief and concise manner. I guessed that O'Leary had kept his own counsel concerning the matter of the red rosette, as well as certain other matters, for the points touched upon during my testimony, as well as during those that followed, were practically the same points that O'Leary had covered during his own informal inquiry. And every member of the household stuck religiously to his original story. I don't know what the coroner thought of Mittie's testimony concerning Isobel's threat to kill Adolph, but the reporters scribbled furiously.

Altogether, though the inquest dragged out for some time, there was nothing new that came up. I was beginning to think of making my escape to the tower room, when all at once Eustace put his handkerchief over his nose, gurgled something in an embarrassed fashion, and was given permission to leave.

And before I realized what I was doing I was on my feet and following him, brushing aside an intercepting policeman. At the door I caught O'Leary's voice, explaining in soothing accents that Miss Keate was returning to her patient.

By the time I had reached the main hall Eustace had disappeared. Had he gone to the tower room, where the jade elephant was hidden?

I ran through the intervening rooms and, reaching the door of the tower room, stood there for a moment on the threshold, holding the green curtain aside and searching the room with my eyes and panting. My patient lay on the bed, unseeing, unconcerned with the business of life, still breathing with slow, painful gasps. And there was no one else in the room.

I had won over Eustace, then, if his goal had been the tower room.

But when I approached the table on which lay the old violin my feeling of self-congratulation collapsed.

The violin lay on the table beside the case. The case was closed, but when I opened it I saw at once that the green elephant was gone!

It had been there when I accompanied Grondal to the library. Every member of the household had been in that room all the time intervening since I had left the tower room. Eustace had left the library but a moment ago, and I did not believe that he could have had time to reach the tower room, extract the toy from the violin case, even supposing he knew where it had been hidden, and escape before I reached the tower room.

But the elephant was indubitably gone. And Eustace was the only person who had left the library.

Was there some power of evil at work in that silent old house whose gifts transcended purely human ability?

Ashamed of my fancy, I shrugged away the absurd and highly unhappy thought. Human hands had lifted the violin, had opened the case and laid themselves upon the elephant. But it was true that something that was evil and dark and scheming was abroad in that hushed old house.

I did not return to the library, thinking that if I

were needed they would likely send for me. But I was not needed, and a little before lunch time O'Leary came into the room. He looked tired and dejected and sank wearily into an armchair.

"Nothing," he replied to my question. "Nothing that we did not already know. I am disappointed. Frequently during the inquest something crops up that is news— some flaw, some inconsistency in the stories told. But—" He paused and the weariness in his face gave place to a keenly alert look and he straightened up in his chair—"what is it, Miss Keate? Surely that gleam in your eyes has a meaning. What is it? News?"

"That's as may be," I said. "Here is the matter of the green elephant as it stands now, but whether it has anything to do with the case or not is another thing."

He listened with growing interest while I told him of the elephant, shook his head when I came to the disappointing close of my story, and walked over to the table to examine the case. He looked at the violin carefully, too.

"It is an old thing, isn't it? No fingerprints that I can see, but there must be some, of course. I'll see if we can get the fingerprints."

"You'll get mine," I said, none too pleased.

"I've no doubt we shall," he returned abstractedly. "Now for the case. Nothing here. And no elephant."

After a moment he returned to a chair.

"It does seem to me, Miss Keate," he said rather pet_ tishly, "that you could have kept that elephant once you got your hands on it."

"Oh, doubtless," I remarked with some acerbity, "carrying it around in my pocket? Or in my hand, so

everyone could see it. And me—" I added bitterly—
"likely being shot by somebody who wanted it!"

He was eying me dreamily, not at all affected by that
possibility.

"Do you know," he said, "I shouldn't be at all surprised if that is what happened to Adolph Federie. He
might have got hold of the elephant and was shot because—because he had it, by someone who also wanted
the thing. You said it was there at the foot of the
tower stairway when you found it first?"

I nodded.

"And the murderer, seeing he could not gain possession of the elephant after it had rolled from Adolph's
dying hand, owing to the danger of your catching him
in the act, as well as owing to the pressing need for his
immediate escape, left the toy elephant and thought
he could secure it at a later and less dangerous time."

"'He?' Do you think a man shot Adolph Federie?"

"I used the pronoun in a rhetorical sense," said
O'Leary coldly. "Please follow the point at issue,
Miss Keate."

"But," I objected, "that green elephant has been,
I suppose, there on the mantel for anybody to take,
absolutely unguarded. If anyone wanted it, he could
have got hold of the thing a hundred times since Mr.
Federie's illness."

"Providing—" Lance O'Leary's gray eyes became
all at once very clear—"providing he knew what he
wanted." He looked satisfied, as if he had come across
a very leading clue, though for the life of me I couldn't
see that matters were helped any. What did he mean?

I was on the point of asking when my eyes fell on my wrist watch and I reached for my thermometer.

"Anything else, Miss Keate?" asked O'Leary.

There were the blue beads, of course, and the strange footsteps we had heard on the bare corridor floor above us during dinner of the previous night. First I told him of the footsteps as dryly as I could while I took my patient's temperature. My voice was quite steady, I am sure, but when I had finished I found that I had put the wrong end of the thermometer in my patient's mouth.

O'Leary watched me as I withdrew the thermometer, shook it again vigorously, and placed it between Mr. Federie's open lips, right end up this time.

"So Kema says she was not upstairs at all during the meal," mused O'Leary. "And Grondal was in the pantry and followed the other men upstairs. You are sure that everyone but Kema and Grondal was at the table?"

"Certainly. That is, everyone but——" I stopped abruptly, annoyed at my half admission.

"Everyone but—Adolph, I suppose you were about to say. You amaze me, Miss Keate. Dead men can't walk."

"You might think otherwise if you stayed in this house overnight," I snapped. "And, in any case, my ears are good. And I heard footsteps! Of course, it might have been your policemen playing leapfrog."

As if in response to a cue the curtain over the doorway was thrust gingerly aside and a policeman, the same who had endeavored to reassure us about the troublesome footsteps, peered into the room, brightened up when he saw O'Leary, glanced toward the table as if to be sure it held no more demi-tasse cups, and, re-assured, stepped into the room.

"What is it, O'Brien?" asked O'Leary.

"I was only wanting to know if me and Shafer was to be on duty here to-night, sir?"

"I think it likely," said O'Leary dryly. "You had the day off, hadn't you?"

"Yes, sir. The chief told me to talk to you, sir. But, Mr. O'Leary—" the man seemed to be struck with a fit of uneasiness—"Mr. O'Leary, sir, I was only wondering if—well—if two men was enough!" He blurted out the last words hurriedly and stood shifting from one foot to another, fumbling with his cap and eying the slender gray man before him with absurd anxiety.

"I think two are enough. Surely you aren't afraid?"

"Oh, no, sir. No, sir. Not afraid." O'Brien paused to swallow and his face looked none too happy. "Only —well, the truth is, Mr. O'Leary"— he leaned forward suddenly and spoke in a hoarse whisper— "this is a very devil of a house, sir. The Old Man himself is in it!"

O'Leary did not smile.

"Why do you say that?"

O'Brien gulped again.

"I don't know. I'll swear I don't know. I wish I did. If it was something I could lay my two hands on or give an honest whack with my club it would be all right. But—but there's a feeling. I've turned around a dozen times, thinking somebody was staring at me and—have

never seen a human eye. It's—it's—there's a feeling."
He stuck, quite red but positive.

"By the way, O'Brien, what is this about footsteps,
during dinner last night? Were you upstairs when it
happened?"

The policeman's frank young face looked relieved.

"Oh, that was nothing, sir. Just a fancy, I think.
Maybe them folks at the table heard something—the
wind blowing in the trees, or somebody walking around
in the kitchen—and one and all jumped at the idea it
was footsteps up there on the second floor. I was upstairs at the time, sir, down there at the south end of
the main corridor, patrolling the house as was ordered,
and Shafer was outside making sure that all the doors
and shutters was fastened. I was there in the hall when
them two young fellows and the fat old duck with
spectacles and this Grondal fellow all came tumbling
up the stairs wanting to know who had been walking
along the back hall and what not. We all ran from the
stairway down the main corridor there and turned into
the hall that runs along the back wing. But, of course,
there was nobody there, sir. Nor in any of the bedrooms.
We even took a peek in the attic. We agreed that it
must have been that old heathen cook—you know, the
old woman with the gold earrings. It satisfied them and
the ladies. But between us, Mr. O'Leary, I think they
just imagined them footsteps."

I could restrain myself no longer.

"Imagined it!" I snorted. "Imagined nothing! I've
got ears and ordinary good sense. I tell you someone
was walking up there."

Lance O'Leary stood, a slim alert figure.

"I'll just see what Kema has to say. Come with me, O'Brien."

"Wait, Mr. O'Leary, there is something else." He paused while I drew the blue beads from the pocket to which I had carefully transferred them when I changed my uniform, and O'Brien watched me, his mouth hanging open, while I explained how and where I had found them and from whose dress they had probably been torn.

For some reason or other the knowledge seemed to please O'Leary inordinately, for he made me repeat the whole thing, and when I added somewhat diffidently my theory that the shot might have been fired from the door of the tower room his eyes began to shine and his whole aspect took on that tense, alert look that I knew so well.

"Miss Keate, you are invaluable," he said. "I'll take the beads, please. Now, we'll investigate those ghostly footsteps."

Grondal, bringing at my request a tray with my lunch on it to the tower room, told me that the funeral was to be at three o'clock at a downtown funeral establishment. I thought it a very sensible arrangement in view of the existing circumstances.

Something after one o'clock, when I was beginning to look forward to a long sleep during my hours off which began at two, Lance O'Leary came into the room again. His carefully tailored gray suit, his smooth brown hair, the effect he gave of modern, well-groomed prosperity, seemed incongruous in that cluttered, smothered old house, with its air of decay, and its damp, stale atmosphere and, most of all, the feeling of grim.

secret hatred and contention that lurked in the very air we breathed.

He began to inquire more particularly about the footsteps we had heard and remarked finally, rather waspishly, that he'd be inclined to doubt the whole thing had I not been one of those who heard the sound. His manner was such that I did not know whether to be flattered or insulted.

"You see, Kema told me that *she* was upstairs walking along that hall and came down by way of the back stairway, thus avoiding the policeman and others. And when I asked her why she changed her mind about it, after telling you she had been in the kitchen all the time, she pretended she couldn't understand me. Now, then, to which of us is she lying? Probably to me, since she has time to think the matter over. In any case, her change of front is interesting."

"Do you think it possible that someone—some outsider—a thief or housebreaker—could have got into the house?"

He looked at me oddly.

"Anything is possible, Miss Keate. But consider— the police were all over the house yesterday, searched every nook and cranny, and found no one besides the members of the household. And we have had a guard on the place every moment since then. He would have to be endowed with supernatural powers to get in and out without being detected. And—though, as I say, almost anything is possible, still we have to stick to the natural and let the supernatural go by. O'Brien insists that he heard no footsteps; but, so far as that goes, he could have heard nothing, for these thick old carpets muffle sounds. The only way in which you people could have heard the footsteps was by being, as you were, directly under the bare floor. Ah, there you are."

He turned as Grondal silently entered the room.

"You sent for me, sir?" asked Grondal.

"Yes." O'Leary surveyed the man thoughtfully for a moment, and when he spoke his words were so quiet and clear and yet so hard that they were like crystals dropping on stone. "The night Adolph Federie was shot you came down the back stairway after you heard the bell from this room. Who was the woman you passed—on the stairway, I think?"

The butler's face grew livid, the scar standing out distinctly. He ran his tongue over his lips.

"Who was it?" asked O'Leary again.

Grondal blinked; his eyebrows had come closer together so that I only caught a dark gleam from his eyes. The green velvet curtain a few feet back of him billowed lightly, as if in a draft.

"It was—Mittie Frisling," said the butler then, and at the same instant the curtain billowed again and I felt no current of air. Was something moving back of that curtain? In much less time than it takes to tell it I had pushed the butler to one side and drawn back the folds of green velvet. I was just in time to see Mittie Frisling vanish around the corner of the little passage. The one glimpse of her wispy back hair and bulging shoulders had been unmistakable.

"Mittie Frisling herself," I said to O'Leary, who had stepped quickly to my side.

At the words Grondal whirled to face me, and there was no denying the fact that the man was unpleasantly affected, for his eyes had a trapped look and he turned them uneasily to O'Leary.

"I'm sorry she heard me," he said. "Miss Mittie has —a bad temper. Her father was that way, too."

"You knew her father, then?"

I think Grondal repented his half confidence.

"In a way, sir. He was a—an acquaintance of Mr. Federie's."

"He must have been something more than a mere acquaintance, since Miss Frisling came here to live immediately after her father's death."

"How did you——" Grondal stopped so suddenly that he almost choked and said: "Yes, sir."

"Why did you give the impression that Miss Frisling had been here only a few days, when in reality she has been living here for some weeks?"

"I felt that Mr. Federie would want me to protect— that is, to—to keep——" he stopped in midair, so to speak, and O'Leary after waiting a moment said crisply:

"To what?"

"I answered to the best of my ability, sir," said Grondal smoothly, recovering himself, and not another word regarding the reasons for Mittie Frisling foisting herself upon the household could O'Leary get from the old butler. I use the word butler, by the way, in a very broad sense, for Grondal was a kind of general factotum.

"Why did you refuse to tell me of passing Miss Frisling on the stairway the night of the murder?" asked O'Leary presently.

"I thought it best," replied Grondal in an unperturbed way.

O'Leary's eyes were suddenly a dark slate color, like the threatening gray of storm-laden clouds, but he is not a man to give vent to his emotions.

"Exactly where were you when you passed?"

"About the middle of the stairway, sir. My hand touched her bare arm in passing. It gave me—rather a start."

"She said nothing?"

"Sort of—gasped, sir. I think she was startled somewhat, also."

"It's quite likely she was," agreed O'Leary grimly. "How did you know it was Miss Frisling?"

Grondal hesitated.

"I hardly know, sir. But it wasn't Madam Isobel— I was sure of that because she uses a perfume that has a heavy and penetrating scent. And it wasn't Miss March because Miss March would not have been afraid and would not have scurried away and—well, I should have known Miss March. It was Miss Frisling, sir; I am sure of that."

"Another thing, Grondal"— O'Leary spoke sharply as the man turned toward the doorway as if to indicate that, so far as he was concerned, the interview was at an end—"what do you know of the green elephant?"

At the unexpected question Grondal stiffened, ran a quick tongue over his lips again, and his eyes darted from O'Leary to me and back to O'Leary again.

"Green elephant?" he said. "Oh, do you mean the little jade curio that belongs to Mr. Federie?"

"Certainly."

"Why—er—nothing, sir. Except that it is a little work of art that Mr. Federie is very fond of and that

it—seems to have disappeared." He looked at the
mantel. "Someone must have taken it away."

"*Who?*"

Grondal did not falter.

"I couldn't say," he replied with barefaced deceit,
and, though O'Leary questioned him adroitly for a
moment or two, he could get nothing more from the
man.

"There is nothing else you are holding back because
you 'think it best'?" asked O'Leary finally, and Grondal flushed a slow, painful red, somewhat to my surprise, for I had supposed him entirely impervious.

"No, sir," he said at once. And it was not until
much later that we knew how flatly he was lying.

After he had gone O'Leary turned to me.

"I'm willing to bet my new car—and it's a beauty,
too—that this fellow could tell me a thing or two,"
he said disgustedly. "Well—I'll get it eventually,
maybe."

"How did you know he passed Mittie Frisling on the
back stairway?"

"Your precious blue beads, dear lady; look here."
He drew cautiously from his pocket the dejected little
cluster of beads I had given him, and three others,
unstrung. "One of these—" he went on, pointing to the
three small blue dots on his palm—"one of these was
about halfway up the back stairs. This one had rolled
into a crack in the floor of the corridor along the back
wing upstairs—quite near the door of Adolph's sitting
room, by the way. And the third—" he paused as if
to give his following words more emphasis—"the third
was in that vacant bedroom upstairs not more than

twelve inches from the spot where we found the revolver that killed Adolph Federie."

I shrank back a little, my eyes staring in dreadful
fascination at those three innocent-looking blue beads.
And in dismay I recalled that it was actually I
who had set O'Leary on the trail of the beads. True,
he would have found them sooner or later, in all likeli-
hood, but still it occurred to me that if Mittie Frisling
were convicted of this crime because of the evidence of
those little blue beads I should probably never enjoy a
peaceful night's sleep again.

"Don't feel badly, Miss Keate," admonishedO'Leary,
quite as if he knew the line my thoughts were taking.
"These things must be. If Mittie Frisling is capable of
committing this crime she is equally capable of suffering for it. That is one of the first lessons a criminal
investigator must learn. Now, then, I've some things
to do this afternoon. There'll be a man up to get the
fingerprints off the old violin during the afternoon,
and I shall be in again this evening. You'd better have
Kema or Grondal stay with your patient during the
afternoon while you take a rest. There are still a
couple of policemen about the place, so you need
not feel alarmed. Ah—how do you do, Doctor?"

Lance O'Leary departed as the doctor entered.

Dr. Jay looked after him admiringly.

"So that is Lance O'Leary," he said, a touch of awe
in his voice. "I didn't think he was so young. Say, he's
a good-looking fellow, isn't he? Wonder who's his tailor.
I had him all doped out as a stocky, thickset fellow with
a cigar and plug hat. Do you know, Nurse," he went
on, turning to his patient, "I always thought I'd like

to be a detective—carry guns, chase down clues, trap the villain, cover yourself with glory! And instead I carry a stethoscope, am routed out at all hours of the night—it's a hell of a life if you ask me." He broke off abruptly. "Where's the chart? How's everything? Looks like our patient is going to make a go of it."

Kema promised readily to sit with old Mr. Federie while I rested. She had not intended to go to the funeral, she told me impassively, hinting that her duty was to the living. A commendable resolution, which I should have admired more whole-heartedly had I been sure that she had had nothing to do with Adolph's taking off. But I was sure of that concerning none of the household, and the only things I had against Kema were her remarkable stolidity and the calm she had displayed in the matter.

Once upstairs in my own room I plucked Genevieve from the bed, where he had made himself comfortable on the soft folds of my black silk kimono, and deposited him in the corridor. I hated to touch the creature, and the feel of his coarse fur clung to my fingers disagreeably, and the more vigorously I shook the kimono, the more closely a few tawny hairs stuck to it.

From my window I watched the funeral party leave, straggling in twos and threes toward the tall gate beyond which were two taxis waiting, their bodies making bright spots of yellow amid the surrounding grays and browns of the dreary world.

Isobel went first; she had a small black cloche pulled low over her eyes and wore a shabby but opulent-looking mink cape. Even at a distance she appeared to maintain an elegant, fine-lady appearance which, I suspected, no amount of poverty or trouble could ever quite subdue.

The day had turned very cold, with the damp chilliness that penetrates one's very bones, and March, too, was wrapped in fur—a soft gray squirrel coat that looked new and smart; she, too, wore a small dark hat and loose white gloves that gleamed coldly as she laid her hand for a moment on the latch of the gate and then withdrew it as Lonergan opened the door of the nearest taxi. He managed to get in beside her, and Eustace, looking exaggeratedly fashionable beside Elihu Dimuck's sedately clothed presence, was forced to take the second taxi. He and Dimuck had to wait a moment or two for Mittie Frisling, who came scuttling down the path, feathers flying from her hat and fringes emerging from under a hideously checked purple coat. Grondal followed her and sat in front with the chauffeur, and the two cars started slowly off along the muddy road.

It seemed strange to me that Lonergan should have gone; probably it was in an effort to accompany March rather than to show any respect for the dead man. What was Lonergan doing in that house, anyway? His friendship for Eustace was not, so far as I could see, of a nature to warrant either his presence in the house at such a time or his anxiety as to old Mr. Federie's state of health.

I relaxed at once and deliciously; it was the first time since my coming to Federie house that I had felt at ease—and I might add it was also the last time. I decided drowsily that my ease was due to the fact that the warring, contentious elements were out of the house. Out of the house and away—to attend the funeral of a man whom *one of them had killed!*

This brought me sitting upright, staring into the pressing gray shadows about me, and effectually robbed me of any feeling of ease. The murderer must be one of those seven people who had gone, ostensibly in sorrow and grief, to make a last gesture of respect to Adolph Federie—or Kema.

Before I could go to sleep, after that, I arose and propped a small chair firmly under the doorknob.

But I believe I had not slept more than an hour when I awoke suddenly, every nerve in my body tingling, my heart nearly leaping out of my mouth, and a cold perspiration on the backs of my hands.

Muffled a little, but yet clear, a sound was coming from below. Someone was playing the piano, touching the tinkling old keys with practised hands. And it was the tune, faint but horribly clear, that was Eustace's favorite—"La Furiante."

I don't know how long I waited as if frozen, listening breathlessly to those weird minors, the thudding, beating bass notes surging threateningly under the wailing, weeping, furious chromatics. It was a devilish thing and stirred me in spite of myself.

But the thing that finally brought me to my feet was the recollection that Eustace was not in the house.

With my own eyes I had seen him leave!

CHAPTER IX

In a moment I found myself, wrapped in my black kimono and without shoes, slipping cautiously into the green corridor. Away down at the south end of the hall, past March's room, I could see a bulky shape in a blue coat silhouetted against the window. The policeman seemed intent on watching something outside and in no way disturbed by such an innocent-seeming thing as a little music. I walked softly, and it pleased me as well that he did not turn.

But as I reached the stairway, without any warning at all the music broke off in the middle of a phrase. There was no crash, no discordant note, no final chord. It simply stopped as suddenly and inexplicably as it had begun, leaving the strain of music suspended.

It was so unexpected that I hesitated for possibly fifteen heart beats, one hand clutching my kimono about me and the other pressed against my mouth as if to keep my heart from leaping out.

Not a sound came from below.

A small inner voice urged me to call the policeman, but I disregarded that caution and instead descended the stairs alone, cautiously but swiftly. There was not a soul in the entrance hall, and I hurried around the corner of the stairs. The curtain over the library door was already pushed back on its great brass rings and pole and I could see the whole room.

And there was no one to be seen!

It gave me an unpleasant little shock, although in my heart I had expected nothing less.

What fingers, then, had touched the yellow keys on the old piano, whose dark polished lines loomed up majestically at the end of the silent room?

It was then that I made what I afterward realized to be a rash and hasty decision. I would search the whole house!

And I did.

I peeked first into the tower room, but my patient was in no need of attention and Kema appeared to be dozing in her chair.

In some twenty minutes I had finished my search, even including the store closets off the kitchen entry, the servants' rooms, the several vacant bedrooms, the trunk room, Adolph's suite, and, in fact, the whole house except the attic and the locked bedroom above the tower room. But I was richer only in the knowledge that it was a musty, dusty, old-fashioned house, poorly ventilated, wretchedly lighted, and remarkably clumsy in its out-dated elegance. There was not even a cellar, and coal and wood were stored in a kind of shed not far from the back door.

As I did not wish to be interrupted I had walked very lightly during my peregrinations of the upper hall, and the policeman did not so much as turn his head, which, though it was what I wanted at the moment, did not incline me favorably toward the policeman. It did

not seem to me to add anything to our safety to have
a policeman about who was, to all practical purposes,
stone deaf.

However, as I came out of March's room, the door of
which was not six feet from him, the door creaked,
he gave a sudden start and whirled.

" 'Tis the Evil One himself!" He gasped, crossed
himself, looked closer, muttered something under his
breath that was not devout, and approached me.

"What are you doing?" he demanded roughly.

By this time I had recalled my unconventional attire,
and on putting a modest hand to my hair I encountered
the curlers about which I had wrapped portions of my
front hair. They were rather long and protruded stiffly
in two prongs above my temples, which, combined
with the flowing black lines of my kimono—well, at
any rate, the policeman's frightened remark was not
flattering.

"I was looking for the murderer," I snapped. "And
for all the good you are doing, standing there mooning
out of the window, we could all be murdered in our
beds."

Walking on my stockinged heels with as much dignity as I could muster I approached and entered my
room. He called something after me, but I clicked the
door on his voice, which was plaintive rather than
apologetic.

I looked at myself thoughtfully in the mirror for a
moment or two before I crawled into bed once more.
I had gained nothing for my pains and had nearly
ruined a new pair of silk stockings, for they had col-
lected an amazing amount of dust besides getting

snagged on the clasp of an open traveling bag in Mittie Frisling's room.

As I dropped off to sleep I reflected drowsily that the attic and the locked bedroom were the only places I had not searched, and that if a ghost wanted to take refuge in either place he was welcome to do so and I should be the last to interfere.

But the diabolic tune of "La Furiante" troubled my dreams and I awoke tired and oppressed with a sense of dread.

It was close to six o'clock when I went downstairs again, somewhat refreshed by a too-cool bath and a spotless and unwrinkled uniform whose white, starched folds rustled soothingly to my ears.

"La Furiante" met me as I reached the hall, but it was actually Eustace at the piano this time; I glanced into the library to make sure. On the piano stood a cocktail shaker, the only modern note in the house, and an empty glass stood beside it. Isobel sat near by, still in her hat, holding another glass between her large, jeweled fingers. At a window stood Deke Lonergan; the very set of his shoulders was inimical, and his crisp blond hair caught lights from the hanging lamp above him.

In the light of more leisurely reasoning it seemed to me that Eustace had probably detached himself from the funeral party for some reason and had returned to the house. But upon my discreet inquiry of March, I found that Eustace had been with the others the whole time, and I wished I had not asked!

There was no change in my patient's condition, and Kema had followed the directions I had given her with scrupulous care.

Dinner was a horrible meal, with Mittie Frisling sniffling now and then and dabbing at her swollen eyes—which, if what I half believed of her were true, was the very height of hypocrisy—Isobel indecently unconcerned and eating with a healthy appetite, Elihu Dimuck peering at each dish in his nearsighted way and bearing himself in a gingerly reserved manner as if contact with the others might contaminate him, Deke Lonergan saying nothing, Eustace smoking continually, and March a still, white little statue. It was a horrible meal, as I say, but still nothing untoward occurred, if we are to except the depression and the heavy silence—a silence that, somehow, was charged with unnamable meaning and that held us all in its portentous grip.

Something to my disapproval they took coffee in the tower room again, but, after all, their presence could not disturb my patient, so I said nothing. That thick silence still enfolded us; it was as if no one dared speak. I was glad when, quite early, Isobel made a motion to leave. The others followed, still in silence, only their eyes alive and shooting furtive, uneasy looks at each other and all about the old room.

March lingered to bid me good-night in her gracious way.

More than once during the preceding hour I had seen her eyes go toward the mantel, and as the others were straggling out of the room she said in a low voice:

"Have you seen a small green elephant? It is a curio that Grandfather usually keeps there on the mantel."

At a momentary loss for a reply I hesitated, and she continued slowly:

"He always said it was to be mine in case of his death.

He was attached to the thing and—particularly wanted me to have it. He has said many times that it is to go to me. Or rather that, in case of his death, I was to take it immediately." She was looking at me thoughtfully, and as if she were a little puzzled by the urgency of her grandfather's wish. "To-night I happened to notice that the elephant was gone. It is just a little thing, about so high." She measured with her firm' young hands. "Have you seen it, Miss Keate?"

"Yes," I said. "It was there on the mantel. But it seems to have disappeared. I don't know what happened to it." Which was true enough, in all conscience!

"Disappeared!" she repeated. Her blue eyes grew steadily darker and the firm lines of her mouth and chin began to show under the soft white flesh. "Disappeared! Why, then——"

"Coming, March?" said Eustace from the doorway. "I'll light you through the passage."

She hesitated, gave me a look that held something beseeching and anxious in it, stepped under Eustace's arm and the folds of green velvet, and I could hear the low, diminishing murmur of their voices.

Shortly after that Lance O'Leary came in. He looked tired, less coolly invincible and more humanly young and worried than was his custom. He dropped into a chair, passed his hands over his face in a weary gesture, and then stretched them out toward the fire.

"This is a barn of a house," he said disgustedly. "No earthly good to anybody, built like this! Away out there in the back entry is the craziest old telephone I ever saw. I don't know how the telephone company came to overlook it. The cook says that old Mr. Federie consented to have it installed years ago only to enable her to order groceries. No furnace, no lights—nothing but curtains and haircloth horrors for furniture." He shivered. "This place has got on my nerves a little to-night."

"I thought a detective had no nerves," I commented, a bit maliciously.

"We are nothing but nerves," said he. "Especially when—when we can't accomplish anything. I'm not getting the right—slant on this thing. There's something I have missed. The clue to the problem—is right in my hands. I feel that it is. But I can't—get the right combination." He made a restless, seeking motion with his hands, his sensitive fingers stretched out as if groping for invisible currents. "And that isn't all," he continued with a somber expression that I had never seen on his face before. "I feel a sort of premonition of—of danger. As if—as if there's more to come." He stopped abruptly, gave me a glance that was half defiant and half ashamed, and suddenly, as if a cloak had dropped over him, he was the Lance O'Leary I knew, his eyes clear and yet impenetrable, his countenance quiet.

"I have something to tell you," I began somewhat diffidently. "While the others were at the funeral this afternoon, I heard—that is, I thought I heard Eustace playing the piano. It couldn't have been Eustace because he was at the funeral, but it was that tune that he always plays."

Lance O'Leary was leaning back in his chair, his eyes half closed but singularly keen.

"Explain yourself, Miss Keate."

I did, of course, so far as I could, but could reply little enough to his sharp questions.

"You are sure you didn't dream all this," he suggested, and upon my justly indignant denial he stared for some moments into the flames without making any comment.

"There is one possibility," he said slowly as if lost in thought. "And that, if true, would be—amazing," he concluded in a hushed voice, and rose to stand with his back to the fire.

"The wind is rising," he said in an abruptly matter-of-fact way. "I don't like the way it is whistling around the house."

I didn't like the wind myself and said so at once.

"It rattles these old shutters till they sound like—like bare dead bones rattling against each other." I had not expected to say just that and the words coming from my own lips surprised me.

He caught the expression on my face, I suppose, and smiled a bit wryly.

"There your subconscious expresses itself, Miss Keate. Do you want me to stay here to-night?"

"Do you think—anything will happen?"

"No. No. But, of course, we can be sure of nothing. We could take a thousand precautions and still——" He did not finish his sentence but shrugged lightly.

"I am not afraid," I said slowly. "There are still policemen here?"

"Yes. One upstairs and one down, with instructions to keep a constant patrol of the house."

"And Grondal will sleep on the couch as he did last night?"

He nodded.

"Well, I don't know that I have any reason to be more frightened than anyone else——"

"I'm willing to bet that the others have got their doors locked and bolted," interrupted O'Leary, adding somewhat grimly: "I'm sure I should have."

"That is the trouble," I said. "There is no door to lock down here and, besides, it happened right over there on the tower stairway! But last night was peaceful enough," I concluded airily with an ease that I did not feel. "I'll telephone to you if I do not like the looks of things."

"Very well. By the way, Miss Keate, I wish you would—er—keep your eyes open to any keys that are lying around unguarded. The key to that bedroom above is still gone and looking for the thing in this house would be like looking for a needle in a haystack. You see whoever has that key——" He stopped and I whispered:

"Is the murderer?"

"Well, it is possible," said O'Leary cautiously. He looked about the room. "Did the fingerprint man get here this afternoon?"

"I don't know."

He crossed to the violin, scrutinized it carefully, and seemed satisfied.

"Not that the fingerprints will be apt to tell me much," he murmured in a disgruntled way. "Lord, Miss Keate, I wish I had no feelings! There's something, a kind of impalpable foreboding that makes me want to—to shout a warning!" He stared gloomily at the fire, and I went to my instrument case and shook out a couple of tablets from the bottle of soda bicarbonates that I always carry.

"It is probably your stomach," I said coolly, though I felt very much the same thing myself. "Take these tablets and you will feel better."

"I did have a pastry at dinner," he admitted, eying the tablets in the faintly resentful manner that comes over a man with the approach of a medicine-armed and resolute woman. "How do you take them? In water or just swallow them?"

Without waiting for water he swallowed them rapidly, one after the other. I think they stuck a little going down, being rather large, for he swallowed several times in a labored way and gave me an ungrateful look as he said good-night.

Grondal must have met him in the passage, for the butler came in at once, blanket over his arm and Genevieve at his heels. But the slight comfort that his presence gave me was marred by the untimely reflection that Grondal was as apt to be the murderer as any.

I endeavored to console myself by the thought that, at least, during the previous night he had offered no evidence of violent intentions. And Genevieve, for once, curled up on the mantel and went to sleep like a Christian tabby cat.

But with silence in the room, the moaning of the trees, the rattling onslaughts of the wind against the old shutters, and the various creaks and rustles and sighs that come at night upon an old house that has seen much of life and death, all combined to set my nerves on edge and keep my eyes traveling around and around the old room, lingering in shrinking fascination on the angles of the tower stairway. The panels below it gleamed dully, and at last I allowed myself deliberately to follow with my eyes the narrow steps of the stairway, step by step, the slender banister at one side and the faded green wall of the tower on the other. Beyond the second turn the stairs were lost in shadows and the slender railing vanished beyond the ceiling.

It was not more than ten-thirty, I think, when I settled into the big chair at the bedside, and at one o'clock I was still alertly wide awake and alive to every night sound, every creak of old woodwork, every sigh of the fire, every rustle of forgotten drafts.

I stirred then. My patient's pulse, always erratic, had dropped, which meant a stimulant and that at once.

The water on the fender was barely warm, and I was obliged again to go to the kitchen for boiling water. The errand was no pleasanter than that of the previous night. If anything, it was worse, for the murmuring and sighing of the wind made the great dark rooms and billowing curtains seem fearfully alive and cognizant of my intrusion. My little candle flickered feebly in the drafts and cast crawling shadows, and by the time I had reached the kitchen and turned up the wick in the lighted lamp Kema had left on the table, my knees shook, and my hands were as cold as ice.

The water on the stove was not quite boiling, so I took off one of the lids of the old-fashioned range, stirred up the fire, and set the kettle directly over the blaze. And in the little pause, while I waited, all at once I heard footsteps in the entry back of the kitchen, then a subdued buzz that sounded rather like a quiet and ladylike coffee grinder, and someone spoke in a cautiously lowered voice; there was a moment's silence and then the murmur was repeated.

I tiptoed to the door and put my ear to the keyhole just in time to hear that brief phrase repeated a third time.

"Main 2662, please."

It was someone at the telephone, of course, and the coffee-grinder sound was caused by the turning of the old-fashioned crank affair that signaled to central.

"Father?" went on the voice in carefully guarded accents. "Yes—yes. I'm still here. They won't let me leave. No, I haven't got it yet."

There was a long, listening pause. I was sure that the speaker was Deke Lonergan, and all my curiosity regarding that sullen young man returned as I applied my eyes with no success, for the entry was completely dark, and then my ear with more success, to the keyhole.

All at once Deke Lonergan gave a sort of groan.

"That's bad," he said. "All right, then. I'll have the money by morning. I'll do anything to get it. *Anything!*"

There was a kind of hot desperation in the last word. He clicked up the receiver, and after a little I heard him walking along the entry to the back stairway. He seemed to be attempting to go quietly, but he stumbled a little on the bottom step, I think, and I could hear the treads creaking.

The water bubbling merrily on the stove recalled me

to the business at hand, and I hurried back through
the shadowy rooms, administered the necessary adrenalin, and thought of nothing but my patient's heart
reaction for the next hour. Then, reassured, I let my
mind wander to Deke Lonergan. What money? And
how did he propose to get it by morning?

I puzzled over those questions for some time, but, of
course, could come to no explanation regarding it—
which failure, by the way, was to give me considerable
chagrin later on, for the explanation was so simple,
so obvious, that it seemed impossible that I should not
have grasped it.

The fire had sunk to smoldering, sulky ashes by this
time; the moaning and wailing of the wind through the
evergreens had died suddenly to a somewhat ominous
calm, and the lamps were burning a little low. I was
conscious of the increasing dimness in the room before,
I realized the cause of it; probably in the excitement
of the day Grondal had forgotten to fill the lamps with
oil. With the abrupt ceasing of the winds, all the little
night sounds of the house stopped, too, and there was
a silence not unlike that heavy, moveless stillness of
death.

I must rouse myself, I knew—shake myself from the
curious lethargy that held me, replenish the fire, call
Grondal to fill the lamps.

But a singular sensation of waiting that had all at
once pervaded the hushed old walls possessed me also,
and I sat stiffly, as if frozen, my tongue feeling large
and clumsy, and my forehead and the backs of my hands
were suddenly moist. The last flame in the fireplace
succumbed to the crowding ashes, the lamps burned

lower, and just as one of them sent up a sudden wisp of odorous black smoke a board creaked in the room over my head.

It creaked and creaked again.

Someone was walking in that locked room above!

My heart was thudding so heavily that I could scarcely hear, but I strained my ears and I was certain that I heard, pressing lightly and stealthily on the old flooring above, the sound of cautious feet.

What was prowling up there?

And all at once Genevieve rose lithely to his full gaunt height, fastened his shining eyes on the stairway, and began to twitch his tail nervously from side to side.

I think the very extremity of my terror served to clear my head. At any rate, I got cautiously to my feet and crossed the room to Grondal's couch, so carefully that not even a fold of my starched skirt rustled, and put one hand on his arm and the other on his mouth.

He awoke at once, and though he jerked away from my detaining hands, still he did not cry out. I suppose the terror in my face told him something, for I said nothing, but simply pointed overhead. And as if to explain me there came again that cautious, furtive sound.

Grondal rose, taking care to ease himself off the couch so that the old springs would not twang, and turned at once to the tower stairway.

Was the man going up those stairs?

That is exactly what he did. I shall never forget standing there as if paralyzed, watching him go, step by step, lithe and silent as any panther, around the first turn—then step by step past the place where Adolph Federie died, on beyond the second turn, and so, as I craned my neck to follow him with my terrified gaze, gradually out of sight, his face first and then his rounded shoulders and body. The last thing I saw fully was one dangling yellow hand.

And he did not come back!

CHAPTER X

FOR long moments I stood there waiting and listening as if my life were at stake. But, so far as I could tell, there was no movement in the room above. The lamps burned lower and were smoking now in good earnest, and I knew that I must see to them—get other lamps or light candles. There was still not a breath of wind and not a sound to be heard. Even Genevieve seemed frozen to a gaunt yellow statue with two fiery eyes that reflected lights from the dying lamps.

Gradually panic was overwhelming me. It did not come all at once, but slowly and dreadfully.

Something had happened in the room above. Why did not Grondal return? Was it because he—*could* not?

And suddenly Genevieve leaped to the floor and, with his bushy tail and gaunt body low to the floor, slunk swiftly to the curtained doorway and disappeared, and the last remnant of courage I possessed was shattered.

Lance O'Leary had told me to telephone to him in case of need. I gave one last glance up that dark stairway and started toward the doorway, thrusting the curtain aside with shaking hands. In the dark passage I began to run; I stumbled at the turn and fell against the wall and somehow kept on. In the dining room there were chilly streaks of moonlight coming through the cracks in the curtains and looking like cold, dead fingers reaching out to clutch at me. The room beyond those faint streaks was blacker.

Somewhere was the door into the butler's pantry. My shaking hands groped in the blackness, met a panel, and pushed. It gave a little and, swinging the door wide, I entered the pantry. The door closed behind me and I felt for the shelves and table that would guide me to the kitchen door. There had been shadows in the dining room; here it was completely dark save for the faint penciling of light under the door to the kitchen.

And, as I started toward that door, from somewhere in the surrounding blackness came a slight sound.

It wasn't a rustle; it was just a breath of sound. I stopped dead still, stricken by a dreadful conviction. Someone was in that dark pantry with me!

And suddenly my outstretched hand touched something that moved. It felt rough like heavy cloth; it moved away, and my touch met bare flesh and fingers for a fleeting fraction of a second.

Then there was a sudden, bold rush of motion, the door into the dining room swung, I caught the barest glimpse of a black bulk of shadow between me and the pale streaks of moonlight, and the door closed again, and I was left in that black void, trying to scream through a throat that seemed paralyzed.

It was stark panic that sent me stumbling through the pantry and into the kitchen, where the fire glowed redly through the open draft of the fire box and the lamp on the table burned dimly.

Somehow I found the telephone in the back entry

beyond the kitchen. And even then I could not remember O'Leary's telephone number and could only gasp in response to central's bored inquiry: "Police—police!"

My teeth were chattering so that I could scarcely reply to the masculine voice that after æons of time came through the instrument, but I did manage to insist upon Lance O'Leary's being told that he was wanted at Federie house. It was after I hung up the receiver that I remembered that there were already two policemen somewhere in the old house. But a sixth sense assured me that I had done wisely.

My hand was still clutching the receiver when without warning an electric torch was flashed full in my face. "Was that you at the telephone?" demanded a voice beyond the bright circle of light. "What do you want the police for? Why didn't you call me?"

It was one of the two policemen, of course.

"There is something—" my voice emerged as only a hoarse whisper and I tried again—"there's something the matter. In the tower room. Where have you been?"

"Hey, there, miss, don't go to fainting."

"I'm not fainting, you fool. In the tower room. There was somebody upstairs. Grondal went up and he didn't—" my voice broke in what was almost a sob—"he didn't come back. *Hurry!*"

The glare from the electric torch made the shelves in the pantry, the vast table, and many chairs in the dining room all loom up with ghostly distinctness. We said nothing as we ran. In the narrow passage I fell behind, and as he thrust the green curtain upward I stood on tiptoe to peer around his shoulder.

The room was dimly lighted, the lamps smoking furiously and filling the room with the rank, suffocating smell of burning wicks. And over on the green couch, directly under the tower stairway whose railing gleamed darkly, a figure was hunched.

"There he is," said the policeman, stepping aside to let me pass. "You just got scared."

I was staring past the smoking lamps at the hunched figure there on the green couch. It was Grondal—and yet—and yet—— Slowly, one step at a time, I advanced.

The figure on the couch did not move.

I shot a glance at the policeman who was following me. His face was a sickly green and his breath was whistling between his teeth and his eyes were bulging.

I went on until I was within a yard of that curiously stolid figure. I stopped, then put out my hand, reached closer, and bent to force myself to look.

"It is Grondal," I heard myself saying in a still voice. "It is Grondal and he is dead. He has been strangled. With a—a violin string."

Then all at once I felt hideously sick and dizzy, things began to circle giddily about me, blending together, and the floor opened to swallow me.

The next thing I was conscious of was the sound of many voices, oddly blurred and all talking at once. The flickering of lights hurt my eyes as I tried to lift my heavy lids.

Someone was saying over and over again in a high-pitched voice: "Who did it? Who did it?" and with the words I remembered what had happened.

I opened my eyes again. Someone must have shoved

me into a chair and I was lying uncomfortably across the arm of it; my neck was cramped and I sat upright. Many lights, candles, and lamps were casting competing flares of light that threw the whole room into sharp relief. The excited voices were coming from a cluster of kimonos and bathrobes and blue coats over there under the tower stairway. Beyond them the green plush foot of the old couch, with a blanket huddled on it, protruded significantly. Eustace and Lonergan and Dimuck were there, all three firing questions at the policeman. Isobel was leaning past Dimuck's shoulder; she clutched a bright Chinese shawl over her nightgown and had thrust her red hair wildly back of her ears. A second policeman was there, too, and he and the one who had, with me, found the body were arguing heatedly as to what should be done. Mittie Frisling was hovering over the fire, sniffling and wringing her hands, and March was kneeling on the floor at her grandfather's side, holding one of his helpless hands in both her own, and shivering violently, her face as white as the counterpane.

Kema came into the room, carrying a pitcher of water; she gave me an unconcerned glance, though I think I needed as much attention as anyone, and went to March, making her drink some of the water.

I rose, crossed to the bedside table, helped myself to a drink of water, straightened my cap, and felt better.

By that time the policemen seemed to have come to some conclusion, for, after a peremptory word to the men, they hurried from the room.

"Why didn't they go up the tower stairs!" I cried. "That is where the murderer was! In the room above."

"What do you mean?" asked Eustace quickly.

"I heard him. I'm sure I heard him."

Then as everyone stared blankly at me I added: "And I'm going up to see that room!" I looked dubiously at the three men. "Mr. Dimuck, will you go with me?"

He shrunk back a little at my abrupt question, pulling his yellow bathrobe more tightly about him and blinking stupidly.

"I'll go with you," offered Isobel, unexpectedly. I shook my head. I did not want Isobel. I could not trust the woman.

In the little pause Mr. Dimuck appeared to have grasped my purpose.

"Surely," he said. "Surely. I'll go with you. You feel that there may be something in that room? Or someone hiding?"

"There *was* someone," I said. "But I don't suppose he is there now," I added with a touch of scorn as the Dimuck man withered a little. "And, anyway, I want to see that bedroom."

"Oh, Miss Keate," breathed March, continuing in a firmer tone: "I'll go with you, too."

"No, you won't!" cried Eustace rudely. "If that old maid wants to take a chance with her life she can, but you aren't going to!"

Deke Lonergan, who had been sitting in a sort of dazed way on the foot of the couch, glanced at the grim figure hunched there, shuddered, and got up.

"It won't matter if we just—straighten him out—and put a sheet or something over him, will it, Eustace?" he said uneasily. "I—well, I can't stand seeing him like that. It makes me sort of—sick. I'll go with you Miss Keate."

"No," I said with decision. "You and the head of the house—" I indicated Eustace with as contemptuous a gesture as I could contrive—"you and the head of the house stay here. There is no danger so long as we stay together. You see"—I looked very slowly and deliberately about the room, lingering at every pair of eyes— "one of us right here in this room killed Grondal. No outsider could get in the house," I went on coolly, unheeding Mittie's strangled scream, and Isobel's suddenly glittering eyes, and March's still white face. "And since we are all here there can be no one in the room above. So, you see, there is no danger."

March was standing.

"Miss Keate," she said in a voice of stifled horror, "do you know what you are saying?"

Eustace was approaching me, his brightly striped pajamas incredibly gay in that somber, ugly room, with the garish lights flaring from everywhere, and the haggard white faces, and the secretive curtains and the narrow tower stairway—and the grotesquely huddled figure on the couch behind him.

"You are out of your mind," he said, a very devil of rage in his even, restrained tone.

"Nonsense," I retorted crisply. "Don't think you can frighten me, young man. And it is no news that one of you is the murderer. You know very well you have been thinking it every waking second of the last two days. You can't see how you watch each other, but *I* can see it. How you speculate—Is that the one? Did he do it? Did she? Was hers the hand that held the revolver? And now you'll think—whose hand knotted that violin string?" My voice was shaking and I stopped.

"The woman is mad," muttered Isobel. Her large fingers were groping absently over the mantel; whether for cigarettes or to find some missile to hurl at me I did not know. At any rate, she kept her strange eyes, fury in their hazy depths, fastened on mine.

"*She was in the room!*" screamed Mittie suddenly, pointing a vicious forefinger at me. "She was in the room when Adolph was killed. And she was in the room when Grondal was killed. She did it!"

"You may consider yourself discharged, Miss Keate," said Eustace, his voice smooth and low and very deadly.

"Discharged, fiddlesticks!" I snapped. "It takes a better man than you to——"

"*Eustace!*" March's voice cut into my words. "*You forget yourself! Is this your place!*"

Dark red surged into Eustace's face, quite as if he had been lashed by a whip.

"My place is certainly to protect you from this crazy woman's charges," he said sullenly, his dark eyes slits of malice.

"When I need your protection I will ask for it," said March very deliberately; her blue eyes were like swords and her black brows were straight and implacable. "Miss Keate stays, of course. And, Miss Keate, if you and Mr. Dimuck wish to examine the room above, do so, by all means. I——" she paused to sweep the faces before her with a coldly scornful look—"I will see to it that no one leaves this room while you are gone."

Eustace stepped aside to let me pass, his manner partaking of that of a whipped dog that yet shows his teeth; I believe it was the first time I had seen him without his mask of debonair sophistication.

Dimuck followed me—reluctantly, I think. He had said nothing during the ugly little scene, but now as we started up those narrow steps he began to mumble in disjointed exclamations of a mingled disapproval and shocked distaste.

I could feel the eyes of those in the room below watching us steadily as we mounted the narrow steps and rounded the first sharp turn. I stepped gingerly past the spot where Adolph's body had lain and came to the second turn. The remaining steps looked very dark as they went past the area that was lighted from the lamps in the room below.

"Will someone hand me a lamp?" I asked, leaning over the banister.

Lonergan passed a lamp to Dimuck, and as its wavering light fell on the steps yet before me I took a long breath and went on, feeling, in spite of myself, that there might be something waiting there at the head of the stairs to clutch at me as I emerged from the stair well.

The stairway ended in a small room that looked like a neglected study. There were bookshelves along the wall and a railing straight across the room dividing the tower well from the room; I glanced over the railing and could see the green couch with its dreadful burden and the top of Deke Lonergan's head.

It was a bare little room, and I motioned to Elihu Dimuck to precede me into the bedroom adjoining. He did so, holding the lamp very high so that his bald head caught glistening highlights and his thick eyeglasses winked. I think he did not relish the expedition, for his face had lost its round pinkness and his cheeks looked like shriveled apples.

The bedroom in which we found ourselves was a long room, running clear back to the east wall, and our lamp made only a feeble effort to combat with its shadows. It was not so cluttered with furniture that we could not see at a glance that there was no one in the room. I knew, of course, that there could be no one, since everyone in the house was accounted for, but nevertheless I looked in the tall wardrobes, two of them, and under the high old bed that was still tossed with bedclothing as when Lonergan had sprung out of it following the shot that killed Adolph. Mr. Dimuck gave me a curious look as I motioned him to hold the light while I peered under the bed, but he said nothing.

To a detective the room might be full of clues, but, though I was positive that the murderer of Grondal had been in that room within the hour, I saw nothing to indicate his presence. I walked slowly back to the bare, marble-topped table that stood in the center of the room and leaned upon it with my hands, staring at the door that led to the corridor of the second floor. Its broad, dark panels stared back at me blankly.

Dimuck set the lamp on the table beside me and walked over to the door.

"I wonder if it is still locked," he said.

Just as he spoke I moved a little away from the lamp chimney, whose light was flaring in my eyes, and somehow, in moving my hand along the top of the table, I caught it on something sharp that looked like a tiny splinter of broken glass. I withdrew my hand hastily to examine the jagged inch-long scratch and thus did not realize that the Dimuck man had taken the glass

doorknob in both fat hands and was shaking and turning it vigorously.

"It's still locked——"

"Stop that!" I interrupted sharply, taking my hand
from my mouth. "Take your hands off that!"

He let his hands drop and looked at me in dismay.
"Why, what is the matter? What have I done?"

"What haven't you done, you idiot!" I cried irritatedly. "You have destroyed the fingerprints on that
doorknob. That's what you've done. If there were any
there," I added to myself, pausing to suck the bleeding
place on my hand again.

"Did you hurt yourself?" he asked, courteously over-
looking the "idiot."

"Just a scratch. Of course, you have left a beautiful
set of your own fingerprints for the police to find."

"*My own!*"

I dare say I am small-minded, but I did enjoy his
discomfiture.

"My own fingerprints!" he exclaimed, looking in
mingled horror and dismay at the doorknob opposite.
"Dear me! Dear me! My dear Miss Keate, do you suppose they'll think I did it?"

"I'm sure I don't know," I said dryly.

"Ah, Miss Keate. I thought I'd find you here. What
is the matter with your hand?" It was Lance O'Leary,
of course, advancing from the tower stairway.

"I scratched it on something here on the table." I
glanced vaguely at the mottled gray and white, and
Elihu Dimuck burst into a shower of apologies anent
the doorknob.

O'Leary listened barely long enough to understand what was troubling the man; then he interrupted curtly:

"I understand. Will you go downstairs, please, Mr. Dimuck, and send O'Brien up here? No, stay here, Miss Keate. I want to talk to you." As Dimuck's agitated yellow bathrobe disappeared down the tower stairway, O'Leary resumed:

"Tell me all about it, Miss Keate, and if you ever cut quick corners in your life, do so now."

And I did. That is to say, I told him the story of the night, including Lonergan's conversation over the telephone, my conviction that I had passed someone in the butler's pantry when I was hurrying to call him, O'Leary, and of course Grondal's ascent into the room in which we stood and the reason for it, and I think the telling of the whole thing did not take more than five minutes' time.

O'Leary stood there quietly while I talked; he rapped out a question now and then or nodded impatiently; his gray eyes shone with a kind of phosphorescent gleam and his fingers tapped the table lightly.

"All right, Miss Keate, thanks. You'd better go down now and put some iodine on that hand of yours. Where was it you scratched it? Oh, I see."

I was glad enough to have an excuse to leave and did so at once. On the tower stairway I passed a policeman, O'Brien, who was ascending. He moved aside to let me pass, and I had to put my foot directly on a darkish stain on the stair carpet where Adolph's body had pressed.

The hour or so that followed was like the aftermath

of a horrible nightmare. My patient's condition was unchanged, and it seemed strange to me that he, there in the room where the things happened, should know nothing, first of his son's violent death and then of the equally ugly death of his old servant.

Everyone remained in the tower room; I did not know whether it was owing to their fear of being alone or to my own furious arraignment of them. Policemen came and went hurriedly; O'Leary came down the stairway and bent for some time over Grondal's body, and we sat, a silent, huddled group, watching the subdued bustle that took place before the ambulance came and orderlies in white duck came again into the room. As they walked slowly toward the curtained doorway, carrying a stretcher between them, I wondered if other thoughts echoed mine. Two bodies had already gone from the tower room. Would there be a third?

Kema broke the rather dreadful stillness that held us as the green velvet dropped slowly into place and the sound of the slow, measured footsteps ceased.

"I'll make some coffee," she said in a calm way, billowing to her feet.

"That is right," agreed March. "And—Kema!"

The old woman turned to face her young mistress; her coarse black hair shone and her yellow eyes were inscrutable as ever between the dangling gold hoops at her ears.

"Yes, Miss March."

"Oh—nothing," said March lamely, but a glance of—well, it was undoubtedly significant, but of what I couldn't guess, passed between them, and Kema nodded once, quite as if she understood March's unspoken words and was gone.

Some fifteen minutes later she was back, steaming
coffee on a tray. I was standing beside March as Kema
offered her coffee. The old cook leaned very close to the
girl, and I'm sure she said something that sounded like:
"It is all right."

As I say, it sounded like that, and certainly March
seemed to be oddly relieved at the assurance, for she
took a long breath and leaned against the back of her
chair and began to look less like a blood-drained little
ghost.

About six o'clock O'Leary returned to the tower room
and began to question us, more sternly this time, and
hurriedly, and with less consideration for our feelings.
This, too, was something like the affair of Adolph's
death, so recently passed and yet unsolved, and gave me
a peculiar sense of repetition. However, I think, if anything, the matter of Grondal's death was more horrible,
for it brought home to us the unpleasant fact that there
was still an active menace haunting the old house. If,
in order to accomplish unnamable ends the deaths of
Adolph and Grondal had been necessary, who could say
what would be next? Or rather, who would be next?

It was not a nice thought.

It was impossible that one of that tense still circle was
guilty. And yet—one of them must be!

Our furtive looks at each other, the ugly speculation
that lay back of every pair of meeting eyes, our haggard
faces, our startled motions when a log slipped in the
hearth, or Isobel flicked ashes from her cigarette, or
Dimuck cleared his throat, or old Kema padded in and
out of the room—all gave witness to the fear we had of
each other. One does not as a rule connect crime, and

ugly, sordid crime, at that, with one's nearest associates—with the people who live in the same house, eat at the same table, share the same daily routine with one's self. And I may as well state here and now that there is nothing more aptly calculated to make the stoutest hearted shake in his boots!

Was it young Lonergan, sitting there not more than five feet from me, staring with moody eyes at the fire? Certainly it might have been, for his conduct needed explanation. Was it Eustace, lolling at ease on the green couch, with a callous disregard for what it had so lately held that would have done credit to a Borgia? Was it Elihu Dimuck fidgeting politely in a straight chair, crossing and recrossing his knees, rubbing his nose, passing a white handkerchief over and over his bald, shining head?

Or was it Isobel, curled now in an easy chair, her bare feet drawn up under the gaudy folds of the Chinese shawl, her streaked hair in a disheveled mop, her cheek bones sharp without the softening outline that her hair usually offered, her eyes clouded, and a perpetual cigarette between her lips, that were pallid now without their usual red salve? She had the capacity for it, if nothing else.

My eyes went on to Mittie. She was huddled bunchily under a beflowered cotton crêpe kimono that had seen better days and did not adequately conceal her shapeless figure, her hair hung in wisps, and her light eyes were staring from brown pockets and looked distracted. At the moment, her appearance was such as to make almost any act of desperation seem quite conceivable.

March was standing beside Mittie; she was straight

and white and very grave; she had not the look of a criminal, but she had resolution and there was always the scarlet rosette.

Or it might even be Kema who was squatting comfortably on the floor. There was a latent savagery in that dark, inscrutable face, though for what purpose she should set out on a career of violence was beyond my understanding.

I believe that they had been expecting O'Leary to return and make some kind of informal inquiry, although no one stirred when he returned. But at the end of some thirty minutes it appeared that everyone save myself had been peacefully and innocently asleep in his bed when the murder occurred, and only two things of any interest developed. One was that Deke Lonergan said nothing of his midnight trip to the telephone and the conversation that took place. And the other was the unexpected tale that Mittie, who was questioned last, told.

"I was asleep. The police whistle woke me, and as soon as I heard it blowing so shrill and loud all through the house I knew that something terrible had happened," she said. "I jumped out of bed and ran into the corridor. And I know that Eustace was not in his room, as he said he was, because I saw him come out of the trunk room!"

Eustace moved at that, shot her a malevolent look, and turned to O'Leary.

"It is perfectly true," he said. "I preferred not to tell you because, well—I have as much regard for my own skin as the next man, and it doesn't sound any too good for me! But, of course, you would tell if you could, Mittie." He paused—to collect himself, I thought. "It was this way. I awoke possibly ten minutes before the murder was discovered—that is, before we heard the police whistle. I thought I heard voices in the bedroom above this one. So I slipped out of bed and into the corridor and went to the door—the door that was supposed to be locked." He paused again.

"Go on," said O'Leary.

"Well, I did hear voices, very low—just a sort of repressed jumble of words. Whoever was in there—I could tell there were two of them—seemed to be quarreling, and the only words I heard distinctly sounded like 'I will have the money.' I'm not sure, but that is what it sounded like. I think they began to fight. I could hear the sound of a struggle and then a heavy, dull noise and —gasps."

Mittie squealed and O'Leary asked dryly:

"And you made no effort to enter the room—stop the trouble?"

"Yes, I did. Naturally I waited a moment or two while I listened. I wanted to—get my bearings. And— I don't suppose you will believe it, but it is true— I had my hand on the doorknob and the door was unlocked. I was on the point of entering the room when something made me glance over my shoulder, down the hall, and I saw——" He cleared his throat and looked ill at ease. "You will not believe it, but I saw a shadowy sort of figure moving down near the head of the stairs. It seemed to be running and vanished into the trunk room before you could wink. I didn't stop to think. There was something about the way the thing was running that—well—I left the door and ran after it and into the trunk room. It was black as tar in there and I couldn't hear a sound. But I kept on waiting, thinking I'd hear it moving about or—something. And after what seemed a long while I heard the police whistle and ran out." He shot another wicked look at Mittie.

"Who was in the corridor when you came out of the trunk room?"

"Mittie Frisling, at first. We started for the stairway. Then Dimuck and Deke were at our heels and then Isobel and March. We all hurried helter-skelter down the stairs and to this room."

"Then if one of them had preceded you into the trunk room you might not have seen him come out and into the corridor with the others?"

"No," said Eustace reluctantly. "But someone in the corridor surely did."

It appeared, however, that no one had, and I didn't know whether O'Leary believed Eustace's highly colored story or not. I could tell nothing from his tone or aspect.

"About how long were you in the trunk room?"

"I thought it was about ten minutes. I can't be sure. I wasn't exactly—easy, you know. I had no idea as to whom I had followed into that room, or what he might do."

"'He?'" queried O'Leary gently.

"You mean, was it a man or woman?" Eustace spread his delicate fingers helplessly. "I haven't the least idea. It was just a—running shadow. The corridor up there is very dark, you know. Only a candle or two to light it. The old gentleman—" he cast the face on the bed a disrespectful look—"that is, Grandfather, would never permit any modern improvements. He seems to distrust them. Perhaps you've noticed that we have no electricity."

"Yes, I have noticed that," said O'Leary. "You are sure it was ten minutes that you waited there in the trunk room?"

"No, I'm not sure of anything. It might have been only three or four minutes. I was—well, I was—scared."

"Could you identify the voices in the bedroom?"

"No," said Eustace decidedly. "Never in the world."

"You are very positive about that," commented O'Leary softly. "Could you tell whether they were the voices of two men or two women—or a man and a woman?"

"Well"——— Eustace hesitated. To make his lie sound more plausible, I thought acidly to myself. "It was my impression that both voices belonged to men. But one of them might have been a woman's voice. A woman who was excited or frightened. It was that voice that said 'I will have the money.' And I suppose, of course, that the other voice was—Grondal's."

There was a curious little hush. I glanced about me. If Eustace were telling the truth one of the strained white masks that were our faces covered a fearful secret. Was any face more desperately intent on Eustace's words than another? My eyes went from one to another, half in eagerness, half in dread, lest I should surprise an ugly secret. But each was haggard, fearing, pale—and completely unfathomable.

"You did not rouse Mr. Lonergan when you got out of bed?" inquired O'Leary.

"No," replied Eustace smoothly. "You see, Deke

was sleeping in the room across the hall. There was a vacant bedroom there, and he decided last night to use it and not to share my room."

"Eustace snores," remarked Deke suddenly and flatly without taking his eyes from the carpet.

Eustace looked faintly embarrassed at this, which was a source of mean gratification on my part, and Isobel smiled thinly.

"Then you are sure that the bedroom above this one was, at that time, unlocked?"

"Positive," said Eustace, regaining his customary aplomb.

"And while you were in the trunk room anyone could have come into the corridor from that room, locked the door behind him, and made his escape without your seeing him?"

"I suppose so."

"How long were you gone from the room, Miss Keats?"

"Why, I—it's hard to say. Possibly ten minutes."

"Long enough for the struggle, of which Mr. Federie tells us, to take place, for Grondal to be killed, and the murderer to escape through the bedroom upstairs?"

"Y-Yes. I think so."

"You heard nothing, no sounds of a struggle, before you went to the telephone?"

"Not a sound."

"Then it all took place, apparently, after you had left this room and before you returned to it. The murderer, whoever it is, had luck on his side this time."

O'Leary paused, his clear gray eyes shining with a strangely lucent look as if they saw far beyond ordinary limits. "*This* time," he repeated slowly and gently enough, but his voice had an undercurrent that was icy cold and implacable.

For a long moment there was silence in the room. Then Lance O'Leary rose, looked at his watch, and spoke in a matter-of-fact way. "That is all—now. You will all want to rest and have breakfast. There will be an inquest at eight o'clock. That gives you two hours. I shall have to ask that no one leave the place until I permit you to do so."

The dismissal was plain, to be sure, but scarcely peremptory enough to warrant the hurried way in which they, one and all, made for the door. It savored of a release; the room wasn't cheerful, of course, but I had the impression that it was O'Leary they wanted to escape rather than the ghost-ridden room.

"There is something I want to tell you," said March, halting the others with an imperative hand. "I have decided not to find another manservant until—until this trouble is over with. I think a stranger or two would only complicate matters." She glanced at O'Leary who nodded approvingly.

"Nonsense, March!" cried Eustace. "I'll send right away to an employment agency. We'd better get a man and an extra maid. I'll see to it."

"I said *I* had decided," said March in a tone that made no doubt of the matter. "And in the meantime—we will share Grondal's work between us. That is, *you* will share his work."

There was an instant's pause.

"And what will you do, March?" asked Isobel silkily.

"I shall see to it that the work is done," returned March, and meant it. And she quelled the little storm of protest that arose with as supremely insolent assurance as that of any pirate captain.

I smiled a little, as they finally straggled through the doorway, and Mittie Frisling's half-hearted grumbles died away in the distance. But the smile left my lips as I turned again to see the gloomy room, the lamps and candles pale and sickly in the dreary streaks of daylight. Two of the lamps had gone out—the two that had smoked so furiously—and the strong odor of burning oil wicks still lingered in the room. And there was no Grondal to clean the lamps and unlock and open the shutters.

Over there on the green couch I could still see, and always shall be able to see, a dreadful vision of the hunched, silent figure that did not move or speak.

CHAPTER XI

TWICE DEAD

LANCE O'LEARY was standing near the couch, looking thoughtfully at its faded, puffy, green plush upholstery.

"Mr. O'Leary," I began without preamble, "I want a good electric torch, a big one, and two policemen in this room to-night. Either that or I and my patient go to the hospital. This thing has gone too far."

"You shall have them, Miss Keate," he said at once. "I'll give you a revolver, too."

"Oh, I don't want a revolver." I shrank back from the ugly thing he was already holding out toward me. "I'm more afraid of the revolver than—that is, I'd prefer a good, stout stove poker. And I'll stay, of course. I have never yet left anything unfinished."

He smiled but said nothing, and I watched him poise the revolver on his palm and look at it contemplatively for a long moment before I asked the question that was trembling on my mouth.

"Have you found anything? Do you know who did it?"

"Well," he said slowly, "I have made a little progress." He spoke in the cordial, friendly way he used toward me, which always made me feel as if we were friends of long standing. As, indeed, we were. "A little progress. It is a strange case, though, Miss Keate. You see, I feel sure that Adolph Federie and Grondal each met his death for the same reason and thus presumably by the same agencies. And Grondal—was killed twice."

"Twice! Why—why, what do you mean?"

"Twice," he repeated. "Somehow he received a blow over the heart that, according to our medical examiner, was sufficient to kill him almost at once. And yet within apparently the same ten minutes he was strangled with a violin string. Now, then, were there two people intent upon his death? Or did the same man who struck the first blow follow Grondal when he staggered downstairs to drop, dying, on the couch, and, fearful that death might not result, twist the violin string about his neck to make sure?"

"You say the 'man' who struck the first blow?"

"Yes, although it might not have been a man. Eustace seems to think it was a woman. It was a heavy blow such as might have been made by—" he glanced about him—"by a very heavy pair of fire tongs, for instance, or, better, a flatiron. He could even have fallen or been pushed, if with sufficient force, against a corner of—that mantel, for instance, if it were lower and received such a blow. It probably took place during the struggle Eustace told of. Of course, that was only the first, hurried report of our medical examiner. A later one may throw a clearer light on it. By the way, who plays the violin?"

"Eustace. At least I have not heard anyone else."

O'Leary walked over to the table and looked thoughtfully at the old violin.

"One string is gone."

I thought rapidly back to the night when Eustace had tuned the thing.

"There were four strings on it when Eustace played it. The night we heard the footsteps while we were eating. I distinctly remember Eustace tuning it. I thought he would never get it right and I remember the four notes."

"Then it is a possibility that the string came from here," commented O'Leary. "A weapon chosen on the spur of the moment. Well, if you can tell me who took the string—but, of course, you can't."

"Mr. O'Leary, have you no clue at all?" I asked desperately.

"Yes. I have a clue." He smiled wearily. "You gave it to me. But as to where it will lead I have only a small hint. Find me the possessor of the key to that upstairs room, Miss Keate. And find me——" He stopped abruptly, as if struck by a sudden thought, and presently continued soberly: "It is a bad business. I've got to worry the thing out some way. There is always a reason. A motivating force somewhere." He paused again, frowning a little. "Of course, you'll remember that Mittie Frisling heard Grondal tell of meeting her on the stairway the night Adolph was killed. But I scarcely think she would choke him with a violin string on account of that."

"He was worried, though, when he found that she had overheard him," I protested. "And Eustace said it might have been a woman up there with Grondal."

"And Eustace also said that the person who was there with Grondal said, 'I will have the money.' Did it strike you as being very similar to Lonergan's promise over the telephone?"

"Oh. I—why, yes, of course." The connection was clear once O'Leary had pointed it out. Too clear. I rather liked young Lonergan in spite of his sulks.

"Worth considering, at least," said O'Leary. "Don't worry about the inquest. It will be of necessity merely a formality." With a little nod of farewell he walked to the door. There was something gone from the usual alert ease of his walk and in its place a less buoyant look of steadiness and of dogged purpose. It is difficult to think of slender, quick-moving Lance O'Leary as being dogged, but there it was nevertheless, as if his task grew more difficult and more distasteful with every hour.

The morning passed rapidly.

Autos came and went busily—police cars, reporters, and many curious sightseers who splashed along the muddy road to stare and point through the tall iron gate with morbid satisfaction. And eight or ten boys, newsboys and street urchins, I suppose, perched along the top of the brick wall staring through the fog with ghoulish delight and looking like wet, draggled little sparrows until a policeman ordered them away.

Once Eustace let loose a fury upon several reporters who got into the house, which sent them scurrying, intrepid though they are, as a class, for besides his temper, which was ugly enough, Eustace unleashed Konrad. Only a fool or an idiot would linger in the neighborhood of such a dog as Konrad, and reporters are neither. This drew a protest from March; Isobel, happening into the hall, had her say in the matter; Mittie came galloping from the library to fling hysterical insults in Isobel's direction, and before I could reach the upper hall—I was going upstairs for fresh bed linen—Dimuck and Kema and Lonergan had turned up and they were all embroiled in one of those sudden, bitterly passionate outbursts that characterized the strange household.

I ascended the steps rather slowly, as becomes one of my age and weight, and heard the whole thing which ended only when March, her voice like a whiplash, ordered them all back to work.

The inquest was, as O'Leary had predicted, a formality; this fact did not prevent it, however, from being a very unpleasant formality, and I was relieved when it was over and it had been decided, with what struck me as rather marked expedition, that Jem Grondal had come to his death at the hands of a person or persons unknown.

The doctor was waiting for me when I returned to the tower room after the inquest. He had heard the news as, according to him, all B—— was ringing with talk of the two murders, and he was bursting with questions. Old Mr. Federie was distinctly better, he said, but I think it was only his very lively curiosity that kept him from ordering me and my patient to the safe confines of the hospital. The doctor lingered for some time, but a telephone call finally came for him from St. Ann's and he tore himself away.

The rest of the day following Grondal's death is characterized in my memory by several events, chief of which is, of course, my ill-advised trip to the attic and what came of it.

After the doctor left I lingered in the tower room, caring for my patient and straightening the disordered room. It seemed very strange not to see Grondal going and coming with his antiquated carpet sweeper and duster, and when Eustace came in with an armload of wood, with Lonergan trailing after him, picking up the numerous pieces of wood that fell, and carrying a little broom with which he swept the hearth—and swept it most untidily, I must say—I found that I actually missed Grondal with his dark face and scar. He had made himself an important part of the household, an almost indispensable figure, and I began to feel that in suspecting the man I had cruelly misjudged him.

His death, too, had appreciably narrowed the range of suspects. And it was in thinking of these suspects that an amazing possibility occurred to me. It was equally amazing that it had not occurred to me sooner.

Was it possible that there was someone hiding in that great old house? Someone who had managed thus far to evade detection by ourselves and by the police?

I don't know whether this alarming idea was simply in answer to the need for a logical explanation of the ugly tangle, or whether it had been growing in my subconscious mind ever since the episode of the footsteps. At any rate, there it was, and I considered it cautiously and, I hoped, reasonably.

There were, first, those mysterious and unacknowledged footsteps. I did not for a moment believe that Kema had told O'Leary the truth when she said she herself had been upstairs, walking on the bare floor of that back corridor, for when she had talked to me I had been positive that she had not lied. Then there was that diabolical music coming from the library the day when everyone save Kema, my patient, and me had been at

Adolph's funeral. I had certainly not touched the piano, it could not have been my patient, I was equally sure that Kema was not thus gifted, and I did not even consider the policemen, one of whom had been under my eyes at the time. True, it strained credulity a little to take it for granted that some intruder—a professional thief, though he had apparently stolen nothing, or perhaps some unknown Federie enemy—should happen to choose to play the tune that was Eustace's favorite, and to play it with the same wickedly sympathetic touch that Eustace used, but I shrugged away from that line of thought.

There was, too, the matter of the vanishing toy elephant; this theory would explain its disappearance from the violin case at a time when everyone in the house had been under my very eyes. If such a secret intruder were actually in and about that old house, where assuredly there must be a multitude of hiding places, was he there with the connivance of another member of the household? And who *could* such an intruder be?

The question of his possible identity was highly problematical, and I did not try to guess its answer. But I knew that if there were such a person he must have had some help in getting in and out of the place, locked and guarded as it was. And immediately certain things occurred to me—the dog's barking at dinner that first night and March's agitation; and the second night Konrad had barked, too, just at dinner time again, which would be the best time in the world for someone to make an unobserved entrance into the house. March's surreptitious errand through the storm the night of Adolph's murder—had that been to lead someone past the furious dog and to a hiding place outside the house which she knew would soon be searched? And Kema—why, of course, Kema was in the secret! Had she not covered March's flight by lying most villainously to the police? And had she not denied her presence on the second floor, the night we had heard someone walking there along the bare corridor and later, doubtless apprised by March of the need, had told O'Leary that she herself had walked there above our heads. Kema, whose tread was as noiseless and stealthy as any wildcat's!

Well, it was a fantastic idea, of course, in view of the fact that the whole house had been under police guard for some two days and nights and presumably thoroughly and completely searched. But I reminded myself that the truth is often unlikely, and by two o'clock, when March came to the tower room and offered to stay with her grandfather while I took my hours off, I was in a fever of impatience to prove or disprove the amazing possibility.

"I don't mind staying in the room," said March as I politely protested. "I am not afraid to be alone. And, anyway, there has been a very large policeman dogging my footsteps all day. I am sure he is somewhere within hailing distance." Her words were a bit flippant, but I think it was only a manner assumed to hide her horror and distress. There were faint purple shadows under her eyes, and she started nervously at every sound.

As I reached for the electric torch O'Leary had left for me on the table she clutched suddenly at my arm.

"If—if I could keep from seeing them! Grondal all huddled over there on that couch. And—and Uncle

Adolph on the stairway! It's his eyes. Uncle Adolph's!
I keep seeing them. All the time." She twisted around to
cast a shuddering look toward the couch and the angular
stairway and all at once flung both hands to her eyes,
pressing them hard against her face as if to shut out
the fearful memory that haunted her. She stood there,
shaking and trembling and drawing long, tremulous
breaths

"Don't!" I said sharply, taking her cold little hands
from her face and holding them firmly. "You are the
only one in the house who can keep things going. Without you it would be a madhouse. You've got to keep
up."

I think my words might have sounded more convincing had not Eustace's voice returned to my ears, saying
with that faintly ironic inflection: "A Federie hand is
born to fit the curve of a revolver," and "You afraid!"

But she stopped shivering and lifted her head; the
taut lines of her mouth and chin and the terrible anxiety
that lay in her darkly blue eyes were not nice to see in
so young a face.

"You are right," she said, a touch of pride in her
tone, though it was cold and even and joyless enough,
too. "One must take these responsibilities. I am the
head of the house while Grandfather is ill."

The hint of a bygone feudal age impressed me a little
in its very inconsistency. There the child stood in her
slim, smart little dress, her slender legs graceful under
suave silk hose, her dark short hair in misty little curls
and waves that were so soft you wanted to touch them
with your hand as you do a baby's hair, and with a
stern mouth announced that "one must take these re-

sponsibilities." What kind of family were these Federies?

"Don't wait, Miss Keate," went on March, keeping tight hold on her voice. "I am all right. It is only that— *that* happening to someone you know, someone in the family—and right here in the house where I have lived all my life——" She stopped abruptly, as if she dared say no more, and her eyes flickered nervously toward the stairway. Then she moved her head with an impatient little movement as if to tear her eyes and thoughts from that dread destination, and moved to a chair near her grandfather.

Well, for my part, I thought that almost anything that was sufficiently dark and evil might happen in that grim, muffled old house, but it did not become me to say so, and after giving March a few directions as to the care of my patient I took a firm grip on the flashlight and departed. As I pushed through the curtained doorway I collided forcibly with a policeman who must have been standing directly behind the curtain. He was inclined to be somewhat peevish about it, wanting to know in injured accents why I didn't look where I was going. He was standing on one foot, massaging the toes of the other as he spoke.

At the sound of the little commotion March came to the door, and the policeman, looking at once embarrassed and resentful, followed me across one of the drawing rooms. At the door of the second one I glanced back just in time to see his substantial bulk tiptoeing stealthily around the door into the little passage again.

In the entrance hall I came upon Mittie Frisling, something, I think, to her discomfiture, for she was doubled up with her knees and elbows on the floor and her head down, squinting in an effort to see under the great walnut chest that stood against the north wall. Her slippers with their run-over heels had slipped back and the heels of her stockings needed mending. She did not hear me until I was within three feet of her when she looked around rather wildly and sneezed several times.

"I was looking for something," she said, pushing the hair away from her face with two very dusty hands.

I regarded her coldly and went on. As I was ascending the stairs I glanced over the railing, and it gave me a little start to see one of the green curtains over a doorway opposite move slightly and Isobel's face appear in the space like a painted mask. She was watching Mittie with a kind of savage, stealthy ferocity and did not see me at all.

As that day and the next wore away I was to perceive that everyone in the house seemed to be "looking for something," for I never saw such a frenzy of restless runnings-about and searchings and secretive expeditions into closed rooms as went on in that house. But of that, later.

I did not pause to consider that if my theory were correct I was undertaking a very dangerous mission. I did think once of waiting for O'Leary's counsel, but decided against it. I am willing now to admit that I acted hastily, but that is my nature.

Without any hesitancy I took my way to the trunk room.

There were two reasons why I chose the trunk room: it led to the attic and I had not entered it the day of Adolph's funeral when I had explored the rest of the house. If the house had had a basement I should have started there, but it had none.

Furthermore, Eustace had said that he had seen someone enter the trunk room during the previous night, and while I did not wholly credit Eustace's tale, still there were little marks of truth about it.

I happened to look at my watch as I stood for a moment at the door, getting up my courage to enter. It was exactly ten minutes after two. And I did not emerge from that room until after six o'clock!

It still gives me cold chills to think of how and where I spent the intervening hours.

I took good care that no one should see me enter the room, a fact that I was to regret later on. And when I had whisked inside the door and closed it behind me I pressed the little button on the electric torch and turned the gleam of the light here and there.

It was a large room, high ceilinged, dark, and shadowy, with roughly plastered walls, but the name "trunk room" was only a fiction, for so far as I could see there was not a trunk in the whole room. Instead it was crowded with a heterogeneous collection of rubbish such as accumulates in an old house. There were plenty of nooks and corners where someone might lie concealed, but I decided to take a look in the attic before my courage, which had begun to dwindle the moment the stale, moldy smell of the place met my nostrils, had entirely ebbed away.

The steps that led to the attic were not prepossessing, being nothing more than a kind of ladder with flat, narrow steps instead of rounds, and not a sign of a railing other than the side pieces. I did not like the looks of it; neither did I like the looks of the dark opening into the attic. But I turned the light once more about the room, advanced to the sinister-looking affair, and started resolutely upward, clutching the side of the ladder with one hand and holding the flashlight, which was heavy and substantial, in the other. It seemed a long time before I reached the opening above, but I finally did and stopped there with my feet on the ladder and my eyes just above the floor of the attic.

Fortunately, or rather unfortunately as it proved, the trapdoor of the opening was pulled back on its hinges and held by a rope which was fastened to a hook in a near-by studding. The rays of the light revealed none too promising a sight, but I went on, crawling with some difficulty through the opening before I really took stock of the situation.

The house was bad, but the attic was worse. Far worse!

It was an enormous place, stretching away in three different directions, into very dark shadows. It was not wholly floored, and there were loose planks leading out toward the massive black outlines of chimneys here and there, and tiny gray windows at the far ends of the place. Long cobwebs, hung with the dust of years, clung to the beams and gave the place a ghostly, wraith-like appearance, and there was a dankly musty odor that suggested mildew and decay and was most unpleasant.

I stood there for a time, turning the light here and there about the cavernous blackness and staring wildly into the shadows that its gleam scarcely penetrated. All at once some small black creature darted from a corner and began swooping in swift circles about my head, making glancing shadows among the thin rays from the light which completed my demoralization. My courage didn't ebb away; it was simply gone and I was desperately and horribly afraid. My knees were weak, my hands and face felt damp and cold, and my heart was racing furiously, its rapid thuds seeming loud in that hushed place.

There was a claptrap of broken-legged tables, chairs with sagging springs, old lamps festooned with dust and cobwebs, and such things as gather in the attic of an old house. Quite near me was a piano stool upholstered in faded red plush; it was of the type that screws around, which pianists of thirty years back used to twirl with much éclat before they sat down to render musical selections. It was the nearest thing at hand, so I sat down upon it, feeling actually as if my knees could not hold me upright another moment. The bat, for such I judged the circling thing above me to be, bothered me and I ducked my head nervously every time it swooped past me and wondered when the creature would dart into my hair and tangle itself there, as I've always been told is its nefarious habit.

I tried to take longer breaths, but my heart pounded as furiously as ever, and it occurred to me that if the murderer were concealed behind one of those great chimneys he might suddenly step out and confront me. Or, worse, he might even now be crawling stealthily toward me, ready to spring. And with the thought I felt something crawling on my wrist, looked down and saw an enormous spider with furry legs. I sprang to my feet with a stifled scream and brushed wildly at the thing with the flashlight. I broke the crystal of my watch and the button on the light slipped, leaving me in impenetrable darkness, and I stumbled, catching at the top of the piano stool as I fell.

And I found the elephant!

Yes, I did.

It was hidden under the torn plush of the stool, and when my groping fingers touched its smooth, cold surface and followed its delicate outlines to the ears and curled-back trunk, I knew immediately what I had found. The piano stool had seemed extraordinarily lumpy, I recalled dazedly, when I sat on it, but I was then in no frame of mind to note such a thing as mere discomfort. Somehow, in clutching at the stool, my fingers had found the long rent in the upholstery, encountered the elephant's polished surface, and—there it was.

At once I comprehended the importance of what I had literally stumbled upon, and simultaneously I perceived the danger of my position. I was afraid to turn on the flashlight again and thus illumine myself, and my only desire was to escape. The opening into the room below was near me, and it was an easy matter to find it.

Now it has always been difficult for me to descend a ladder, particularly to get started. Darkness and fright confused me a little, too, and what with feeling into the darkness below me with my foot for the first step and being quite sure that something would reach either up from the trunk room to clutch my foot, or down from the attic to choke me, and with holding the flashlight in one hand and the cold little elephant in the other, and with trying to balance myself on the narrow little steps—what with all that it is no wonder the thing happened, though, to this day, I don't know just how it came about.

But all at once, without the least warning, the trapdoor came down. It was only owing to the fact that I had lowered my head in a fruitless effort to peer into the blackness below me that I escaped being brained then and there. The door made quite a thud as it hit and clouds of dust must have risen, for I had difficulty in breathing. But the really terrible thing was that somehow in its descent it had caught a fold of my dress and held it fast.

And there I was.

I transferred the elephant to my teeth and pulled and tugged and pushed, but could neither lift the trapdoor nor release my uniform. And it was no use trying to tear the garment as it was one of a new set I had recently had made of the firmest cloth, warranted to wear. I was held as in a vise in the most awkward position in the world.

Suppose I should lose my balance on the ladder and dangle in mid-air suspended by that outrageously solid uniform! Suppose there was someone hiding in the black void below me! Suppose no one missed me and I hung there a prisoner for hours above that stifling, ghostly room! Below that still ghostlier attic! A hundred such suppositions surged through my mind before all at once I stopped trying to free myself and froze into immobility, straining my ears to listen as if my life depended upon what I should hear.

From somewhere below me in that black void came
the sound of a cautious, stealthy movement!

It is no exaggeration to say that the blood fairly
curdled in my veins, for that is exactly what it feels like,
and is due, I suppose, to your heart seeming to stop.
It came again—an unmistakable rustle and sound of
something moving in the corner just below me.

And in a very frenzy of cold terror my hand grasped
the flashlight tighter and hurled it in the direction of
that cautious sound!

I had acted instinctively and the instant the flashlight
left my hand I knew that I had made a mistake. Especially as there was a kind of thud and then dead
silence.

What was there? Who was it? Was he waiting till I
felt secure enough to descend the ladder? Did he know
I was a prisoner there? Was it one of the family? Was it
the mysterious intruder I had expected to discover?
Why did he make no further sound? Had I managed
to strike him with the flashlight?

It is true that I have usually a good aim, especially
with a fly swatter, but still I did not think that in the
dark my impulsively chosen weapon could have hit its
mark.

But, above all, what could I do?

After æons of time, during which no further sound
came from the corner below me, I struggled out of my
uniform. It was the only thing to do and I did it cold-
bloodedly; it was buttoned from hem to collar, else
it would have been impossible.

Then, free from the trapdoor, I debated whether or

not to make a sudden dash for the door into the corridor. If the thing, whatever it was, had been in the far
corner of the room, I should have risked it, but, as it
was, he could reach the foot of the ladder before I could
do so. That is, if he were not knocked senseless by the
heavy flashlight, and I considered it highly improbable
that the thing had come near him.

After a period of time that might have been shorter
than it seemed I turned very cautiously around and sat
down on one of the steps—if you can call it sitting. And,
believe it or not, I sat there for three mortal hours!
Cramped, cold, numb. Afraid to go down and afraid
to go up. Alternately afraid I had killed the thing below
me and afraid I had not!

Three hours of sitting on a ladder under such circumstances is a hideous ordeal, and a woman of less than an
iron constitution must have toppled over at the end of
the first hour. But it is surprising to what lengths of
endurance we can go under the pressure of grim necessity.

During the last hour or so I began to feel that if the
thing below me were actually the murderer of Adolph
Federie and Grondal, I would almost rather risk a sudden death than be overtaken by a lingering one, as I
certainly should be if I sat on that ladder much longer.
I remember that I had figured out a quite touching
scene to take place when they found my lifeless body,
with the green elephant clutched in my cold hand,
showing that I had been faithful to the last. And I was
glad that I was wearing my best crêpe de Chine under-
slip.

It was just then that without warning the door into,

the corridor opened. The faint light streaming into the shadows had silhouetted against it a broad, squat figure. "Kema! Kema!" I cried. My voice was hoarse and cracked.

She made a quick motion as if to close the door, and I cried again, hoping as I did so that the thing that lay below me had no revolver: "Kema, wait! Open the door! Call the police!"

She uttered an exclamation, which I lost in my attempt to scramble down the ladder. Somehow I managed to stumble on numb feet to the corridor.

Someone was approaching us down the green gloom of the corridor from a half-open bedroom door; it was Elihu Dimuck and he hurried his steps as he saw me.

"Call the police," I kept repeating. "There's someone in that room. Call the police!"

"What is it? What has happened?" cried Elihu Dimuck, and Isobel coming from the head of the stairway paused to survey me with a gleam of insolent amusement in her eyes. Behind the lace drapery of the gown she wore I saw Kema's dark arm reach out stealthily and close the door to the trunk room.

"What on earth!" said Isobel. "Really, Miss Keate, did you—forget your dress?"

"Get the police," I insisted, uneasily conscious of my petticoat, and then became aware of a curious silence. All three of them, Elihu Dimuck and Kema and Isobel, were looking steadily at the green elephant in my hand!

Well, it was a good ten minutes before the two policemen, whom Mr. Dimuck finally summoned, searched the trunk room and presumably the attic. They found nothing. I think they did not even believe my story and had the impression that they made only a half-hearted search of the place, attributing the whole affair to my nerves. Nerves, indeed!

I remember that I retreated with some dignity, under their somewhat curious gaze, to my own room. I groped for matches, lighted the lamp, and stared at the little elephant which I still clutched firmly in one hand. I turned and twisted it. But again I was baffled by its green smoothness. The very simplicity and triviality of the thing defeated me. It was like shaking a doll and demanding that it babble secrets of life. The only thing I knew certainly was that it must have some meaning.

Perhaps if I had had longer to examine the elephant— but I did not have much time. I must hurry to dress and go downstairs. I must find O'Leary.

I met my face in the mirror and laughed wildly.

My hair hung in wisps about my grimy face, my cap perched perilously over one ear, I was streaked with dust and perspiration, several gray cobwebs floated eerily from my hair, and my best petticoat was all barred and blotched with dust.

It was no wonder the policemen had given such half-hearted credence to my story, for if any woman ever looked entirely demented I did at that moment.

I laughed again rather hysterically.

A fine-looking corpse I should have made, I must say!

CHAPTER XII

A MATTER OF HISTORY

On going downstairs I wrapped the green elephant securely in the scarf I was knitting and sallied forth with the roll of orange wool under my arm. I took the roll of wool to dinner with me, too, and kept it on my lap during the entire meal.

I suppose that meal was as uncomfortable as all the other meals in that gloomy dining room, but I was hungry and tired and I concentrated on the food. Isobel served, slapping things down with an air of insolent nonchalance calculated, I think, to irritate March, and slipping into her place between courses and having to be asked to remove the plates. At dessert she balked entirely.

"It is stewed prunes again," she said languidly. She rose and trailed out of the room, murmuring over her creamy shoulder as she went: "If any of you want stewed prunes you can go and get them yourself."

Mittie, it appeared, did want them and got them and created a little diversion by choking on a prune seed and having to be patted on the back. I did the patting and, having no love for Mittie, may have patted rather vigorously. At any rate, the prune seed flew out with an explosive little pop and landed on Eustace's plate. His face darkened in a flash; he threw down his napkin, shoved back his chair so forcefully that it crashed over, flung out a word or two that I shall not repeat, and left the room without even a glance of apology toward March.

March's eyes flashed from under stormy eyebrows; Elihu Dimuck made a deprecatory gesture with his two pink hands, and Deke Lonergan laughed. It was a hearty, ringing laugh of purest delight and quite astonished me, for it was the first time I had ever seen the man cast aside his cloak of sulky brooding. March gave him a curious look and lowered her satin-smooth eyelids slowly and deliberately, and he leaned toward her suddenly, blond hair catching highlights from the tall candles, and gray eyes darkly intent as he said something I could not hear distinctly.

Not caring myself for prunes I left the dining room, going by way of the little passage toward the tower room.

I walked along rather slowly, holding the roll of knitting under one arm, thinking of Eustace's vile temper and having no premonition of danger. I was just passing the curtained door into the drawing room off the passage and was about to turn into the tower room when without an instant's warning the green velvet curtain over the drawing room doorway was flung over my head and shoulders and twisted there. I struggled violently, but the roll of knitting was dragged from my grip and I was left alone, pulling at the curtain and trying to scream through its stifling folds.

It was over and done with in a quick moment or two, and it couldn't have taken me more than a few seconds to extricate myself from the enveloping folds of velvet.

Apparently no one had heard the struggle and my stifled cries. The passage and the drawing room were dark, and I ran to the tower room, seized a lamp, and hurried back. By the time I held the lamp high in one hand and under its light objects in the drawing room took on shape there was no one there. But in the middle of the floor, bright against the dull carpet, lay a spot of brilliant orange wool.

I picked it up; the needles were dangling, stitches had been pulled out, and a long thread of orange yarn went almost to the opposite door and back again in a long, raveled thread. But the green elephant was gone.

Again!

Twice I had had the thing in my hand and twice it had been taken from me. The first time I had been careless, it is true, but at that time I did not comprehend the importance of the toy. And this time I had not been careless.

There was no use sounding an alarm, for any one of that household might conceivably have taken the thing. Feeling singularly disorganized, I retreated to the tower room where I soothed my shattered self-esteem by picking up stitches in my knitting, thought very bitter thoughts, and gradually resumed control over my shaking nerves.

It was there that Lance O'Leary found me some thirty minutes later. He gave me one look, sat down, folded his arms, stretched out his feet to the fire, and said severely:

"What is all this the policeman upstairs has been telling me? Come, now, Sarah Keate—just what have you been up to?"

Nothing loath, I told him the whole story, and when I finished he was sitting bolt upright in his chair, surveying me with a look that held mingled awe and apprehension.

"You are a dangerous woman," he said. "You are an active peril. But may I touch you for luck?" He reached over and lightly touched my hand.

"Luck!" I said scornfully. "Luck? When I've had that silly curio in my very hands and not only failed to find anything of importance about the toy but actually permitted myself to be robbed of it?"

"Luck because you are still here, alive and uninjured," he said very gravely.

"Then you think the man in the trunk room might have been the murderer?" My heart quickened.

"At any rate, there was someone there who took good care that he shouldn't be seen. Though, of course, he might have been as frightened as you were. You think it was some outsider, no one of the household?"

"Well—" I hesitated—"my theory was that it was some intruder. Not a thief, perhaps, for nothing apparently has been stolen except the green elephant, but some—intruder. That is what I started out to prove, if I could. And when I stumbled onto the elephant itself in the attic and knew that someone was in the trunk room I just took it for granted that I was right. But, of course, I'm certain only that it couldn't have been Kema or Isobel or Mr. Dimuck. And another thing, whoever was there took good care not to be found by the policemen, but they did not make a very thorough search. I think they didn't wholly believe my story, and I dare say it does sound improbable."

"Not if they knew you as I do," murmured Lance O'Leary. "Then Kema and Isobel and Dimuck all knew that you had found the elephant?" He rose and started toward the door. "I'll be back in a few moments, Miss Keate."

And it was not more than a quarter of an hour before he was back in the tower room, an enigmatic look on his face.

"For once everybody has a perfect alibi. They seem to have all taken a fancy for the tower room here, and between four and five o'clock this afternoon every one of them were here having tea, which Kema served. And between four and five o'clock this afternoon you were— sitting on a ladder. Also, to-night when the green elephant was taken from you—and you are lucky that you weren't strangled in the process—at that time everyone save Isobel and Eustace were in the dining room. So either Eustace or Isobel took the elephant or—the fellow you thought was in the trunk room. I hope you'll not think I'm blaming you when I say that you carried it rather obviously—obviously, I mean, to anyone who knew you had the thing."

"At least I did find it!" I remarked waspishly, and O'Leary smiled.

"You did, Miss Keate."

"Then you believe that there is an outsider about the place? What on earth is his purpose?"

"It is just possible," assented O'Leary. "But if I knew the motive of these crimes I should have the criminal in my hands. If there is anyone hiding about the place, it is with Miss March's assistance; that is why I have had her watched so closely. Of course, I might have had out twenty men or so; there must be countless hiding places about the house, and it would take that many men, I think, to lay our hands on the gentleman. Finesse is better than force, as a rule."

"H'm! I must say, I think it would be better to search for the man and lock him up at once."

"On what grounds, Miss Keate?" inquired O'Leary gently. "And, anyway, there may be no such person. Can you be absolutely sure that he was below the ladder there in the trunk room during those hours when you heard no sound or stir?"

"I certainly am sure," I snapped. "I should have seen him open the door to the corridor if he had done so. I should have heard his first move."

"You didn't close your eyes from weariness, for instance? It was very dark, you said—if there happened to be no light in the corridor, couldn't he have got to the door and out without your seeing him?"

"No," I said positively. "He could not. Its being dark didn't affect my ears, and I could have heard a pin drop."

O'Leary sat down, drawing the worn pencil from a pocket and beginning to roll it between his slender, well-cared-for fingers.

"There are things about this business that I can't—can't get a grip on. The night Grondal was killed I had a kind of feeling of danger, but there was nothing definite. Lightning seldom strikes twice in the same place, and I had nothing to warrant my saying to the chief, 'Here, I want a whole detachment of men at the Federie place to-night; my nerves tell me that something may happen.' You see, Miss Keate, it is an affair that is a little out of the ordinary. Usually in criminal investigation the crimes occur within circles that are criminal circles, or that touch criminal circles. Tips come to us. We can lay our hands on men who can tell us things. And usually the issues at stake can be discovered. But this business is entirely different. It appears to be wholly within a family connection. And I cannot discover the motive. Unless I found a hint of it this afternoon." He passed his hands over his face with a wearied gesture.

"Do you suppose, Miss Keate, the time ever comes in a man's life when he can look back on a completed task and see that he has made no mistakes?"

"It has been only a day or two," I said dryly. "What do you expect? Some of these cases drag out for months. What was it you discovered this afternoon?"

"In the first place, I found that the tradesmen— grocers, butchers, and all—that deal with Mr. Federie are always paid in cash. Never by check. Grondal, it appears, went around every month with a pocketful of silver and bills and paid everything, taking receipts. This looked strange, and pursuing the matter I found that there is not a bank in the city that has ever done business with the Federies. And that, furthermore, the only deed on record that shows the Federie name is the abstract for this house, made out in 1880 in the name of Deborah Federie—that was old Mr. Federie's wife, I found—and it was transferred at the time of her death to March Federie, who was then exactly six years old. As a family they are singularly obscure; this old house, the manner in which it is furnished and all would lead one to think that years ago they were of some importance. But I could discover nothing of interest

about them even from the old-timers here in B——,
until I went to old Miss Van Guilder."
He paused, looking at me inquiringly. I knew old
Miss Van Guilder as everyone in B—— knew her; she
was an eccentric old lady whose memory was surprisingly clear and whose chief interest lay in the historical
foundations of B—— where her father had been an
early judge.

"Even she knew nothing of the Federies that we did
not know. But she did unearth some old newspapers,
and among them I found a singular reference to the
Federie house. I didn't dare clip it, for she was watching
me sharply, but I copied it. It seems to have been made
in the robustly jocular spirit employed by the early
newspapers in this part of the country. Listen to this:
'The magnificent new Federie mansion is nearing
completion. We have been told that masks and pistols
will be discarded during meals. Verily the wages of sin
is wealth. Travelers are warned to take other than the
Aufengartner Road.' And it was dated February 9,
1880."

"What does it mean? Let me see it!" I read with my
own eyes the rather amazing item, copied in O'Leary's
neat handwriting. "Why—it sounds very much as if
they were—*thieves!*"

O'Leary nodded, gray eyes faintly amused.

"Highwaymen, bandits, whatever you want to call
them. Editors were free with their words in those gal-
lant days, and I rather believe this gentleman was
speaking the truth. I trust it was only a coincidence
that he died suddenly within the next month, according
to a later notice I found." He eyed the face of old Mr.

Federie. It looked flushed, of course, but the slight dis-
tortion of mouth was disappearing and the features
were rugged and fine against the white pillow. "Can
you imagine him, Miss Keate, sallying forth in the dark
of night, masked and armed, and ordering wayfarers to
'Stand and deliver!'"

Well, I could imagine it readily enough as I looked
at his indomitable eyebrows and domineering chin and
nose. While I had had strange patients I never before
had an ex-highwayman and I hope it is no reflection
on my character to say that I regarded him with the
liveliest interest from that moment on.

"But even if we are to accept this defunct editor's
words as truth and concede that the Federies were
bandits, and add to this the fact that they pay their
bills in cash which argues a supply of money somewhere
about the house—then what do we have? Nothing.
Someone might be determined to get hold of that money
and in the doing so must needs murder two men. But
it isn't reasonable. Adolph had no money. Grondal had
none. This silly elephant isn't reasonable, either. I have
learned more about art in the last few days than I ever
knew in my life before, and there's nothing I can discover that would lead me to think that the curio is
in itself valuable. I've read, talked to jewelers, the
curator of the museum, and every collector in B——,
and I've come to the conclusion that if the elephant is
really jade it is fairly valuable as a piece of art, but by
no means of a value to cause a man to commit murder
for its possession. No, it must have another meaning."

"March said it was to belong to her after her grandfather's death," I said thoughtfully. "She has been

inquiring for it. And I caught Mittie Frisling down on her knees in the hall, looking under that big walnut chest. Of course, she might not have been looking for the elephant. But, Mr. O'Leary, what about the man who is hiding in the house? Aren't you going to arrest him? It seems to me we are all in danger so long as he is left at large."

"Always assuming that there is such a person. There, there, Miss Keate! Don't look so indignant. Just trust me for another day or so. I have things to do that—take a little time. And I'll tell you this: You, yourself, gave me the only real clues I have."

He would say nothing more on the subject, and though I racked my memory I could not recall any occurrence which seemed to hold a particular or clinching significance.

"In assuming that both murders were committed by the same person and for the same motive, I believe that I am correct. And I think that the solution of the affair lies right here in this old house. Oh, I don't mean any hidden stairway or secret panels or anything of the kind," he interpolated with a half smile, as I supposed I looked the curiosity that I certainly felt. "I mean among the rather curious members of the household. I shall not say family, for that would exclude Mr. Dimuck and Miss Frisling and Kema and young Lonergan. At various times during the last day or two I have questioned the people in the house, separately and collectively, and I think that almost every single one of them has lied to me in some degree. Yes, even your Miss March—oh, you need not try to conceal your partiality for her, Miss Keate—even your Miss

March is concealing something, though she evades an out-and-out lie with a dexterity that does credit to her lawless ancestry. The lies have been almost as interesting as the truth, but from now on I'm going to have the truth. And Mittie Frisling is the first who's going to come across," he concluded somewhat flippantly.

"I shall bring her in here to talk, Miss Keate, if that is all right."

I nodded perhaps a bit enthusiastically, for he smiled a little as he left the room.

While waiting for them to return I busied myself with my patient. I have often thought how fortunate it was, in view of the startling developments of the case, that my patient required as little care as he did; had it been pneumonia, for instance, or a surgical case or one of heart disease or, in fact, almost any other affliction, I could scarcely have left his side. But, as to that, later events proved that had he been conscious at least some of the trouble would not have taken place.

His condition was improving. I remember that as I stood there with my fingers on his pulse I looked idly at his hand—a rather nice hand, wrinkled with age and with prominent veins and tendons, but well shaped and the hand of a man who knows his mind. How many times had it held a menacing revolver, or looted travelers' pocketbooks? "The Federie hand is born to fit the curve of a revolver." If this were true Eustace had spoken with justice.

It all fitted in rather well. The magnificent house, the labored respectability when once the Federie before me had decided to take to more lawful ways, the books, the pictures, the knickknacks, all evidences of what was called refinement in those strenuously artificial days. The old man's stern bringing up of his sons, his refusal to countenance their misdeeds, his feudal rule of family, natural in one who had controlled a bandit gang, and his rigid clinging to the formalities and ceremonies of what constituted his idea of a respectable life—all this was what one would expect. "Defense mechanism," I thought wisely to myself.

The days when the Federie house must have been built were lawless ones in our part of the country if tales of those early times can be believed. Of what moonlight expeditions could this man, whose wrist I held, tell? What flurries of horses' hoofs, shots in the night, shrieks and oaths from overturned stagecoaches, gold and silver and jewels glimmering in the starlight! "Masks and pistols will be discarded during meals," the departed editor had said with grim sarcasm. And "travelers are warned to take other than Aufengartner Road."

I had to take the man's pulse three times before I could be sure I had counted it with due attention. I was changing the ice pack when Mittie was ushered into the room. She gave me an unpleasant look from her light eyes, but took the chair O'Leary offered her without demur.

"Now, then, Miss Frisling, I'll have the truth, please," he began without preamble. There was a certain steely edge in his quiet voice that sounded forbidding. "Look at me, please. You stood behind that green curtain over the door the night Adolph Federie was shot. You saw him fall. You turned and ran through the back of the house and up the back stairway. You hurried along the corridor of the back wing, turned

Into the main corridor, and dodged into the vacant bedroom near at hand to avoid meeting anyone in the hall
as you would have if you had continued down the hall
to your own room. You left a revolver in that room!
You shot Adolph Federie!"

At his first words Mittie had turned an ugly greenish
yellow, and as his inexorable voice went on her fat hands
began to writhe in her lap and her light eyes grew wild
with panic.

"I didn't!" she cried hoarsely. "I didn't."

"You did. You stood back of the curtain. You saw
Adolph on the stairway over there. You raised the revolver and——"

Mittie began to shriek.

"I did not! I did not! Grondal told you that! I heard
him!" She half rose from her chair, her head thrusting
forward and her eyes glittering. Then she sank back
with a cowering movement. "Oh, I did stand there
back of the curtain. But *I* didn't shoot him. It was
someone from up there. From the tower stairway. I
saw him fall. He—he clutched at the air. The elephant
rolled down the stairs. And Adolph fell. And rolled
a step or two. He—he clutched at the air, I tell you."
She was shuddering and panting, now, and Lance
O'Leary, with a curious look on his face, watched her
carefully.

"Why were you standing there at the curtain?" he
said presently when she had quieted a little.

"Because I—I wanted to find out if Mr. Federie was
really sick and not able to speak. He had promised me—
something. And then they said he was sick. I watched
the nurse. I thought I would wait till I thought she was

asleep and then I would slip into the room and speak to Mr. Federie. And I saw Adolph come down the tower stairway; he came very cautiously, a step at a time. The nurse didn't hear him; her face was in the shadow and I couldn't see it. Adolph went to the mantel and looked at everything there and finally picked up a little green elephant that stood there. He looked at it under the lamplight for a moment or two and then he did something to it—I don't know what. It looked like he was unscrewing something about it, for I could see his elbow move. Then he had a little piece of white paper in his hand and he bent over, there under the lamp, and seemed to read it."

"Just where did he stand?"

"There, by that table."

"So he could be seen from the top of the stairway," murmured O'Leary rather absently. "Go on, Miss Frisling."

My interest had quickened, if that were possible, at the mention of the green elephant, and I stole a look at Lance O'Leary. He was leaning forward, his eyes shining with that strangely lucent look, his whole being intent on the words that came in rushing, spasmodic little bursts from Mittie's pale mouth.

"And then all at once he sort of—jumped and looked upward toward the second landing of the tower stairway. And I think he put the little paper back inside the elephant and screwed the thing together again. I couldn't see very well because he turned so that he stood with his back to the lamp. And then he walked back to the stairway so quietly I could not hear a sound. And it was just as he reached the turn of the stairway

that—that—I can't tell it! *I can't tell it!* I've seen it
ever since. Over and over. But it was Isobel. I know it
was Isobel!"

Again O'Leary waited until Mittie had stopped beating her hands on her fat knees and had taken a limp
handkerchief from her bosom and was dabbing at her
eyes.

"How long have you known Isobel?"

"Since Adolph married her. He was too good for her."

"How long have you known the Federies?"

She held her handkerchief suspended while she shot
him a swift look in which a new alarm seemed to leap.

"A—long time."

"The truth, Miss Frisling."

"Since—since I was a child."

"What were your father's relations to Mr. Federie,
that you have a claim on him?"

"A—a claim? Why—why, he was just a friend."

"How old was your father when he died?"

"Up—up in the seventies."

"You have doubtless heard him tell tales of his youth
in this part of the country. How he belonged to——"

Mittie jumped up. I think she knew what was coming.

"So was Mr. Federie," she cried incoherently. "And
the Federies took almost all the money when the—the
gang broke up. And they have still got it. My father
was one of them, but you can't do anything to *me! I*
haven't anything. When Mr. Federie dissolved them,
he took almost all the money. He said he was the leader
and it belonged rightfully to him. But he always sup-
ported my father. And—and me."

"So upon your father's death you felt justified in coming to old Mr. Federie here to—blackmail him?"

"I only wanted what was mine."

"It never occurred to you that your threats were empty? That it would have been impossible after fifty years to find witnesses or evidence that could convince any court in the country?"

"I only wanted what was rightfully mine," she repeated, adding spitefully, "The Federies have always thought they were so much! That March with her high and mighty ways! And they were no better than the rest of us. All robbers! And March is the granddaughter of—a *thief!*"

"Let's say highwayman, Miss Frisling. After all, it is half a century past. By the way, are there any other surviving members of the gang?"

"Only Mr. Federie," said Mittie. "Since Grondal—died."

"Does the present generation of the Federie family know its history?"

"You mean March and Eustace? I think Eustace had a hint of it from Adolph. But I'm sure that March does not know it—*yet.*" There was an ugly satisfaction in the threat of the last word.

"You knew Adolph Federie—rather well?"

Slowly the ugly look died out of her queer, light eyes.

"Yes," she said slowly. She sat down again and her puffy fingers began to fold and refold a bit of her dress. "Yes. I knew him. Rather well."

"When was that?"

"Years ago. He used to come to see my father. And—and me. Then all at once he married Isobel. We were not even invited to the wedding." Her voice was torpid, almost stupid, as if any glow of resentment had burned out long ago. But she still hated Isobel!

"We were never invited to this house. Not since I can remember, and that is——" She left the point of her age untouched and went on: "I never saw March Federie until she came home a few days ago. I came here when Father died. Adolph and Isobel came, too. Adolph—didn't remember me." Her flat voice stopped rather oddly, without a period or a note of finality. Her whole frowsy, inept life, its fires banked with brooding, was summed up in the dull, emotionless words: "Adolph didn't remember me."

And she had seen him die. She had seen his hand clutch futilely into the air.

One of his hands had got March's red rosette in its frenzied clutch.

CHAPTER XIII

A BEAD BOX

"GRONDAL, of course, knew the whole thing?" said O'Leary.

"Yes," replied Mittie simply, her dull eyes on the fire.

"And what were you looking for this morning that you thought might be under the chest in the hall?" She did not look at me.

"The little green elephant, of course. Adolph had it in his hand when he was shot. I think—" she wrinkled her forehead in a puzzled way—"I think everyone else is looking for it, too. But I couldn't find it. Anywhere."

"Why did you think everyone is looking for it?" She shrugged lifelessly.

"They are looking for something," she said, and stopped.

"You saw no one on the tower stairway above Adolph? Think, Miss Frisling. A hand—the revolver—the shadow of a—skirt?"

She shook her head.

"I saw nothing but Adolph. Isobel must have been above him, out of sight on the stairway. It was all so sudden, so unexpected. One instant Adolph was there, walking up the steps. The next——" She shuddered and covered her face with her hands.

240

The green curtain wavered and lifted; Eustace cast a quick, sharp glance about the room and entered. "Good-evening, O'Leary," he said. "Ah, Miss Keate, how is Grandfather?"

"A little better, I think."

He looked thoughtfully at me, his dark eyes secretive. "Is there a chance that he will recover his speech soon?"

"Why, yes, I think so. But we cannot know definitely when—or even if he will do so."

"I hope you'll remember to call me at once, Miss Keate, when there is a change for the better. It is most important. And, by the way, Nurse, there was a little green elephant on the mantel when you came. It has been missing for a day or two. It was of no particular value in itself, but—Grandfather is attached to it. I should like to find it. He may want it when he recovers consciousness. It was a little jade trinket. Do you know anything of it?"

"No," I said flatly, avoiding O'Leary's eyes. And, as far as that goes, I did not know anything of it at the moment. The thought struck me that Eustace himself might have taken it from me; it would be like him to try to cover his possession of the elephant with an inquiry such as this.

"If you should happen to find the elephant, give it to me at once." He spoke in the distantly polite manner he would have used toward a maidservant and crossed to a chair, sitting down casually and asking O'Leary how the investigation was going. In a moment or two Isobel drifted into the room with Elihu Dimuck and presently March came in also and sat down beside me. After a little Mittie rose, left the room, and returned with the little tin box in which she kept her beads, and I idly watched her fingers weaving glittering black beads, the four small knitting needles catching dull gleams of light. Gradually her hands ceased trembling. Deke Lonergan came to the tower room, too, lounging to a chair near March. He seemed engrossed in his own problems, though, and said nothing until Genevieve stalked gauntly into the room and, in misplaced affection, jumped to Lonergan's knee. And then he only uttered a startled and disgusted exclamation and thrust the cat violently to the floor.

A policeman coming to the door interrupted the somewhat desultory conversation that was going on between Eustace and Dimuck with an occasional word from O'Leary, who seemed to prefer listening to them to talking himself. The policeman's eyes sought O'Leary's and he held a white something under one arm.

"Nothing, sir," he said, as if giving a report. "Nothing but this." He extended the white something, holding it gingerly by the tips of his fingers.

It was my own uniform. His eyes shifted to me and became suspicious and faintly reproachful.

"I found this, too, sir," he added, holding out O'Leary's flashlight. "They both was in that room."

"I'll speak to you in a moment, O'Brien," cut in O'Leary's voice. He gave me a glance that held a gleam of amusement as he crossed the room. I could hear a low murmur of voices as he and O'Brien walked away through the passage.

It was a long evening, with little said, and the air of tense restraint that hovered over the whole house made itself manifest in the long silences. It was quite as if any sudden word would release all the surging, pent-up emotions that were held in reserve and set them into fierce, clashing turmoil.

I knit rapidly, the little click-click of my needles carrying on a sort of duel with the subdued tinkle of Mittie's beads. It was about ten o'clock, I think, that I ran out of yarn and went to my own room for a new skein. I took a candle and walked circumspectly through the gloomy rooms and corridor and I listened every second for any untoward sound. When I opened the door of my room I stood there quite motionless for a moment or two, staring with all my eyes at the amazing disorder that, since I left the room just before dinner, had overtaken my neatly arranged possessions.

For the room had been thoroughly and completely ransacked. Its entire contents were flung recklessly about—fresh uniforms tossed in a heap on the floor, and a bottle of lavender water on the bureau was on its side, with the liquid meandering gayly over the top of the bureau. It only goes to show the state of mind I had reached when I admit that I did not even set that bottle upright, and the next day I found quite a red spot on my hand where the hot wax had dripped from the candle.

I turned and marched downstairs again; I did not remember the yarn until I had reached the tower room, where the others were sitting as if they had not moved a muscle since I had gone. O'Leary was not present and, of course, I did not mention the matter. It was clear to me, however, that someone had been seeking the green elephant, probably before it had been taken from me, for naturally there would have been no need to search for it afterward. My thoughts went from one to another of that still, restrained group sitting about the fire and waiting for my patient to speak. But I might say here and now that my wildest speculations did not even approach the truth!

Along toward eleven o'clock they rose by unspoken consent and started away. Lance O'Leary came into the room again as they were leaving.

"I suppose I need not advise you people to—er—lock the doors of your bedrooms at night?" He spoke in the easy tone in which he would wish them pleasant dreams.

There was an instant's pause. Then Isobel said harshly:

"Lord, no!"

O'Leary stood aside to let the singular little procession file past him.

"I am going to stay here in the tower room to-night, Miss Keate," said O'Leary.

My spirits lifted at once; I had been dreading the long, dark hours of the night to come.

He eyed me contemplatively for a moment before he added in the most casual way in the world:

"I had better tell you that I—I believe you are in grave danger."

"*I!*"

"You."

"But—I don't know anything about this business!"

"You had the elephant."

"I have it no longer. But my room, some time after I left it between six and seven o'clock this evening, was searched from carpet to ceiling." I waited for his comment in some trepidation. No one likes to be told that he is in grave danger, especially when it seems to be true.

"I didn't expect it quite so soon," said O'Leary quietly after a moment. "And only Kema, Dimuck, and Madam Isobel knew that you had the elephant —*and* our—what shall we call him?—the man in the trunk room. Of course—Eustace may have guessed that you knew something of it. Well, this proves that at least two people are determined to find the elephant."

"Why? I don't understand. I thought that my room was likely searched before the elephant was taken from me."

He looked at me impatiently.

"You went almost directly to dinner, leaving your room at about a quarter to seven. From six-thirty till dinner time Miss March and Madam Isobel, Eustace, Dimuck, and Deke Lonergan were together in the library, and Kema was in the kitchen preparing the meal. You were all together during dinner and immediately afterward the elephant was taken from you. No one of the household had had a chance to search your room until *after* the green elephant was out of your possession. Still it was searched."

"Oh," I said rather flatly.

He sat down, relaxing into an attitude of thoughtful musing.

"But don't be unduly alarmed, Miss Keate; just keep your eyes open. As I say, I shall stay overnight and will be right here in the room. So that is the secret of the green elephant, and the paper it contains is so

important that Adolph Federie was shot rather than
be permitted to have it in his possession. Adolph must
have stumbled onto it; old Mr. Federie's partiality for
the elephant would draw his attention to it."

"Do you think Isobel shot him?" I asked in a small
voice. There were cold little shivers traveling up and
down my spine; if Adolph had been killed because he
had the elephant—why not I? True, I had not had the
wit to discover its secret, but the murderer would not
know that.

O'Leary shrugged.

"Time will tell. Time and a good bit of drudgery. I
wish my work were as magically swift and simple as
it is made out to be. You see, Miss Keate, there is a
difference between the discovering of the guilty man
and the securing of evidence that will convict. And I
want to secure evidence that will result in conviction,
not in acquittal on legal grounds. I don't mind telling
you that"—he lowered his voice so that I barely
heard the whispered words—"I might even make an
arrest right now, but it would be based for the most
part on supposition and I must have definite evidence."
He paused and added thoughtfully: "Definite evidence."

I longed to ask the identity of the person whom he
would arrest on supposition, but reflected that had he
wanted me to know he would have told me.

"But why did not the person who shot Adolph take
the green elephant?" I asked after a moment's thought.
"Perhaps it was Isobel, after all. Perhaps the green
elephant had nothing to do with it."

"But, on the other hand, Miss Keate, suppose he was

shot because he had the elephant and had read the paper it contained. Mittie says the elephant dropped and rolled down the stairs. The murderer would not have dared follow it and secure it, knowing that you were here in the room and that the shot would rouse you. He probably figured that the curio had remained in safety on the mantel for several days, ever since Mr. Federie's illness began, and that few, if any, knew of the significance of the thing. Hence it would be a simple matter to slip into the room sometime later and take the elephant."

"I wish old Mr. Federie could speak," I said. "He knows the secret the elephant holds."

O'Leary nodded.

"Doubtless. But even then we might not secure the —evidence to convict."

"I never thought of the thing being hollow," I re- marked in chagrin. "But there is nothing about it to suggest such a thing. You can't see the mark where it opens—unless—it might be in the folds of skin around the neck and under those big, fanlike ears."

"We'll see when we get our hands on it again, Miss Keate," said O'Leary briefly. "Find me the elephant again, Miss Keate. And find me Adolph's diamond. And find me the key to the bedroom upstairs."

It was purely coincidence that just as he spoke the flame in the lamp started to smoke. I moved hastily to adjust the wick and my sudden gesture upset Mittie's bead box which she had forgotten and left on the table.

Hundreds of shiny little beads showered to the floor; they must have been three inches deep in the little box. The box went, too, face downward. I bent to pick it up. And, as I lifted the box, there on the little heap of beads lay a key.

"Here it is," I said nonchalantly, and to my own surprise, for the words came out of my mouth entirely without volition on my part.

And the astounding thing about it was that it did prove to be the key to the locked bedroom just above our heads. O'Leary had leaped up the tower stairway, tried it in the lock, and was back again triumphant before I had finished picking up the beads, which Genevieve was nosing tentatively.

"What did I say about you a little while ago?" inquired O'Leary jubilantly.

"You said I was a dangerous woman," I said dryly. "You said I was an active peril."

"I take it all back," he said. "I eat my words. You are a marvelous woman. You really do have the most extraordinary way of——"

"Did I leave my bead box here?" interrupted Mittie's voice inquiringly. She advanced slowly into the room. Her colorless hair was in curl papers and she wore a draggled crêpe kimono. I might say, here and now, that one of my most vivid memories of Federie house has to do with the varied and peculiar negligees in which its inmates appeared; as the thing went on I even wondered why they undressed at all, for there was only one night during which we were undisturbed.

O'Leary neatly palmed the key, and I replied to Mittie's question.

"Here it is," I said. "I knocked it over. There were quite a lot of beads in it and I don't know whether I got all of them back again in the box or not."

She looked anxiously at the box and stirred the contents with her forefinger.

"Miss Frisling," said O'Leary sternly. "In this box was the key to the locked bedroom upstairs. How did it get there? How long have you had it? Did you lock that door?"

Fortunately I had not quite relinquished my hold on the bead box, else I should have had to help pick them up again. Her hands fell slowly as she stared at the key he held before her; she moistened her pale lips and her light eyes looked rather wild.

"In—in my bead box?"

"Yes."

"You—found it *there?*"

"Certainly. Explain it, Miss Frisling."

She shook her head slowly.

"I didn't know it was there. I don't know how long it has been there. I've left the box everywhere— on the library table and, oh, just any place where I was working with my beads. I don't know anything about that key, Mr. O'Leary. Really I don't."

And though he questioned her closely she reiterated her denial and at last he let her go, though I don't know whether or not he was convinced of the truth of her statement.

"At any rate, we have the key," he said as the green curtain fell into place behind Mittie's pudgy figure. "Whether Mittie has had it all along, or whether the same hand put it there that put the violin string around Grondal's neck and for the same purpose —to detract suspicion from the murderer—in any case we do have the key."

My thoughts went back to the horror of the previous night.

"Poor Grondal," I said soberly. "Did they discover what he actually died of?"

"Yes. The blow over his heart killed him and that blow must have been a lucky accident for the person who was struggling with him, for Grondal, despite his age, was a strong man. Our medical examiner thinks that Grondal staggered down the tower stairway and collapsed on the couch. The murderer stole down the stairs after him, saw his helpless condition and slipped the violin string in a noose about his neck in order both to help—finish the job—and to complicate matters. The murderer must have been wholly desperate in his need to stop Grondal's mouth forever, otherwise he would not have taken such a chance. At any second you might have returned to the tower room."

"And all that time I was getting to the kitchen and trying to telephone. He worked fast."

"Yes. The whole thing, struggle and all, took only a few moments."

"If I had remained in the room I might have saved Grondal. I might have given him something——"

"Stop, Miss Keate. You did exactly right. You could not have saved him. Come here, closer to the fire. You are shivering. You must try to rest as much as possible during the night. I may need your help to-morrow."

"My help? What do you mean?"

But though I was all eagerness he would not explain. We talked for some time of the different aspects of the case, but, though O'Leary may have seen his way clear, to me the affair was wholly baffling. There seemed to be clues enough, certainly, but they pointed in widely different directions, and I did not think that everyone in the house had banded together for the purpose of doing away with Adolph, unpopular though he was, and poor old Grondal.

Feeling secure in O'Leary's presence, and less disturbed by Genevieve's green stare from the mantel than I had ever been, I dozed off finally, rousing when necessary to care for my patient, whose condition, by the way, was steadily improving. Once when I glanced across the room O'Leary was sitting at the table, head bent thoughtfully over a piece of paper, and once he was coming quietly down the tower stairway, pausing to lean over the railing above the couch. The sight set me to shuddering violently, and I heaped the fire with wood and stirred it till the flames leaped furiously and nearly scorched myself in an effort to get warm.

"By the way," said Lance O'Leary, breaking into my none too cheerful thoughts. "Your uniform is in your room upstairs. And here is the electric torch again. But I must warn you that O'Brien regards you with the darkest foreboding. It is easy to see what he thinks of females who leave their dresses dangling from ceilings."

He chuckled a little and held out his slender hands to the blaze. And it was just then, without any warning at all, that a scream arose from somewhere in the old house.

It was a horrible, high-pitched scream that rose and rose, piercing the dank old walls and muffling curtains in a fearful crescendo of stark terror.

It rose and fell and rose again, and then O'Leary was bounding up the tower stairway and I after him, through the little room at the head of the stairs, through the deserted bedroom and, as O'Leary unlocked the door with swift fingers, into the upper corridor. A candle or two was burning dimly along its green length. Doors were opening, matches were sputtering, and other voices were rising. And in the middle of the corridor, down by the main stairs, stood a bunchy figure. We sped toward it. It was Mittie Frisling, her curl papers making grotesque shadows and her hands writhing together, still screaming. Isobel joined us, I think, at the intersection of the back hall; at any rate, she was at my elbow when we got to Mittie. Others were crowding around, too, a couple of policemen running up the stairs, Eustace and Lonergan and March and Dimuck, and above the pandemonium of excited voices Mittie kept on screaming. Her eyes were screwed tight shut as if she dared not open them, but she was apparently unhurt, and it was March finally who put a glass of water to her lips. Mittie began mechanically to drink and choke and drink again, and we presently got intelligible words from her.

And I must say they were rather extraordinary. For the first thing she said when she opened her eyes and looked at us was:

"*I saw Adolph Federie!*"

There was an element of quite terrible conviction in her voice.

My hair stirred at its roots and I cast a swift glance up and down the green gloom of the long corridor. Involuntarily we all moved a little closer together and a kind of shudder went over the whole group.

"*You—did—not!*" I said jerkily. "You—couldn't have!"

"I did. He was standing right there." She pointed to Elihu Dimuck, who moved rather hurriedly to one side. "He stood right there. I saw him just as plain as I see you."

"Come now, Miss Frisling, you are over-tired—hysterical," suggested O'Leary; his voice was very quiet but too well controlled.

"I did see him," persisted Mittie. "I saw Adolph Federie. I came out of my room. I was going to the bathroom to get a drink. See, there's the glass." She pointed and, sure enough, on the floor near by was a broken tumbler. "And just as I got here he *appeared*. Just appeared. Right there at the head of the stairs. And then I shut my eyes and started to scream. But I ·*saw* Adolph Federie."

Again there was that terrible conviction in her voice. It held us all for a silent moment. O'Brien happened to be facing me across the little circle about Mittie, and as I saw his dropped jaw and staring eyes a wild little quiver of mirth ran over me and was gone. And at that instant Konrad, outside, began to bark long, deep-throated barks that we heard distinctly through the walls between.

The sound produced rather astonishing results. O'Leary hurled a sharp word or two at the policemen which sent them running heavily down the corridor, and March went dead white, turned as if to follow the policemen, faltered for a fraction of a second, and without a word or a sound dropped flat to the floor.

Deke was at her side three feet in advance of Eustace and he gathered her up in his arms and lifted her and simply stood there, his face as white as hers, while he called her name over and over again in frantic anxiety. Eustace paused, his outstretched arms falling slowly to his side and his eyes narrowing viciously, and I stared at March's bare feet, slim and pink and childish looking, dangling there below the dark silk folds of her dressing gown and thought stupidly that the girl would take her death of cold, running about the drafty old house without slippers.

Then as I roused myself and started toward them to tell Deke to take her to her room, March's eyelids fluttered and opened and Deke Lonergan, his heart in his eyes and himself utterly oblivious of our presence, bent his head suddenly and pressed his mouth against March's and held it there.

Well, it was quite a kiss.

It lasted a long time and made me feel quite warm and tingly just watching it. Mittie thrust her face past my shoulder to stare avidly at the two; Isobel shrunk back a little, her face all at once pinched and old; Elihu Dimuck clucked suddenly rather like a startled hen, and the sound seemed to rouse Eustace from the cold fury that had gripped him.

He took a single step forward.

"Suppose you leave that, Lonergan," he said in a cold voice that was as deadly as the sharp edge of steel. "Can you walk, March? I'll take you to your room."

Lonergan lifted his tousled blond head. His whole face had changed; it was gay, triumphant, and his eyes were brilliant.

He tightened his hold on March.

"I'll take her," he said calmly, though his breath was uneven.

But March would have none of either of them. In a flash she had regained her air of command and, though Deke Lonergan set her on her feet with as tender care as if she were a young baby, she surveyed us all with a deliberate, imperious blue gaze that held nothing of emotion or embarrassment. However, her lips were very red and soft and looked exactly like crushed rose petals.

I sighed a bit regretfully as, with her habitual air of authority, March advised Mittie to return to her room and go to sleep and intimated that the rest of us would do well to do likewise; I should have liked to see the tender little scene repeated. But O'Leary had vanished; Eustace, his dark eyes still venomous, stuck at March's elbow as she walked to the door of her own room, and I recalled my patient and high time I did so, left alone in the tower room. As I passed Deke Lonergan I looked sharply at him; he was soberer now, but still exultant. He looked straight at me.

"She kissed back," he said dazedly. I think he had not the faintest idea that he was speaking aloud. "What do you think of that! She kissed back!" Then he blinked, looked at me with seeing eyes, became annoyed and rather embarrassed, and whirled away.

I made my way unmolested back to the tower room, found that all was well, and sat down to consider the situation.

Love-making and a ghost!

It could not have been a ghost, of course; Mittie had

only had a nightmare. And yet—the conviction in her voice, the terror in her screams returned to me, and by the time O'Leary came back to the room I was sitting as stiff and cold as a ramrod, whatever that is, staring at the forbidding shadows of the angular tower stairway and simply quaking like jelly in my inside.

He was noncommittal to my inquiries and said little, simply sat and stared into the fire with grave eyes and an uncommonly intent expression on his face.

The rest of the night passed quietly enough. Dawn found my patient decidedly better, Lance O'Leary as calm and unruffled as the summer sea, and myself feeling the need for a good night's rest. I don't mind admitting that I have reached an age where peace and a certain amount of tranquillity are rather necessary to my disposition and looks, to say nothing of my digestion. It is true that I have a somewhat snappish disposition and nothing to boast of in the way of looks, but I do value my digestion.

As I say, Lance O'Leary looked as if he had just stepped out of a bandbox, and there was a kind of alert decision about him that led me to think that perhaps his night's cogitations had borne fruit. I remember that before leaving he questioned me again and at some length regarding Adolph's death, going over and over every phase of it, and wanting to know such minute details as how Adolph was lying, exactly where I found the elephant, and every little frightened exclamation of suggestion that was made when the others came into the room and saw the body.

He wound up by handing me a revolver.

"Take this, please, Miss Keate. I want you to do

something for me. You know how to fire it, don't you?"

"I dare say I could find out," I remarked, holding the cold thing gingerly. "Do you pull this?"

"Yes, but don't do it!" he cried, skipping nimbly to one side. He caught my hand and turned the thing so that its nose, or whatever you call it, pointed downward. He gave me a curious look that was dubious and respectful at the same time. "I don't know whether I can trust her with this or not," he said doubtfully as if to himself. "Promise me this, Miss Keate, do not fire it under any circumstances unless I tell you to do so. And, when you do fire it, be sure to point at the floor."

"Very well," I promised readily, for I had not the least desire just then to experiment with it.

He still eyed me a little doubtfully, looking, indeed, rather shaken for some reason or another and putting a hand on his stomach as if to be sure it was still there.

"Mr. O'Leary, sir," said O'Brien from the doorway, and at O'Leary's nod he entered.

"Yes, O'Brien."

"Me and Shafer was arguing about your orders, sir. I said that you told us to leave the back door unlocked and unguarded during the day and to watch the rest of the house like our necks depended on it, but make no arrests. Wasn't that right?"

"Exactly."

"Yes, sir. Yes, sir. That's what I said all along, but Shafer said it was against reason. That you said——"

His eyes wandered to me, he gave a violent start and, to my astonishment, began to lift his arms toward the ceiling. "My God, sir! Do you see what that woman's got!"

O'Leary turned, looked at the revolver which I possibly held in an awkward way, and sprang toward me. "Didn't I tell you to point it at the floor?" he demanded with much vehemence. "That's all right, O'Brien. I gave it to her myself."

O'Brien lowered his hands slowly, eying me with a look of extreme disfavor.

"Yes, sir," he said submissively, and retreated with long steps in which there was a hint of haste. Once in the passage, he thrust his head back through the opening in the curtains.

"All I can say, sir," he remarked in a kind of explosive way, as if the words would come out in spite of himself, "all I can say is you're taking your life in your hands." He gave me another dark look and vanished.

"What time is breakfast, Miss Keate?" asked O'Leary soberly, though his clear gray eyes were sparkling.

"Usually about eight."

He looked at his watch.

"Now, then, at exactly seven minutes after eight I want you to aim that revolver at the floor and pull the trigger once."

"Very well. Perhaps I had better set my watch with yours. I broke the crystal yesterday when a spider got on my arm, there in that attic, and it may not have kept good time since."

"'She broke the crystal,' she says coolly, 'when a spider got on her arm in the attic,'" remarked O'Leary softly as if to himself. "You win, Miss Keate. Say, did you ever play poker?"

"Yes," I replied absently, winding my watch. "To

entertain a patient I once had. He grew tired of playing it, though, almost at once. He said he didn't own any oil wells. Did you say seven minutes after eight?"

He did not reply at once, for he was surveying me rather strangely, and I was obliged to repeat my question.

"Er—yes. Yes," he said, clearing his throat. "How much did you win from him?" he added curiously.

Someone running through the passage thrust the curtain aside and burst into the room. It was Deke Lonergan, his top coat over his arm and his hat in one hand.

"Look here, O'Leary, I've got to go. I've got to leave this place. I can't stay here any longer."

"Why do you have to leave?" asked O'Leary, stern at once.

"I've got to go!" repeated young Lonergan as if he were quite beside himself. "I can't stay here. You must tell that policeman to let me out."

"Why?"

"None of your damn' business!" blurted Lonergan, flushing suddenly with anger.

"There you are, my young fellow!" It was O'Brien again, pounding to Lonergan's side. He grasped his arm. "This guy was after walking out the front door, bold as brass. What'll I do with him?"

"Let me go!" Deke Lonergan suddenly twisted away from O'Brien, and all at once there was a scrambled mêlée of coats and arms and legs which ended as quickly as it began. O'Leary, his eyes calm and his face bland as usual, was standing between them, O'Brien was touching gently a red blotch on his cheek, and Lonergan was adjusting his tie and glowering from one eye—the other eye had suddenly assumed a pink-ish-purple look and was rapidly beginning to swell.

"If you can't explain to me why you want to leave, you can stay here," said O'Leary.

"Hell," remarked young Lonergan disgustedly. "I've had enough of this. I'm going to get out. And you can't keep me from doing it!"

"Oh, is that so!" said O'Brien, prolonging the vowels unpleasantly.

"Yes, that's so!" snapped Deke Lonergan.

"That will do, O'Brien," interrupted O'Leary sharply. "And, as for you, Mr. Lonergan—you will stay here. No one leaves this house. Your reason for wishing to leave may be important, but there are few things more important than murder."

With an unintelligible growl Lonergan swooped up his coat and hat from where they had fallen on the floor, gave the hat a bitter look, for someone had stepped exactly on its crown, and hurled himself out of the room. He was followed hotly by O'Brien.

"At seven minutes after eight, Miss Keate," said O'Leary again. "And be sure to aim at the floor. A few bullet holes more or less won't hurt this old place."

Left alone I found plenty to do and decided to go to breakfast after I had carried out O'Leary's request. But it happened that at exactly five minutes after eight March herself brought in a tray with my break-fast on it, saying she thought I might be too busy to come to the dining room and the coffee was getting cold.

Unfortunately she lingered, and I was obliged to pick up the revolver and put my finger on the trigger and carefully aim it at a spot on the floor where I thought any havoc it made would not show much, conscious all the time of her rapidly growing nervousness. She started to speak a time or two, but stopped herself, while I kept my eyes on my watch and at seven minutes after eight I pulled the trigger.

The thing made a horrible racket and startled me so that I forgot to remove my finger, and somehow it shot six times without stopping. Then it stopped, and I laid it rather dazedly on the table, while March took her hands from her ears and looked at me very strangely and others came pouring into the room through the passage, and altogether there was quite a hullabaloo.

"I shot it accidentally," I replied to Eustace's sharp inquiry, not daring to take my eyes from the gun for more than a second at a time, for I felt that it might begin going again.

"Accidentally!" said March in a queer voice, and stopped again.

Just then O'Leary walked into the room, looked about him with barely a tinge of satisfaction in his face, took the revolver in his hand, and said lightly:

"Accidents will happen. But no harm is done, so I'd advise you to get back to your breakfast."

When they had gone the aggravating man said merely: "Thanks, Miss Keate," and walked away, which, in the face of my bursting curiosity, was almost endurable.

CHAPTER XIV

CHARLES FEDERIE

FIVE minutes later Lance O'Leary put his head through the doorway again to say in a low voice:

"By the way, Miss Keate, since your patient is better it will do no harm to give his family reason to hope for the best." He paused and added: "And to indicate that he may speak within twenty-four hours."

He uttered the "twenty-four hours" in a significant tone, and while I did not understand his motive I did not doubt that it was good. So a few moments later, when Eustace and Isobel stopped into the tower room to inquire as to old Mr. Federie's condition, I assured them blandly that he would soon be able to speak.

"Probably during the night," I added, getting into the spirit of the thing.

I told Elihu Dimuck, who fairly haunted the tower room all day and who took more of my time than I could spare with fretting about his anxiety to get back to his business, the same thing, and also Kema who came in with hot water and a newspaper. She took my volunteered statement with her usual impassivity, informed me that Mr. O'Leary had sent the newspaper to me, and padded silently out of the room.

I unfolded the newspaper and found that for the first time that week the Federie affair was not in headlines, for blazoned across the front pages were the words "Construction Company Fails," and below in smaller type "Dekesmith and Lonergan Go to Wall."

That was surely the construction company that was largely owned by Deke Lonergan's father! I read the details eagerly, but could gather little from it beyond the salient fact of failure. This, then, must be the reason for Deke Lonergan's anxiety to leave the house. It explained, too, the conversation with his father over the telephone, that I had overheard. But—*how* had he expected to secure the money that his father evidently needed rather desperately? Had he wanted to get money from my patient? Or had he some claim on the Federies?

Well, O'Leary had doubtless come to some conclusion about it, for he would not have sent the paper to me had he not already seen it. I folded it up again as the doctor, earlier than usual, came into the room. He agreed that Mr. Federie's condition was much better, changed the orders, asked a number of totally irrelevant questions about the progress the police were making, and went away after remarking somewhat tartly that it was all right for nurses to keep quiet about their patients' affairs, but there was no need to be so close mouthed about crime which was common property.

I watched my patient that day with more close attention than had been necessary previous to that, having my lunch sent in to me and refusing to take my hours off. Elihu Dimuck shared my watch most of the long day, sitting near the fire in a chair that creaked every time he moved, fretting and fidgeting, whenever I would listen to him, about getting back to his business, and watching my patient with anxiety. The others seemed no less anxious, for March and Eustace and Isobel kept coming into the room to ask a question or two about Mr. Federie, give him long looks, and wander restlessly about the room, and Mittie huddled over her beads in a corner, and even Lance O'Leary seemed to hover in the neighborhood of the tower room, though at the time, I am glad to say, I did not understand the reason for the rather solicitous attention he gave the room.

By late afternoon, however, they had all drifted away, and as the shadows deepened I began to feel— not nervous, you understand, nor frightened, but decidedly ill at ease. Finally, as I found that my hands were beginning to shake so that I could scarcely hold my knitting needles and my eyes kept going fearfully to the darkening gloom of the angular tower stairway, I decided that the silence and the atmosphere of breathless waiting that seemed to enfold that whole gloomy room were not conducive to quiet nerves and that I might relieve the tension that possessed me if I could find something to read. Accordingly I called Kema, asked her to sit beside the bed and call me if my patient stirred, and took my way to the library. The house seemed all at once deserted, although as I passed through the hall a figure darted suddenly out of sight into the back drawing room. I think it was Isobel but couldn't make sure, and I wondered what she was doing and what they were all doing that the house should seem so silent, so muffled, and yet, strangely, not empty. Rather it was packed to the brim with a kind of impalpable hush of suspense that was definite enough, too.

No one was in the long library, and I glanced along the tiers of books that lined the walls. There were all kinds of books, most of them worn, and I walked slowly along, searching for something that would soothe my tattered nerves. Some of the shelves showed gaping spaces as if someone had been searching the spaces back of the books, and in the tower alcove were stacked the withdrawn books in helter-skelter heaps. I was glancing through these scattered heaps when I was aware that someone had entered the library. It was shadowy there in the alcove, for the shutters were closed over the windows that lined it, and I was concealed by the folds of dingy green velvet that divided the alcove from the rest of the room. I peered through the crack between curtain and wall.

March and young Lonergan were standing in the center of the room, and as I watched they walked slowly toward a divan that stood with its back to the alcove and sat down. Their very first words were such that I—well, I just stayed where I was and I have no apology to make!

"I love you, March," said Deke Lonergan rather hoarsely. "I'm plain mad about you. And I haven't got a cent. The company has failed and it's—my fault." He ended on a sort of groan. He had turned toward her, and the eye that I could see was swollen almost shut and entirely purple, which did not look romantic.

"Deke, does Eustace owe you money?" asked March quite as if it were her business to know and love and loving could wait.

"Well—yes," admitted Deke.

"How much?" The girl's voice was as crisply incisive as if she were conducting a business conference, and I was quite positive that he was holding both her hands and looking very tender out of his good eye.

"A—good deal," he replied evasively.

"Why on earth did you loan it to him?" she asked with a sort of desperate exasperation.

Deke shrugged.

"You know Eustace when he wants anything. I was a fool, of course. I've learned my lesson. But it's too late."

"It's never too late," said March in a shade softer voice. "What did he do with it?"

"Speculated—and lost," said Deke tersely, adding with something like surprise: "You've got the most beautiful eyes. Especially when you look like that."

Upon which I think March closed her eyes, for he leaned over and kissed first her eyes and then her lips—long, lingering kisses. Their warmth must have penetrated March's steely calm, for suddenly she twisted away from Deke and sat facing him. I could see her delicate white profile.

"Oh, Deke, Deke!" she said with a sudden sob. "I've done something terrible. I didn't mean to do it. I didn't know what it meant."

"What do you mean? Don't talk like that, darling. Tell me."

"I mean—these murders!" She brought out the word with tremulous fierceness. "It is all—my fault!"

"March, you don't know what you are saying. Stop it!" He looked horrified, as well he might, and put both hands on her shoulders and shook her slightly.

"If I could only tell you," said March. "But I can't. I promised."

"March, I—" he swallowed hard—"I saw you. I saw you go through the bedroom up there, where I was sleeping with Eustace. Only I wasn't asleep and I saw you. You had—a little candle in your hand and you went down the tower stairway. I—I saw you, March."

She nodded. "I thought you were asleep."

"But, March, why didn't you come back for so long?"

"Why, Deke, I wasn't there more than three minutes. I—" she faltered momentarily and continued— "I was worried about something. So I slipped through your room and down a few steps of the tower stairway so I could see into the room below. But I just stayed a few moments on the stairway and then came back as quietly as I could."

He shook his head.

"Tell me the truth, March. I love you."

"I am telling you the truth. You just didn't know it when I came back through your room. I had blown out the candle on the stairway so the nurse wouldn't see me and wonder what I was doing there. So I had to creep back through your room in the dark. You simply didn't hear me, Deke. And I didn't want you to hear me, of course."

"But, March"—Lonergan's voice was miserable but dogged. "I *did* hear you. But it was an hour or so later. I had gone to sleep, thinking you had gone on down the tower stairway and upstairs again by way of the main stairway. Then the sound of the shot awoke me and—

I heard you come back through my room, *after the shot was fired!*"

It was unfortunate that just then I sneezed. I felt it coming and seized the dusty curtain near me to stifle it, but it was no use. It was a healthy, hearty sneeze, and the two on the divan jumped to their feet and turned startled faces toward the alcove.

With as much nonchalance as I could contrive I picked up a book, walked coolly out of the alcove and toward the door. I did not even glance at the two, but dare say they felt as discomposed as I, which was a comfort.

The hall was gloomy and deserted, but in the first drawing room Isobel stood at a curio cabinet. The glass door hung open, and she was taking up various sea shells and little china figures and rock paper weights. She whirled with a startled exclamation as I entered the room and, seeing who it was, reached forward to clutch my arm. Through the muslin of my uniform I could feel the hot grip of her wide fingers, and their long nails glittered.

"Look here, Nurse," she said, "is that old man going to get well?"

"I hope so, I'm sure," I replied brusquely, trying to pull away.

But she strengthened her grip.

"Soon?" Her high cheek bones and curved nose shone whitely in the semitwilight of the room. "He's got to make some provision for me before he dies. Will he be able to speak soon?"

"Probably," I replied coldly, and pulled away from her. There was suddenly something repellent about the woman—her heavy perfume that struggled with the odor of stale cigarette smoke, her rouges, her lip salves, her white powders, and her trailing laces. Beneath the artificial poses, what was the real Isobel?

Kema rose as I entered the tower room. It was odd that despite Kema's heathenish appearance she had a sensible, matter-of-fact way that I liked.

"He'll talk soon," she said in an unconcerned way. "Likely before morning."

It was not a question; it was merely a statement of fact, and I agreed readily. After lighting a lamp or two and locking the shutters she padded away, and the gloom and terrors of the room closed in on me again. I poked the fire and opened my book, resolving to put March's half confession to Deke out of my mind until I saw O'Leary. The first sentence my eyes fell on brought me sitting upright in my chair with my skin crawling. I looked at the title; it was *The Red Death*, and I simply stuffed that book under the wood in the box, and for all I know it is there yet. Only a decent respect for other people's property kept it out of the fire.

Things were no better after that, and Eustace entering the room with his silently graceful step and Genevieve trailing at his heels gave me quite a start, for I had been watching the tower stairway and did not hear Eustace until he was at my elbow.

"How is Grandfather?" he asked abruptly.

"It's a pity you couldn't let a body know you were about," I said waspishly, settling my cap securely on my head again as I sank back into my chair. "He's better."

Eustace walked to the bed and stood there looking at his grandfather's sternly modeled face. "Will he be able to talk soon?" he inquired. He reached over with an oddly solicitous gesture and pulled the counterpane straight. His hand lingered on it for a moment.

"Probably before morning," I replied. Was that the hand that had knotted that violin string and pulled it?

"To-night," he said thoughtfully. "You haven't found that curio I spoke of? The little jade elephant?"

I shook my head.

"It was to come to me on Grandfather's death," he said clearly. "Call me if Grandfather becomes conscious."

As I followed with my eyes his departing figure, certain suspicions crystallized in my mind. There was not, so far as I could see, a shred of evidence against the man, but could he have been the motivating force back of the tragedies, all along? With my own ears I had heard him urge March to undertake something that she had been most reluctant to do.

Perhaps I had made a mistake in concealing my knowledge of that episode from O'Leary. Yes, decidedly I had.

As if in answer to my thought the green curtain wavered and Lance O'Leary, his gray figure poised and alert, held back the curtain for March to enter.

"Miss Keate is in my confidence," said O'Leary as if continuing a conversation. "And I think we will not be interrupted here. Sit down, Miss March. Here." He drew a chair out into the room, and as March sat the mellow glow from the lamp on the table showed a tired young face, troubled and pale, with the little flush that Deke Lonergan's kisses had brought quite gone.

"Now, Miss March, please trust me. Who is the man you have been hiding in the house?"

I think she had not expected the question, for she gave a start that bore witness to the truth of O'Leary's implied statement. Her eyes, meeting O'Leary's, were incredibly blue under those lifted black eyebrows and her extravagant black lashes were wide apart.

"What—do you mean?" she asked in a voice that strove to be steady.

"Your father and Eustace's father and Adolph Federie all lie in the Federie lot at the cemetery," said O'Leary meditatively. "But Charles Federie—— Has Charles turned up after having presumably filled a gambler's grave for some fifteen years?"

The girl shrank back a little at the name, but said nothing.

"You may as well tell me the truth," went on O'Leary. "I'm sure it is Charles. Grondal implied that he was dead, but I have been able to find no records substantiating the notion. He resembles Adolph, doesn't he?"

And as March yet said nothing, just sat there looking at O'Leary, with her face white and blank and a kind of pinched look around her nose, O'Leary repeated sharply:

"Does he look like Adolph?"

"Y—yes," said March, moving her lips stiffly. There was a faint blue line around them.

"I was sure of it last night, though it is nothing

unusual for brothers to look alike," remarked O'Leary in the quietly conversational manner that has produced such astonishing results. "So Mittie Frisling actually caught a glimpse of Charles last night, instead of— Adolph's ghost. Where has Charles been hiding?"

"In the attic and trunk room. There were quilts in an old box and Kema managed to give him meals."

"How did he escape the police?"

"He hid in the stables—up in the hay loft. He knows the whole place, every twist and turn, of course. He said it was easy." A ghost of a smile touched her lips and vanished. "How did you know this?" she cried suddenly as a sort of anguished alarm came into her face. "Have you got him?"

O'Leary did not appear to hear her inquiry.

"You may as well tell me the whole thing, Miss March. How long has he been here?"

"Ever since the day before Uncle Adolph was killed —the day the nurse came. I let him into the house that night. I promised not to tell that he was here. He was very anxious to see and talk to Grandfather. I had to tell Kema, of course. I—I felt it my duty to let him come."

"And when Adolph was shot you immediately went to warn Charles?"

"I had to get him out of the house. He had said that it was imperative that no one should know of his presence, at least until he and—and Grandfather had been reconciled."

"And—you feared he had shot his brother?"

March's hands went up before her face.

"I—didn't know," she whispered huskily. "Charles

had been away so long. How could I know? But he is a Federie, and I stood in Grandfather's place."

"You wanted him to escape justice?" asked O'Leary sternly.

"I don't know what I wanted," said March wearily. "I didn't want to let him into the house at all without Grandfather's knowledge, but Charles insisted. He said he must be here in the house in case Grandfather recovered consciousness before he died. I hate them all," she burst out suddenly. "All they want is Grandfather's money. They are all scheming and twisting and working. Why, they are even trying to keep the little green elephant away from me."

"Why?"

She shrugged.

"Because Grandfather left it to me, I suppose—or will leave it to me if he—goes. They think it means something. I don't know what."

"Do you know what paper the green elephant holds?"

"Paper?" She looked at him in a puzzled way. "I didn't know there was a paper in it—it might be Grandfather's will."

There was a short silence.

"Have you been worried about Charles's presence here in the house?" asked O'Leary after he had rolled the shabby little pencil he carried up and down through his fingers twice.

She flung out her hands and took a long breath.

"I haven't had a peaceful moment. Even that first night before Adolph was shot I—I couldn't sleep. I kept wandering about the house trying to keep Charles from—disturbing Grandfather. I didn't know—what he might do." She added the last words in a frightened whisper.

There was another short silence; my thoughts were whirling with surmises, for the positive fact of a man hiding about the old place, in conjunction with his turning out to be Charles Federie, presented matters in an entirely new light. One was obliged to rearrange the puzzle to fit this new factor. I believe O'Leary was doing the same thing, for he said contemplatively:

"The dog didn't know Charles, of course, and barked every time he saw him. And the night Adolph was shot you yourself, Miss March, held the dog while Charles escaped."

She nodded lifelessly.

"Your grandfather keeps quite a sum of money somewhere in the house, does he not?"

"Why, yes, I believe he does. It is one of his peculiar ways."

"You don't know where he keeps it?"

"No."

"Or why he keeps it here instead of in a bank?"

"No. He never liked me to question him about things."

"Thank you, Miss March, that is all now."

She rose and turned to me.

"Is Grandfather really better, Miss Keate?"

"Yes."

"Do you think he will speak soon, within a few hours?"

"Very likely."

She gave the face on the pillows a long, affectionate look before she walked swiftly out of the room, her dark

head high and her slender shoulders straight. I think
the child was relieved to have shared some of the load
of anxiety she had been carrying.

"Well, Miss Keate," said O'Leary with none of the
jubilance that I should have expected. "The thing
isn't over yet."

"So it was Charles Federie all the time!" I exclaimed
incredulously.

"Why, of course," said Lance O'Leary as if I should
have known it long ago. "Who else would it be?"

At that moment I recalled my decision to tell O'Leary
of the conversation I had overheard between Eustace
and March before I had even entered the gloomy walls
of Federie house. I cleared my throat uncomfortably
and began. When I had finished O'Leary said nothing,
and after waiting a moment or two I resolved to make
a clean breast of it and went on to tell him of Lonergan's talk with March not an hour ago. My voice
dragged more miserably with every word, for it seemed
to me that I was closing the net around March tighter
and tighter. And I couldn't believe she was guilty.

"It is the money young Lonergan wanted, of course,"
said O'Leary finally. "I wonder how he proposed to get
it——"

"Is Mr. O'Leary here?" It was Mittie who interrupted him. She was blinking a little in her effort to
see past the circle of light made by the lamp into
O'Leary's face. She advanced into the room, glanced
over her shoulder with an indescribably conspiratorial
look, and did not stop until she reached O'Leary. He
rose, and she drew close to him, thrusting her sallow,
puffy face up into his.

"I've got Adolph's diamond," she cried in an excited eagerness. One fat hand was clenched, and she opened it, looking with rather ugly pleasure from its palm to O'Leary's face and back again.

I moved closer. Sure enough, sparkling in the light was the large, dubiously clouded diamond which I had last seen on Adolph's clammy hand.

"It was his," she repeated sharply. "I knew it at once. And where do you think it was?"

She leaned still closer to O'Leary so that he drew back involuntarily from her hot breath.

"Isobel—" she was panting a little now in an excitement that was not nice to see—"Isobel had it all along. I found it in her powder box. See, there's powder still on it." She rubbed it once or twice against her dress and then looked at it again. "It was Isobel who killed Adolph."

CHAPTER XV

"At it again, Mittie?" asked a lazy voice from the doorway. Isobel stood there, one hand on her hip, surveying us with insolent amusement. After an instant or two she walked slowly into the room, her pliant body swaying in the fashion so peculiarly her own.

"What is it now?" she asked O'Leary.

I think he did not like Isobel, or, rather, it might be that he—well, at any rate, he always seemed to be a little on his guard when she was near him, a little less human and more dryly machine-like.

"This diamond," he said in an expressionless way. "Was it your husband's?"

A kind of curtain came down over her dreamy eyes, but she answered readily:

"It was. Where did you find it, Mittie?"

"In your powder box! Where you hid it!" Mittie whirled to face Isobel, and her whole fattish person seemed to quiver and bristle with triumphant malice.

"What were you doing there?" Isobel's voice was harsh and her eyes ugly. "Let me catch you again in my room, Mittie, and I'll wring your fat neck. Just like that!" She gave a sudden and extremely lifelike twist of her large hands and Mittie turned green.

"Just a moment, please," cut in O'Leary's voice.

forestalling the imminent exchange of recriminations. "This is Adolph's ring, then. It was gone from his finger at the time of his death. Will you tell me, please, just how it happened that you have it?"

"Is it so unusual for a wife—a widow," she corrected herself deliberately without the slightest change of expression, "to have a ring of her husband's in her possession?"

O'Leary said nothing, and under his steady eyes she broke the little waiting silence and went on:

"He left it in my room that night, just an hour or so before he was shot. He—well, I had a little money, scarcely enough to quarrel about, but I wanted to keep it. He needed money right away to pay some gambling debts. His father keeps money somewhere in the house, but Adolph didn't know where, and his father couldn't speak. So he insisted on taking my money. I finally agreed to let him have it the next day—it's in the bank—and he pretended it was to be only a loan and gave me that ring as security."

She plucked the ring out of O'Leary's fingers and looked at it, smiling with her painted mouth alone.

"The diamond is like Adolph, glittering but value-less." With a rather horrible gesture of disdain she simply opened her fingers, let the ring drop where it would, and turned and walked out of the room.

O'Leary made no effort to stop her, and Mittie scrambled for the ring where it lay on the carpet, found it, and scuttled after Isobel. I have often wondered what she did with the diamond. It was all she ever had of Adolph, and it was paste.

Eustace and Mr. Dimuck must have met her in the

passage, for they came into the room immediately upon her exit.

"Look here, O'Leary," began Eustace in the arrogant way that was habitual with him. "I think, and Dimuck agrees with me, that you have had plenty of time to unravel this affair. Just what have you accomplished?"

"Suppose we sit down and talk the matter over," suggested O'Leary whom Eustace's arrogance did not seem to affect. I was interested to note that O'Leary's eye had taken on that lucent, clear look that always made me feel he could see through me, clear to my bones, like an X ray.

"There are a few things you can tell me about, Mr. Federie, that might help matters—expedite them a little."

Eustace's eyes flickered warily, but he sat down.

"Certainly," he said. "Certainly."

"Why did you insist that your cousin March was on the main stairs coming down when you ran into the lower hall immediately following the sound of the shot that killed Adolph Federie? She was actually in the main hall downstairs."

Eustace spread his fingers in a cynical little gesture.

"She ought not to have been there at such a time," he said lightly. "Noblesse oblige. She is a Federie; I didn't want it known that she was wandering about the house just then. She could have shot him as well as anyone."

"Is that what you urged her to do, during the afternoon before the murder? You were with her down by the little bridge south of the house."

Eustace stared at O'Leary for a moment, his narrow, dark eyes impenetrable.

"I don't know what you mean," he said finally. "I urged her to do nothing of the kind."

"She didn't want to," said O'Leary, making use of what I had told him. "But under pressure she finally consented."

"I don't know what you mean," repeated Eustace. "Who told you all that?"

O'Leary shrugged.

"It would be wiser to explain."

"I have nothing to explain." Eustace was growing angry. "That is all a lie. Was she actually talking with someone down there? Promising something? Who was with her?"

"Then tell me this," said O'Leary. "What were you really doing so late in the library the night Adolph was shot? The book that was on the arm of the chair and that you said you were reading so interestedly was titled *Fashions in Bead Work*. You were not sitting up until three o'clock in the morning through your interest in bead work."

Eustace hesitated. His fingers groped in his pocket, he drew out a cigarette case, extracted a cigarette, after offering them to O'Leary and Mr. Dimuck, and lighted it slowly. After a preliminary puff or two he decided to answer.

"Well, I may as well tell you. You probably know already. The fact is, Grandfather has always had a dislike for banks, and has kept quite a sum of money here in the house. He was a rich man and—I need not go into the reasons for his feeling as he did. I am not supposed to know, myself, but Adolph told me all about it one time. Grandfather was always close mouthed about such things, and I have no idea where the money is. No one knows, unless it is March, and when Grandfather became ill we were faced with the knowledge that the chances were that he would die without telling where the money is. Which would leave us in a nice fix! Anyway, that night I was searching along the shelves back of the books, thinking there might be some sort of cupboard affair. Oh, there are no secret passages or anything like that in the house. I know every crook and cranny of the whole place. But—I don't know where the money is. And there must be a considerable sum. It is cash, I think, which makes it a dangerous business."

"Did you need money for your own purposes?" asked O'Leary softly.

Eustace flushed a quick, dark red.

"If I did it is none of your business."

"How do you expect to pay back the money Deke Lonergan loaned you?"

"Has he been blabbing? I might have expected it. I suppose he told a great tale. Well, I'm sorry his father failed, but it wasn't my fault. And I tried to get the money for Deke, but you see how things were. If Grandfather dies"—he cast a rather callous look toward the bed—"I'll inherit something, I suppose, though the bulk of it will go to March. That is, if Grandfather becomes conscious and clear minded enough to tell us where the money is."

"Is your grandfather such a wealthy man?"

Eustace flung the half-smoked cigarette into the fire,

got up, and stood with his back to the mantel, facing O'Leary.

"From the way you've been snooping around, Mr. Detective, I'd say you already know the answer to that. Grandfather was the head of the Federie—er—highwaymen some fifty years ago. They were rather notorious in their day. It was an outlaw gang who made themselves rich in a number of ways that won't bear inspection. My great-grandfather was the leader of them; he died suddenly—of pneumonia and in his bed, which must have surprised him—and Grandfather, who was then about my age, took by far the lion's share of the plunder, dissolved the gang, built him this house, married a wife of irreproachable ancestry, bought books and pictures"—Eustace glanced mockingly at the atrocity in oils across the room—"and settled down to a life of respectability. But naturally his family had little to do with their neighbors—or perhaps I should put it the other way around, for the neighbors took the initiative. But years passed, B—— grew to a city, the Federie name was entirely forgotten, and we have never mingled much with other people. My grandfather was never a man to talk of his business affairs, but from what Adolph told me and from what I have seen of the easy way he digs up money for March or Adolph I believe that he has quite a sum of cash here in the house. Don't you agree with me, Dimuck?"

Dimuck gave a nervous little cough.

"This is not entirely news to me," he assured O'Leary. "But it was nothing to me how or where my client, Mr. Federie, secured his money. He seems to have plenty, however."

"Just what do you do for him, Mr. Dimuck? You speak of him as your client; just what does that mean?" Mr. Dimuck coughed again.

"In an advisory capacity, as I have told you, Mr. O'Leary. In an advisory capacity purely. Occasionally Mr. Federie likes to take a little flutter at the stock market, and I, if I may say so, usually watch the markets, though I never invest. Mr. Federie was a very conservative buyer. I have known him for some time. I respect him highly. Yes. Respect him highly. Indeed, I may say that I have a personal regard for him."

"You still have no idea as to what particular business he had in mind when he asked you to come here?"

"I didn't have at the time, Mr. O'Leary. Not at the time. But since these deplorable—these highly deplorable things have happened I have begun to think that possibly Adolph wanted more money than it was convenient for Mr. Federie to give him. At least Mr. Federie might have had some unusually heavy call upon his resources. Yes, something unusually heavy and urgent."

Lance O'Leary, who had been rolling and twisting that obnoxious little stub of pencil between his fingers, drew a piece of paper from his pocket and scribbled something on it which he passed to Dimuck.

Eustace watched uneasily, and Dimuck himself looked rather surprised, but he took the paper and held it nearer his eyes. He looked rather blank, however, as if he did not quite follow O'Leary's intention. Then he handed it back to O'Leary.

"I quite agree," he said rather uncertainly.

"Just what was that?" asked Eustace in a brittle tone.

"Nothing of much consequence," said O'Leary. "Well, Mr. Federie is so much better that the doctor and nurse promise we shall learn from his own lips the answers to any questions and that within a few hours. Did you not say by morning, Miss Keate?"

I came to myself with a little start.

"Yes, yes. We expect him to be able to speak by morning," I said hurriedly.

"Fine." Elihu Dimuck got to his feet and rubbed his pink hands together. "Fine. That is good news, Miss Keate." He beamed approvingly upon me and his heavy eyeglasses winked cheerfully.

"That is all now, thank you, gentlemen," said O'Leary so firmly that they seemed to forget they had come to question him and must have been a little surprised to find themselves outside the tower room and in the passage. O'Leary waited until the muffled sound of their footsteps had quite ceased and then walked across the room, lifted the curtain, and peered along the narrow passage. Satisfied, I suppose, that it was empty, he returned to me. I did not see that anything of any particular meaning had occurred during the little interview just past, but O'Leary's clear eyes were shining brightly and he wore a kind of hair-trigger alertness that aroused my curiosity.

"It will be before morning, Miss Keate. Before morning, I'm sure. Did you notice how Eustace stayed away from the green elephant?" He paused, his eyes going rapidly here and there about the room.

"Decks are cleared for action," he said presently.

"And if you'll just help me, Miss Keate! But there is
a considerable touch of danger about what I'm going
to ask you to do." He eyed me soberly. "And yet, if
I was not sure that I could protect you, I shouldn't
ask you to do it. Can you—do you place sufficient confidence in—my judgment?"

"What is it you want me to do?" I asked bluntly,
preferring not to commit myself.

"It is this—" his voice was low and vibrant with a
subdued excitement—"it is this: First, I want you to
complain of being very sleepy at dinner to-night. I
dare say it will not come hard, for you've not had
much rest lately. Give the impression that you are apt
to fall into a heavy, sound sleep by midnight."

"That will not be difficult," I said grimly. "What
else?"

"Then when you return to this room I want you to
sit in that chair by the bed with your back to the wall
so you can see the tower stairway and the door to the
passage——"

I interrupted him.

"See here, are you expecting someone to come down
that tower stairway? Because if so, I won't——"

"I'll be right here, close at hand, in such a case,"
he said hastily, and with a promptness that would
have been more reassuring had he not glanced somewhat anxiously toward the tower stairway as he spoke
and lowered his voice to a barely audible whisper.

"Sit there," he continued, still whispering. "Sit
there until about half-past twelve. Isn't that the time
you usually get hot water for your hypodermic—or
your packs or whatever you call them? You needn't

expect anything, I think, until after that. Then very
quietly blow out the lamp by the bed and turn down the
wick of the lamp on the table here in the middle of the
room. And you yourself stand over there at the other
side of the bed. There is room to conceal yourself
behind the shadow of the curtain of the bed. Take this
police whistle and keep it in your hand and—can't
you arrange the curtain so it will conceal you and yet
you can see into the room?"

He was around the bed in an instant, pulling and ar-
ranging the stuffy curtains that hung from the canopy
of the great, old-fashioned bed. Unsanitary things that
I had wanted to yank down at my first glimpse of them!

"But is someone—do you expect the murderer to—
to——" I stuck.

"I do," said O'Leary, with blood-curdling nonchalance. "And, when he comes, wait. Wait till he bends
over the bed. Then whistle."

"*What!*"

"Now that your patient is about to recover, Miss
Keate, he is in more danger than he ever was."

"But, Mr. O'Leary, if that is true you must guard
him. I can let you take no risks."

"If I did not feel perfectly sure that I should be able
to protect both of you, do you think I would undertake
such a plan?" asked O'Leary sternly.

Well, I didn't think so, of course, but at the same time
the very thought of the vigil the man was thrusting
upon me and the responsibility of my patient's welfare
that would be mine made cold shivers start up from the
small of my back.

"Surely you don't think that Charles Federie would
—murder his own father?" I whispered in horror.
"I don't know," said O'Leary. "A desperate man will
do anything to protect himself and carry out plans he
has begun so cold-bloodedly. And what we know of
Charles Federie is certainly not to his credit."

"Aren't you going to arrest Charles Federie at
once?" I demanded tartly, little liking the idea of the
man being permitted to roam at large over the house.

Lance O'Leary shrugged his shoulder.

"Miss Keate, can you tell me one scrap of evidence
—not suspicion but real evidence, that we have against
Charles?"

"His behavior is not that of an innocent person!"

"True. But can you point to anyone in the whole
household whose behavior has been entirely that of an
innocent person?"

As to that I could not. I suspected everyone in the
house except March, and had I followed logic rather
than impulse I should have suspected her more than
any of them. Which only shows to what a pass I had
come during those dark days in Federie house, for I am
not naturally a suspicious person. Having nothing to
conceal, myself, I do not suspect others of conceal-
ment.

"I am confident that neither you nor your patient
will come to any harm," said O'Leary. "You see, Miss
Keate, the secret that the jade elephant holds, whether
it is the clue to where the Federie fortune is hidden or
something else, is a secret that is known to Mr. Federie,
for he put it there. March only knows that there is some

value to the elephant. Mittie Frisling knows that Adolph had it in his hands when he was shot and it has disappeared. Adolph found what that secret was and met his death almost within the moment of his discovery. Grondal, I think, learned that secret, too, and likely admitted it, which was his own death signal. Whoever killed those two men knows that with Mr. Federie's being able to speak his own death sentence will be pronounced."

"Suppose it holds only Mr. Federie's will and that March does not benefit. Will you hold her responsible for these murders?" I objected.

O'Leary smiled faintly and shook his head.

"There is something else, Miss Keate. Such a will would never have caused all this. Of course, I can't be entirely sure that I am right, but—well, I'm willing to take a chance on it. Besides—well, we shall see."

He gave a quick glance about the room.

"All right, Miss Keate. Don't be uneasy, for I shall be close at hand." And with that he was gone, leaving me in the gloomy room with the tower stairway twisting into the shadows, a sick man whose life was threatened on the bed, and a cold little whistle in my hand for my sole protection.

"Don't be uneasy," indeed! It was all very well to say, but how could I help being uneasy! My knees were shaky already and I felt exactly as if I had swallowed a brick, and the night had not even begun.

I had no inclination to eat, but when a policeman—it was O'Brien again—appeared at the door of the tower room saying that Mr. O'Leary had sent him to stay with my patient while I ate my dinner I was reminded of O'Leary's request and made my way to the dining room.

That dinner was a rather ghostly replica of my first dinner in Federie house. It was merely accident, I suppose, that March wore the crimson velvet gown again, and the silver ornament in her soft dark hair, and Isobel her yellow taffeta, and Mittie tinkled with blue beads. And there were Eustace and Lonergan and shiny Mr. Dimuck in their customary black and white— Eustace debonair and sleek, Lonergan easy and young, with eager eyes on March, and Elihu Dimuck fumbling nearsightedly with his silver and looking more glisteningly rotund than ever in his formal dress coat with its tails dangling and his waistcoat wrinkled across the front.

The tan candles wavered, Kema padded softly here and there, the place beside me was vacant, and Grondal, with his faded livery and ceremonious airs, was gone forever. March sat straight and stern at the head of the table, Mittie fidgeted and fretted but ate voraciously, the wind outside was rising a little, and once Konrad barked and barked again.

"Charles is crossing the yard," I thought to myself, and March met my eyes coldly and went on with her salad, though her lips were a white line and the purple shadows under her eyes were distinct against her white cheeks.

And all about us rose the great silent house, with its secrets and its terrors. What would the night bring forth?

Genevieve, stalking through the room, sat down beside me. He chose exactly the spot where Adolph's

chair had been and stared at me. I found I had salted
vigorously a slice of baked ham on my plate and had
poured mayonnaise on some creamed potatoes. I rose.

"I am very sleepy and tired," I said. "I must get
some rest. I don't see how I can stay awake during the
night to care for my patient."

"Would you like me to stay in the room, Miss Keate,"
asked Mr. Dimuck, rather half-heartedly, it seemed to
me.

"I will stay with you," volunteered March at once.

"No, no," I refused hurriedly. "You see I expect him
to recover consciousness at any moment."

Knowing what I knew, it was rather dreadful to see
the faces that turned toward me at those words. It was
as if their masks slipped a little and the selfish desires
of each came boldly into their naked faces.

It was March, though, who spoke.

"You said you expected him to be able to speak soon,
did you not, Miss Keate?"

"Yes." My voice was husky. Was I leading one of
those people to a last fearful penalty? But there was
Charles—was he near at hand, in the pantry perhaps,
so he could hear my words? "Yes," I repeated more distinctly.

The masks were back again now, and the desires
hidden and furtive.

"During the night?" asked Isobel.

"Yes," I said again and, stifling a desire to take to
my heels and run, I walked out of the room, feeling all
the way the concentrated gaze of that rigidly silent
cluster around the long table.

I did not know that Genevieve had followed me until

I reached the door of the tower room, when he brushed purringly against my ankles and, as I pushed him away, leaped to the table, sniffed curiously at the old violin case that still lay there, and finally sat down and looked about him with a coolly proprietorial air that drew a startled word or two from O'Brien, who had watched him with distaste.

I think O'Brien was glad to leave, for he looked very unhappy and took his way out of the room with what I considered uncalled-for expedition.

It seemed ominous to me that that night no one came to the tower room. Not even Kema, who had taken over some of Grondal's duties despite March's ultimatum, came near.

Once from the library came the muffled, eerie strains of "La Furiante," but it broke off abruptly after only a few bars, and dead silence came down again upon the ugly old house.

I knit resolutely. The flames flickered and cast glancing shadows, the wind rattled the shutters, the sick man stirred a little once or twice, and about eleven o'clock I found that I had purled three whole stripes instead of knit one and purl one alternately as I should have done. In some disgust I rolled up the wool and laid it on a chair. But as to that, what with keeping my eyes on my patient, the green curtain, and the gloomy stairway simultaneously—which sounds impossible but can be done by one in the state of mind that I was in—what with all that, it is a wonder that I didn't knit the whole thing into knots.

Feeling, of course, that my first duty lay to my patient, I gave him assiduous care, but there was not much I could do for him. I am bound to say that as the night wore slowly on I liked O'Leary's plan less and less And I did not fancy the thick, palpitant silence.

By midnight I was as nervous as a witch, my heart jumping to my throat every time the wind shook the shutters or some old board creaked. And once when Genevieve yawned suddenly and stretched himself I had to press my hand over my teeth to keep from screaming before I traced the sound of the little rustle. When I rose to lower the wick in the lamp on the table, as O'Leary had directed me, my hands were like ice and shaking so that I turned the wick too far down and it sent up a black wisp of smoke before I could adjust it.

Then I approached the bedside table, took a long breath and a last look around the room, felt in my pocket to be sure I had the police whistle, and blew out the flame in the lamp that stood there.

This left the room almost completely in darkness, for the faint light on the old center table was barely enough to give the furniture dim outlines and make a spot of light on the table, which thereafter diminished steadily until the corners of the room and the tower stairway and the curtain over the doorway were almost lost in blackness.

By the time I had reached the farther side of the bed and was squeezing myself into a hiding place back of the bed curtain I was in a cold chill of stark terror.

But for a long time nothing at all happened, and the room was as still as death itself.

My fears, however, did not quiet themselves; they grew worse with every second. And it was with my heart nearly leaping out of my mouth that I saw that a shadow over near the doorway was moving.

The whistle was at my lips before I noted that the moving shadow made no effort to approach the bed, but simply remained in the denser shadows behind a great chair. O'Leary had said wait, and I waited. But I held the whistle poised at my lips.

More fear-laden seconds ticked away, and the shadow back of the chair did not move again. I had begun to wonder if my eyes had deceived me when a slight rustle from the other end of the room brought me staring in the direction, straining my ears for a repetition of that sound.

I heard it again.

And I froze in a very paralysis of panic.

Cautiously, with infinite stealth, someone was descending the tower stairway!

CHAPTER XVI

THE JADE ELEPHANT

WHO was it?

Was it O'Leary?

Did a fold of my white dress show from beyond the curtain? No.

Was the watcher across the room also aware that someone was creeping down the tower stairway?

Down another step and another. Only the soft pressure of feet on that padded carpet, the subdued creak now and then of the old timber, the hushed, barely perceptible breath of motion gave evidence of that slow descent.

At last there was a pause, and then a darker shadow emerged from the gloom surrounding the stairway, loomed up noiselessly between me and the dim lamp, bulked blackly against the red coals in the fireplace, and *was approaching the bed!*

The whistle was at my dry lips.

Another cautious step and another. I wondered if my heart beats could be heard and drew a cautious breath of air into my bursting lungs.

Another step. The shadow was near the bed. It was bending slowly. And all at once that other shadow had flung itself forward and was blended in a furious struggle with the figure already there, and I was blowing the police whistle with all my pent-up force, and its shrill notes were cutting through every curtain and thick wall in the old house, and pandemonium was let loose in the tower room.

Lights, shouts, policemen crowding, people pouring into the room—all this I was only vaguely conscious of, for I was staring across that expanse of white counterpane.

There were three figures struggling there instead of two. One was O'Leary and one was Elihu Dimuck and one was——Policemen shouldering into the mass were thrusting them apart and I caught a glimpse of a face that made me grasp the curtains for support and stand there shaking, for in the glancing lights it looked as if Adolph Federie had returned to the tower room!

But it was Charles Federie, of course. I realized that even as a burly policeman pulled him aside, thrust quick hands up and down his body, and then linked an arm securely through his captive's arm.

"Good." It was O'Leary's voice, panting but keen as a knife. He was putting something long and slender that caught a sharp highlight as it vanished in an inside pocket. "Turn up the light over there, Murphy. Light that other lamp, Shafer. O'Brien, let the others come into the room. Miss Keate, are you all right?"

"Y-yes," I said in a small voice. Somehow I reached a chair and sat down, keeping my eyes on Charles Federie. I comprehended only vaguely that March was at my side, crying over and over again in a stricken way: "Why did you do it? Why did you do it?" and that Elihu Dimuck's eyes were nearly popping out from their sockets and that Mittie and Eustace and Lonergan and Kema were there, too.

Charles Federie, his dark face and pouched eyes defiant, faced us with a policeman hanging on each arm.

Isobel thrust her way suddenly through the crowd and broke the momentary spell, for she came close to Charles, stared wildly into his face, touched his face with the tips of stiffly outstretched fingers, and said at last in a still voice that held as much horror as awe:

"It's Charles Federie."

No one spoke, and Isobel turned toward us, her eyes going helplessly from one to another until she came to O'Leary.

"It's Charles Federie," she repeated in that dazed way. "And he's been dead fifteen years."

And at that Mittie began to scream, Kema padded forward and took March's hand in her broad, brown clasp, and Deke Lonergan sat down suddenly on the foot of the bed and said fervently: "Well, I'll be damned!"

O'Leary's clear voice dominated.

"Sit down here, Mrs. Federie. And you here, Miss March. We may as well have it out now. We can put the whole thing in a nutshell in a few moments, I think. Miss Frisling, will you stop that screaming!"

The sharp rudeness of the request seemed to bring Mittie to herself, for she gulped and subsided. I realized that my mouth was hanging open, closed it with a snap, and walked on somewhat unsteady feet to the bed. My patient was untouched and unharmed, but I remained there, my fingers on his pulse.

"To begin at the beginning," said O'Leary, "Charles

Federie wasn't any more dead than I am. He found it convenient, however, to get out of the country some fifteen years ago and did not see fit to discourage the report of his death. Is that right?"

"Quite right," agreed Charles Federie. At the sound of his voice I gasped, for it was easy and suave and arrogant and so like Eustace's voice that I had to look to be sure it was not Eustace speaking.

"You came here finally, hearing that your father was in poor health, with your mind made up to secure as much money from him as possible. You were only afraid that he would leave a will so that you would get nothing. Your father, of course, thought you were dead."

"Exactly," said Charles Federie. He spoke coolly, but his eyes were going warily from O'Leary to the police and around the room.

"Wait!" cried March. "It is all my fault, Mr. O'Leary."

"You let him into the house," said O'Leary. "And you have not had an easy moment since."

"Oh, I haven't!" cried March. "Not an instant. Since I met him outdoors the afternoon before Adolph was shot. I was out walking, and he came up to me and told me who he was; I knew he was telling the truth, of course, for he is like Eustace and Adolph and all the Federies. He persuaded me to let him into the house that night. And I did. But I tried to watch him. I even slipped through Eustace's bedroom up there and came a few steps down the tower stairway for fear Charles had come into the room and would—annoy Grand-father—try to talk to him. I didn't know that it would make no difference to Grandfather." She cast a sad little glance toward the insensible figure on the bed.

"That is where you lost your crimson rosette off your slipper," said O'Leary, but did not tell her where he had found it. I suppose she never knew that Adolph's dying hand had clutched it from the step where it had fallen. And O'Leary had not seen fit to question her directly about his discovery of the rosette; what a waste my anxiety had been!

"March," cried Deke Lonergan. "What a blind fool I was! Can you forgive me? Remember, I've been half out of my mind with worry over the money I threw away. And I saw you go through the room, you know, and I did not know that you had returned, for I didn't hear you. And when I heard someone slipping so quietly through the room after the shot was fired and locking the door into the upstairs corridor I—well, I just jumped to the conclusion that it was you. I didn't know why you were there, but I wasn't going to tell——"

"You certainly were blind," interrupted O'Leary. "Adolph and—his murderer both went through that room and down the tower stairway and you slept, I suppose, through it all."

"Go on, O'Leary," said Eustace nervously. "Let's have the rest of it." So far, he had not spoken to his newly returned relative, although he had scarcely taken his eyes from his uncle's dark face.

"Very well," agreed O'Leary. "Adolph Federie was shot because he took a small green elephant from the mantel, here, where Mr. Federie liked to keep it. I might mention that upon the disappearance of the elephant later on everyone in the house became convinced that it held the secret they longed to know, and they all started looking for it. But the secret it holds is not, I think, the one you expect." His eyes went from Eustace to Isobel and included Mittie. "Adolph managed to open the elephant and read the paper it contains. Will you give me the elephant, please?" He addressed Charles Federie.

O'Brien's hand was in Charles Federie's coat pocket. There was a brief struggle and O'Brien held a bit of green toward O'Leary.

"Here it is, sir."

It was curious to note the startled little hush as O'Leary took the jade elephant into his hand. Everyone was leaning forward, staring at the spot of vivid green, and a queer kind of sigh went over the room.

O'Leary balanced the thing on his palm.

"A pretty toy," he said slowly. "To hold a man's life."

There was an electric silence. Then:

"Open it," said Isobel harshly.

"Not yet," said O'Leary. "I'll tell you first what happened. Then I will prove it. The murderer of Adolph Federie escaped. Grondal knew that there was money in the house, was fearful lest his master die without divulging the secret of its hiding place, had looked everywhere for a clue as to where it was hidden, and heard Miss Keate mention that she had found the little green elephant at the foot of the stairway immediately following Adolph's death. This drew his attention to the elephant; he took the thing and, I think, succeeded in opening it and reading the paper it held. But Miss Keate recovered the elephant and hid it in the violin case over there. From there, too, it disappeared."

Charles interrupted.

"I took it," he said coolly. "I was on the tower stairway when the nurse hid it. I saw her. In fact, I—well, I watched this room most of the time."

On the tower stairway! Then he had the key, of course, to the bedroom above.

"I thought you had it," I said, addressing Eustace. "You left the inquest so hurriedly that I——"

"You followed me," said Eustace grimly. "I wanted a look at this room when no one was here to watch, but you followed too quickly. I had to give up when I saw you coming."

"The green elephant was recovered again by Miss Keate," went on O'Leary.

"Do you know you nearly brained me with that flashlight?" interrupted Charles Federie, giving me a look of displeasure that was still a little respectful. "It caught me squarely on the head. I had to stay behind a box in the corner for hours. I thought you were a policeman until Kema opened the door of the trunk room. And I had to make a quick getaway to the attic. But the police didn't find me."

"I told you he was there," I said to O'Brien, enjoying my triumph.

"That is how you knew, then, that Miss Keate had the elephant again?" asked O'Leary.

Charles Federie nodded.

"It was easy enough to get hold of it again. Once I discovered it was gone, I guessed, of course, that she had

it and waited till she came from dinner. There wasn't
much that I missed in the house. But I got tangled up in
the yarn it was wrapped in and she nearly caught me."
So it was Charles Federie who had wrapped me in
the curtain and wrenched the elephant from my clasp;
I liked Charles Federie accordingly.

"But in the meanwhile Grondal was killed," resumed
O'Leary. "Killed for knowing too much. For meeting
the murderer in that upstairs room. For telling the
murderer what he knew. The two struggled; Grondal,
luckily for the murderer, was thrust somehow against
the corner of a marble-topped table up there." He
motioned to the bedroom above the tower room. "He
staggered down the tower stairs and collapsed on the
couch and the murderer slipped down the stairway after
him and tied a violin string around his neck to make
sure that what Grondal knew was safe—forever. It
sounds like a feminine crime."

Mittie shrieked, but O'Leary did not pause in his
grim recital.

"The murderer made sure that there would be no
revival for Grondal."

Charles Federie again tried to jerk away from the
policemen and did not succeed.

"Why don't you open the elephant?" he asked
O'Leary. "The head of the thing unscrews."

Lance O'Leary gave him a long look. He held the
green elephant balanced on his hand. Someone near me
caught his breath sharply.

"Open it?" asked O'Leary softly. The fingers of the
other hand caressed the shimmering green lightly. A
policeman back of me stirred and felt for something in

his hip pocket. The room was all at once stifling, and it was difficult to breathe. We were all looking breathlessly at that spot of vivid, clear green.

"Open the elephant?" asked O'Leary. "Very well." His voice became sharp and clear. "Shafer—O'Brien." His eyes flashed from one to another of the bluecoats about us. Then he whirled, his gray figure electric, his hand flinging outward. "Make your arrest!"

There was a sudden whirl of rapidly moving figures, screams, outcries, a confused blending of voices and questions and a furious struggle going on before my eyes. I blinked, took a step or two forward, trying to see past the blue backs, and then as they fell back I think I screamed, too. I couldn't have helped it.

For there between Shafer and O'Brien was Elihu Dimuck, writhing and pulling at the glittering handcuffs that bound him to the policemen, his spectacles gone, his face distorted and livid with rage and fear, and a gibbering stream of black curses coming from the mouth.

"Hey! Stop that!" O'Brien shook his club in Dimuck's face. "Another word out of you and you'll find out how this feels."

"It does no good to struggle," advised O'Leary, regarding the man curiously.

"*It was you!*" cried March. She was leaning forward, her eyes like twin swords until she closed them. She put out her hands blindly.

"Here, dear. Don't look at him." Lonergan had her in his arms, her face pressed against his shoulder.

I stared at Elihu Dimuck. It was the first time I had seen him without the broadly benevolent eyeglasses,

and I was amazed at the difference in his appearance.
His eyes were shrewd, cruel, greedy, and were darting
now from one to another of us with the beady, vicious
look of a cornered rat.

"You can't prove it," he said in a hoarse whisper.
"You can't prove it."

"Ah, but I can." O'Leary revealed an unsuspected
flair for the dramatic. "Before I open this elephant,
before we know the secret that brought two deaths, I'll
tell you how I know that this man is guilty. The night
that Adolph Federie was killed Dimuck came to the
tower room and said before anyone had told him what
had happened: 'Who shot him?' and Adolph Federie
was lying on the stairway on his face, in such a position
that it was impossible for anyone to know that he had
been shot at all. For all Dimuck ought to have known
the man was only sick or had died from natural causes.
But he said at once: 'Who shot him?' That was enough
to interest me in the man, especially after he said that
the sound of the shot awakened him. The revolver was
of a small caliber; with Miss Keate's help I experi-
mented and found that in his bedroom at the far end
of the house *he could not have heard the shot*. Then, I
found four different fingerprints on the old violin. There
were Miss Keate's, Eustace's, Charles Federie's—oh,
yes, we had those from the china doorknob on the kitchen door long ago—and Elihu Dimuck's. Then, after
Grondal's death, he took pains to destroy the fingerprints on the knob of the bedroom door upstairs, which
he must have forgotten in his haste to get away after
he had twisted the violin string about Grondal's throat;
as a rule he was very cautious about fingerprints. I was

convinced, however, when Miss Keate cut her hand. She cut her hand on a small sliver of glass on the table upstairs. And the glass proved to be a broken bit of a lens for spectacles. With the help of various oculists and a good deal of time, I traced that bit of glass and found it was exactly like the lenses in the spectacles with which I discovered Elihu Dimuck had recently been fitted. But apparently Elihu Dimuck's spectacles had not been broken, for he was still wearing them. He had been refitted quite recently, though, so it was not unreasonable to suspect that he yet had his former pair of spectacles, those he had previously worn, before he got the new pair. If he had broken his new pair, he could have gone directly to his room, taken out the old spectacles, which, by the way, no longer helped his vision, put them on, hidden the broken pair, and come downstairs at the sound of the police whistle which by that time was ringing through the house. He must have considered it fortunate that he had the old pair with him, although he could not see so well through them, which, of course, was his reason for being refitted."

A thought flashed over him.

"That is why you wrote that note!" I cried.

Lance O'Leary nodded.

"Yes. I was convinced when, first, I handed Dimuck a note saying: 'Where are your broken eyeglasses?' Had he been able to read it, it would have given him quite a shock, but he could not even read it. Then I found the broken pair hidden under the carpet in his bedroom. That was your greatest mistake, Dimuck. Go and get them, will you, Murphy; they are under the carpet, hidden in the straw padding, near the right-hand side of

the foot of the bed. I left them there so Dimuck would
not know that they were found."

Dimuck was still sawing at the handcuffs.

"You can't prove anything," he reiterated. "You
can't prove anything."

"There is only one thing I am curious about," said
O'Leary quietly. "How did you get that revolver over
in the corner of the vacant bedroom upstairs without
entering the room yourself?"

Dimuck smiled; it was an ugly smile.

"I threw it!" he said with a grisly touch of triumph
in his voice. "Had you there, didn't I! I simply opened
that door, rubbed the fingerprints off the revolver
with my handkerchief, and threw it." A look of terror
came into his face. "No, I didn't! No, I didn't! You
can't prove anything."

"You've confessed, you fool," said O'Leary in a tone
as near savagery as I've ever known him to use.

Charles Federie laughed.

"You're a smart man, O'Leary. Open the elephant."

"Yes." Isobel was leaning forward, her hands clutching the back of a chair and her eyes on the elephant.
"Open it."

"Very well," said O'Leary again. "And we'll see
whether or not I am right."

I think the sight of his slender fingers turning the tiny
green head maddened Dimuck, for he gave a strangled
yell and surged desperately at the handcuffs, and there
was a moment of struggle before he was standing fairly
quiet again.

"The head turns backward," said Charles Federie.
"Take hold of the ears."

No one seemed to breathe while O'Leary's fingers turned and turned and finally the head and body of the green elephant parted. A bit of white showed against the green; I believe that O'Leary's fingers shook a little as he withdrew the small piece of paper, opened it, and glanced at the written lines.

"Listen to this: 'This is to acknowledge and affirm that all properties held by me and registered in my name as undersigned are actually the properties of Jonas Federie. In return for the use of my name in this way I am to receive a yearly salary which is to be deducted each year from the income of these properties, and it to be agreed upon each year between me and said Jonas Federie. All deeds and mortgages are in safety box number 287 of the Savings Trust Bank of B——. At the moment of recording this instrument all properties will revert to the owner.' Signed 'Elihu Dimuck.'"

There was a moment's silence. Then O'Leary added: "This is witnessed by Matthew Frisling, a notary public, and Jem Grondal. And both witnesses are dead. It was a golden opportunity for Elihu Dimuck. Short and to the point as the agreement is, it is perfectly legal and binding."

Charles Federie cleared his throat.

"My father always felt that some legal difficulty might arise if he kept his money and property in his own name. He always felt there was danger, I suppose. Father managed his farms, did all his business through the medium of Elihu Dimuck's name. Dimuck's ownership would never have been questioned if he had succeeded in destroying that paper."

Murphy entered, shouldering his way to O'Leary.

"There's them spectacles, sir," he said.

I stared at the spectacles O'Leary held in his hands; the gold rims were intact, but only a few raggedly sharp bits of glass remained. Even that way the gold rims were broad and substantial and ineffably benign. And what greed, what cruelty, what sordid, ugly crime they had concealed!

"The money, by the way, that is supposedly kept in the house," said O'Leary, "consists of a couple of thousand dollars in bills. It is in a small trunk under Mr. Federie's bed; a hiding place so simple I dare say you never thought of searching it. Mr. Federie is too good a business man to leave a fortune in cash hidden in the house, delightful though the idea is. And, Mr. Lonergan, I have no doubt that Mr. Federie will return to you the money Eustace borrowed and lost, thereby causing you such anxiety. You annoyed me, you know. I could not at once fit you into the puzzle."

"If it's any comfort to you, you annoyed me," retorted Deke Lonergan.

Genevieve, who had been washing his face vigorously during the whole time, jumped down suddenly and stalked out of the room; there was a kind of righteous finality about the very angle of his tail, as if he had done his duty well and was ready to turn to other matters.

"But the key to the bedroom upstairs," I said suddenly. "It was in Mittie's bead box; who put it there?"

"There must have been two keys," said O'Leary, eying Charles Federie. "Dimuck had one. He must have thought it an excellent idea to lock young Lonergan into the bedroom above the tower stairway and retain the key in order to give himself access to the tower room and the green elephant. Then when he grew afraid that he would catch him with the key he placed it in the bead box merely to complicate matters for us. And probably Mr. Charles Federie has an old key to that room."

Charles Federie nodded.

"Here it is in my pocket," he said. "That room upstairs had been mine. Mine and your father's, March, for we were the oldest. And when I left home suddenly the key was in my pocket and—and I've always kept it. By the way, I suppose there is no chance of keeping my presence here a secret?" he asked O'Leary doubtfully, and as O'Leary shook his head Charles turned regretfully to March. "I'm afraid you may have to stand a revival of some old—er—scandal."

"Was it you who played the piano the day of Adolph's funeral?" I asked suddenly.

He nodded, smiling a little.

"I didn't know, then, that I had hit on Eustace's favorite tune. And you nearly got me there in the butler's pantry when Grondal was killed."

"That was a fortunate meeting for you," said O'Leary. "She touched the roughly woven material of your coat at exactly the time the murder took place. And since the others were all—er—in pajamas or bathrobes when they came downstairs, I thought it likely that was you. That is, after I became convinced of your presence—and of your innocence."

Charles laughed.

"I expected the nurse to raise an alarm. I hurried up the main stairway, and Eustace followed me into the trunk room—which was also in the nature of an alibi for me, I suppose."

"Then Dimuck knew all along that the paper was in the elephant?" inquired Eustace.

"How about it, Dimuck?" asked O'Leary.

"I didn't know where it was until—Adolph——" Dimuck stopped.

"But you thought it was somewhere close to Mr. Federie," said O'Leary. "And you watched. And you followed Adolph through the bedroom up there and down the tower stairway to where you could see into the room. Adolph was doubtless looking for a clue as to where the money he thought was in the house was hidden. And when he happened onto the secret of the elephant you guessed what he had found. You knew at once where to find the paper. And that Adolph must die for his knowledge if you were to succeed in your scheme."

"Did Grondal know that this paper existed? You said he witnessed it," persisted Eustace.

"I think he witnessed only the signatures," said O'Leary. "Is that right, Dimuck?" And as the man made a sullen gesture of assent O'Leary continued: "But Grondal, too, was looking for some clue to the fortune you all supposed to be hidden in the house— not for himself, likely, but for the family. When he happened upon the knowledge the elephant contained and came upon Dimuck in the room above to which supposedly only the murderer had the key, he taxed Dimuck with his new knowledge. The two quarreled, Dimuck saying boldly that he would have the money.

And you knew, didn't you, Dimuck, that you must kill Grondal, too? *Answer me!*"

"Y-yes. If I confess—will you make things easier for me?" His ratlike eyes were ugly.

"You have confessed," said O'Leary again.

There was a sudden stir and a muffled stammer of words from the bed. I turned quickly. For the first time old Mr. Federie was looking at me with intelligence in his blue eyes.

"Who—are—you?" He spoke slowly and with labored thickness of tongue.

"Grandfather!" March was kneeling at the bedside.

"March," he said. "M-March—" the words came slowly and with great effort—"the green—the green ———"

"Yes, dear. The green elephant? Here it is. It is safe."

O'Leary stepped quickly to her side and placed it in the old man's wrinkled hand.

"Telephone for the doctor," I said hurriedly to Kema. "Hurry. It is Main 2336."

Well, that is about all. I remember the doctor's arriving in the cold gray dawn and, after he had pronounced my patient out of immediate danger, his almost ghoulish interest in the events of the night. I remember Kema's bringing coffee and how gloriously commonplace and welcome its fragrance and stimulating heat were. I remember the clattering patrol wagon, and how March and I met each other's gaze and shuddered as it drove away from the gate, and how Mittie watched from a window with her nose flat against the glass, and how Isobel sat, superbly at ease in her nightgown and Chinese shawl, and smoked and stared into the fire. And how Lonergan would scarcely leave March's side, and how Eustace and Charles talked and questioned O'Leary over and over again.

And I remember, too, and shall never forget, how gloomy was the tower stairway, and how somberly the green couch loomed in the stairway's morose shadows.

It must have been seven o'clock in the morning before they left me again in the tower room. And as the green curtain fell behind Isobel, who was the last to drift away, O'Leary returned and flung himself into a chair, sighing deeply.

"Well," he said in a dull voice, "your patient is going to get well, and the thing is done."

"The thing is done," I repeated after him. Another day was at hand. I reached one hand to my cap and tucked in straying locks of hair.

"You do not seem hilariously triumphant," I commented.

"I am not." Lance O'Leary's aspect was unutterably weary. "Mine is a terrible profession. Without imagination I would be no good; with it I am too—sensible of what I have done."

"The man was a murderer. He deserved to be caught," I reminded him sternly.

"Yes." He sat thoughtfully silent for a moment or two. Then he shrugged. "Well—anyway, the thing is over."

"Was Dimuck actually intending to kill old Mr. Federie?" I asked, whispering so as not to arouse my patient who had fallen into his first natural sleep. "And was it he that searched my room last night?"

Lance O'Leary nodded wearily.

"Look here." An ugly-looking knife lay in his hand; it glittered evilly. "He dropped this when I got him there by the bed. Wicked-looking thing, isn't it? I spared Miss March the sight of it."

"But how did Charles Federie happen in the room to-night?"

"He came through the door; I was watching him. He admits that after reading that paper he suspected something of the kind. And Charles did not want his father to die. At least, until he had made some arrangement by which Charles would inherit."

"But why didn't Charles come forward as soon as he read that paper and knew how Dimuck would benefit by Mr. Federie's death?"

O'Leary glanced irritatedly at me.

"Charles didn't have the clues we had, remember. To-night I left the bedroom door up there unlocked, baited the trap for Dimuck, and watched from the passage. You watched from back of the curtain at the bed, and Charles from across the room when Dimuck came down the tower stairway. He was desperate, as I knew he would be, else he would not have taken the chance. It meant more than the property that old Mr. Federie should never speak."

Lance O'Leary sighed again, slipped the knife back under his coat, and rose.

"I should like to be able to thank you properly, Sarah Keate," he began.

But I brushed away his thanks, and finally he walked slowly to the doorway and turned there; his slight figure and intent face were poised for a moment against that green background, while his clear eyes lingered on the old room with its secretive curtains and twisting tower stairway. There was something fateful about that silent moment, something curiously significant; then he turned with a little gesture of farewell, and the green curtain fell slowly into place. And all around me lay again the secrets of Federie house.

Well, as I say, that is about all. I found Mr. Federie a lively and entertaining patient, especially after he became reconciled with Charles. But after his recovery I went back to the hospital and have never, since the Federie case, taken a case in a private home. There are no musty curtains and twisting tower stairways here!

I saw something of the Federies and a great deal of Lance O'Leary during the trial, which was a long-drawn-out affair. Not long ago I nursed Lance O'Leary through an appendectomy, and during his convalescence we reconstructed the Federie case with such success that the training nurses refused to enter the room and the head doctor himself came to remonstrate.

"That is all right," said Lance O'Leary. "You may think that Miss Keate is a good nurse, but she is a better detective. The next time I get stuck on a case I am going to send for her."

Which was absurd, of course.